Praise for *Oh Pure & Radiant Heart*

[A] superb, memorable novel"—*Publishers Weekly* (starred review)

"[An] extremely smart . . . resonant fantasy."—*New York Times Book Review*

"Millet . . . boldly fuses lyrical realism with precisely rendered far-out-ness to achieve a unique energy and perspicacity, the ideal approach to the most confounding reality of our era: the atomic bomb." —*Booklist* (starred review), Best Books of 2005

"Lydia Millet is da bomb. Literally . . . Though *Oh Pure and Radiant Heart* possesses the nervy irreverence of Kurt Vonnegut and Joseph Heller, Millet makes the subject matter her own, capturing the essence of these geniuses in a way that can only be described as, well, genius."—*Vanity Fair*

"In her brilliant and fearless new novel Lydia Millet takes a headlong run at the subject of nuclear annihilation, weaving together black comedy, science, history, and time travel to produce, against stiff odds, a shattering and beautiful work."—Jennifer Reese, *Entertainment Weekly* (lead review, A–)

"Thanks to Millet's evocative rendering and impeccable scholarship, the physicists feel real, convincing and even moving."—*Time Out NY*

"An entirely original novel: equal parts funny and chilling, accurate and bizarre."—*Philadelphia Weekly*

"[A] wonderful flight of the imagination, funny and thoughtful and richly imagined."—*Hartford Courant*

"A Molotov cocktail comprised of dreams, history, philosophy and wit, *Oh Pure and Radiant Heart* explodes the rationale for nuclear armament along with any claims of its rationality."—*Oregonian*

"Millet deftly manages this dangerously high-concept conceit with generous, precise, and funny prose. A born storyteller."—*Flavorpill*

"[Millet]does an exquisite job of deploying moments of reason despite

its unlikely plot, and, conversely, it excels in evoking intense feeling despite its preoccupation with science and reason . . . In its smallest moments and its most expansive ideas, *Oh Pure and Radiant Heart* is a beautiful and fiercely intelligent novel, and it provides us with some very important advice: pretend the world is real." —*Ottawa Citizen*

"[A] unique and wide-reaching book . . . [I]ts head soars into philosophical inquiry about love and peace and creative ambition; its heart is planted in the emotional and psychological landscape of its characters and those who have been terrorized by the bomb; and its feet are sunk firmly into the political reality of greed, manipulation, and opportunism." —*Bloomsbury Review*

"Millet is a ferocious writer with a sense of humor that is as dark as it is funny . . . [She] has written a novel with the intellectual heft of Pynchon and DeLillo —only a lot more fun to read." —*Tucson Weekly*

"The creators of the atomic bomb are mysteriously transported to modern-day Santa Fe, where they encounter confusion, celebrity, and infamy. Millet manages this dangerously high-concept conceit with generous, precise, and funny prose." —*Boldtype*, Best Books of 2005

Praise for *Everyone's Pretty*

"With a sharp eye for small details, a keen sense of the absurd and strong empathy for its creations, *Everyone's Pretty* is both prism and truth." —Sarah Weinman, *Washington Post Book World*

"A kaleidoscopic new satire of America's quietly freakish office workers . . . gives voice to a wide variety of life's unbeautiful losers —and makes them sing for us." —*Boston Globe*

"Beating through the pages of this strange little book is a lonely heart searching for intimacy in a crazy world." —*Entertainment Weekly*

"At the still point of its lurid absurdity is a story about America. Like a sobering radio broadcast playing unattended in the midst of a party run amok . . . " —*Globe & Mail*

"A biting send-up of vapid Americana wrapped up in a hilarious novel about five desperate Angelenos in search of redemption." —*Boldtype*

"Juggling an enormous cast of psychos, *Everyone's Pretty* revels in its own religious chaos, the sexually crazed repeatedly clashing with the sexually pure . . . The book impressively teeters on the edge of total inanity, each scene becoming increasingly uncomfortable, then unraveling out of control." — *Village Voice*

"[F]unny, dark and surprisingly tender in unexpected places . . . Millet has many talents as a writer, but one of her greatest is creating scraps of dialogue that sound like the accidentally significant and funny stuff that is the reason people watch reality TV." — *Montreal Mirror*

"Absolutely captivating . . . I picked it up, read it almost in one day — and I was pissed when I had to stop. *Everyone's Pretty* is fast & furious reading that nearly hypnotizes." — *Sex Kitten*

"Millet . . . treats her characters without condescension and with surprising tenderness and respect as they wind their way toward a sort of tattered redemption." — *Elegant Variation*

"*Everyone's Pretty* is so transgressive, so wildly and beautifully dark, that it's like a breath of fresh air in a stale literary environment overrun with too-clever postmodernists." — *Tucson Weekly*

Praise for *My Happy Life*
Winner of the 2003 PEN USA Award for Fiction

"A prodigious feat." — *New York Times Book Review*

"Strange and lovely." — *Village Voice*

"If there were any justice in the world, *My Happy Life* would become not merely a cult book, devoured by a few astonished readers every year, but an exemplar, 'This,' we would say, 'is how to write a novel that is impossible to forget.'" — *Commercial Appeal*

"A heart-rending novel." — *Boston Herald*

"Sad and infinitely touching . . . A courageous and memorable achievement." — *Publishers Weekly* (Starred review)

"A nightmare limned in gold." — *Entertainment Weekly*

"Same breath with Raising Arizona." — *Palm Beach Post*

"A biting critique of the Bush years with all their ghastly blandness and deceit." — *St. Petersburg Times*

"Hilarious and sure to make its mark." — *St. Louis Post-Dispatch*

"The most sardonic and laugh-out-loud funny satire I've read in years." — *Denver Rocky Mountain News*

"Smart and funny." — *Village Voice*

Praise for *Omnivores* (Algonquin Books of Chapel Hill, 1996)

"American appetites — for sex, power, and possessions — are darkly lampooned in this strange, very funny debut." — *Entertainment Weekly*

"*Omnivores* reads like a cartoon with soul." — *Los Angeles Times*

"A world where absurdity reigns and reality fluctuates from the mundane one second to the surreal the next." — *Voice Literary Supplement*

"A hilariously bizarre novel that centers around one teenage girl and the voracious appetites of the three men in her life. Just what you'd hope a young copy editor at Hustler would write in her spare time." — *Buzz Magazine*

"Millet's heroine and her plight draw you in and gnaw at you until you're bloodied, but enjoying the pain." — *Paper Magazine*

"Richly imaginative, acidly absurd, medievally creepy, weirdly delightful." — *Quill & Quire*

How the Dead Dream
A Novel

Lydia Millet

Counterpoint
Berkeley

b12692924

Library of Congress Cataloging-in-Publication Data

Millet, Lydia, 1968–
 How the dead dream / Lydia Millet.
 p. cm.
 ISBN-13: 978-1-59376-184-4
 ISBN-10: 1-59376-184-8
 1. Real estate developers—Fiction. 2. Mothers and sons—Fiction. 3. Loss (Psychology)—Fiction. 4. Human-animal relationships—Fiction. 5. Endangered species—Fiction. 6. Extinction (Biology)—Fiction. 7. Psychological fiction. I. Title.

 PS3563.I42175H69 2008
 813'.54—dc22 2007035242

Jacket design by David Janik
Interior design by Anne Horowitz
Printed in the United States of America

Counterpoint
2117 Fourth St
Suite D
Berkeley CA 94710

www.counterpointpress.com

Distributed by Publishers Group West

10 9 8 7 6 5 4 3 2 1

How the Dead Dream

1

His first idol was Andrew Jackson. He knew the vertical dart between the brows, the jutting chin, the narrow mouth; he knew the windblown coif that perched atop the great man's forehead like a bird's nest on a lonesome crag. Jackson's face was fixed in a somewhat neutral expression and T. spent long hours trying to decide if it suggested idle speculation or a slight annoyance.

Running his fingers over the faded gray lithograph he imagined the once-president, a moment before the portraitist captured his aspect, being taken aback by a gently unpleasant sight: a horse dropping slow, deliberate pats in front of a government building, for instance, or a manservant picking his nose. But his opinion of Jackson was not diminished by this vision; rather he admired the great man for his composure in the face of the trivial. No passing insult could compel him to emote.

Jackson's grave and finely etched countenance came to him in moments of anxiety and calmed his heart. And from Jackson he moved on to Hamilton, whose face was fraught

with nobility and feminine grace despite a nose that was far from small. Hamilton had a homosexual way about him that lent an air of refinement to the ten-dollar bill. Jackson, on the more valuable twenty, nonetheless became a ruffian by comparison; Jackson was a more primitive version of the American statesman, a rudimentary model waiting to be superceded by gayer men with cleaner fingernails.

When he finally learned that Hamilton had, in fact, pre-deceased Jackson he was still not dissuaded in this. History often stumbled.

His allegiance to Hamilton lasted for several months. At times he found himself ranking the girls in his class on a scale of one to ten in terms of their resemblance to the former soldier of the Republic. None came close, he lamented; still he saw a trace of Hamilton's light eyes in the plump face of Becky Spivak and his well-turned mouth on Gina Grosz, a victim of rosacea.

He needed a trace of the venerable and the upright close to him, in the grainy and familiar everyday. If he could detect an edge of arrogant pride in a skinny girl at a swim meet, say, jiggling a bare foot in the bleachers as she stared coolly at the other swimmers, he was pleased; he was reminded of the potential for all shackled beasts to break from their bonds and rise, their ragged wings beating, into the stratosphere. He clung to a vision of forward motion, the breath of hope that could lift individuals into posterity. He told himself every day of this latent capacity for eminence among humans, to the untrained eye so often hard to see. Rise, my sister! Rise, my brother! Soar.

Great institutions and the tall columns and white soaring domes that stood for them—these seemed to him the crowning achievement of his kind. Authority inspired him, resting along the eye-lines and in the closed mouths of the

long-deceased statesmen. The bills themselves he preferred soft and worn, for when they were freshly pressed they seemed nearly counterfeit. He kept the proceeds from his paper route under his pillow and would touch them before he went to sleep and check for them first thing in the morning when he awoke, sliding a hand between the cool mattress and the weight of his head.

His mother knew the currency was sacrosanct and after she changed the sheets would replace the pile of bills with care precisely where she had found it. He was six when he started hiding the stash there at night, and at first there had been misunderstandings; once she left the cash on a book-shelf, open to the elements. Upon its discovery T. was horrified. The bills were naked as babes.

Their confrontation ended in bitter tears and his father was summoned.

"I get to keep it under there. I get to keep it right there! She tried to put it out there by itself! She can't take it!"

"But honey," said his mother, "I'm not trying . . ."

"Angela, let the boy keep his money wherever he likes."

As a younger boy, when his allowance was a mere five a week—a single Lincoln, deformed giant with heavy brows and long ears, or five Washingtons with their sly sideways glance—he had a habit of secreting coins on his person, a thick and powerful quarter lodged under his tongue or discreet dimes tucked into the cheek pouches. He never swallowed and he never choked.

"Such a dirty habit," said his mother regularly. "Do you realize how many strangers have touched those coins? Bacteria!"

He did not dignify this with a response.

Many times she tried to engage him in more serious

discussions, for clearly his fascination with the coin of the realm struck her as unhealthy—though not, strictly speaking, un-American. Both she and his father had extolled the virtues of financial institutions since he first started sucking on nickels, but it was only around his eighth birthday, during a brief early flirtation with Grover Cleveland, that he saw for the first time there might be a percentage in it for him.

She broached the subject in the kitchen, leaning across the table to inspect a stack of pennies beside his cereal bowl as he spooned up puffed wheat, then sitting back to cock her neat, honey-blond head and smile at him.

Beside her his father sat gazing absently out the window, twirling a toothpick between thumb and index finger.

"I just wonder, sweetie, why you feel the need to have the money with you all the time. On your *person*. I mean no one's going to steal it from you, T., if you put it away somewhere. You could keep it all in a piggybank, or something."

"A piggybank? Are you kidding me?"

"*What*, T.?"

"Talk about sitting ducks."

"No one's going to break in, T. We have a security system! So it's just your father and me. Don't you know you can trust us? Why would I steal from my own little boy?"

"It's *money*," said T.

"I would never steal from you, honey. Neither would your daddy."

"That's right, T. I've got way richer guys than you to steal from."

T. fixed on his father a stern and unwavering eye.

"Just kidding, son."

"How about this: your dad can open a savings account just

for you, at the bank. How about that, T.? Your money will be perfectly safe there."

"What if I put all my savings in the bank and a robber comes in?"

His father placed the toothpick carefully on the beige tabletop and reached over to grasp him firmly by the shoulder.

"Banks are insured against theft, buddy. It's called the FDIC. So Bonnie and Clyde or not, you're guaranteed to get your money back. The one damn thing the feds are good for, by God."

"David! *Language*."

His father rolled his eyes.

"Well . . ." He eyed them both sidelong. "Maybe if you put some in there for me and it doesn't all get stolen? Then *maybe* I'll put mine in too."

They exchanged knowing glances that said: such sweet and see-through attempts at extortion! But they did not have the last laugh, for in subsequent weeks T. made several appearances at his mother's book club meetings, hosted in the sitting room, where the ladies sipped daintily at rose hip tea leaving their freshly bought copies of *Brideshead Revisited* uncracked upon the coffee table. When he was called upon to return a greeting from one of them—"Well T.! Aren't you a big man now!"—he would carefully, with a few gagging head pokes like a cat vomiting, open his mouth and rain a wet spew of coins into his cupped hands.

Soon afterward his father made a modest deposit in his name. The account grew steadily as he tucked away the proceeds from lemonade stands, pet-sitting assignments, driveway car washes, charity walkathons, and occasionally the lowball resale of items appropriated from neighbors or

relatives who had incurred his displeasure. His father tolerated his commercial dealings; his mother was more suspicious.

"You told Mrs. Hitchens you were doing a March for Hunger," she said once. "She told me after Mass. She said she pledged twenty cents a mile."

"Hitchens, Hitchens . . ." he mused, stalling.

"It was either a March for Hunger or it wasn't."

"It was definitely a March for Hunger."

"She said you billed her for ten dollars. Fifty miles, T.?"

"It was over a period of several days."

"When did you walk fifty miles?"

"Over, you know. A period of several days. There was a bunch of us from school. We did laps on the track."

"Hmm."

"Well, we kind of counted gym class. For a couple of weeks. Double-tasking made it more efficient."

"I see. And how much money did you raise, T.?"

"Like a hundred forty."

"All of you, T.? Or just you?"

"Just me."

"For hunger, T.? Who's so hungry suddenly?"

"Children, Mom. OK? In Africa. Just for one example. What is this, now you don't like giving to the needy? You're supposed to be a Catholic!"

"So you're telling me that all one hundred and forty dollars went to a group that helps starving children? That's what you're telling me?"

"All the funds went to children. Yes. They did."

Cheerful and popular, he was also cocky. He did not hesitate to punish adults as he saw fit; he remembered slights and took particular exception to condescension. His youth was no reason to presume him stupid, for stupidity was not the

province of the young alone, as he himself had observed through careful study. Indeed there were millions of frail elderly gentlemen, slope-shouldered, weary, and brimful of gravitas, who despite their dignified appearance were dumb as a shot put.

His own grandfather on his mother's side struck him as one of these: the poor old fellow was a half-deaf Ukrainian who had immigrated to Florida not long after the war but never mastered English, and who, when he visited them, struggled around the neighborhood feebly waving his walking stick at fast-moving children and cursing at cars in his incomprehensible native tongue. T. tried to treat him with kindness, if not exactly the respect his mother said he deserved; but the codger constantly stymied his attempts at pretend deference, be it through glaringly obvious pee stains on his tan corduroys, a chronic inability to count out change, or the total opacity of the old man's blithering rage, which delivered itself in seemingly random outbursts of strange syllables.

He did not rejoice in this—far from it. He liked things to be as they appeared. The young were at least smooth-skinned and straight; the old were flabby and wrinkled. At least, he thought, they should pony up some piece of timeless wisdom to make up for their wretchedness: yet most shambled from breakfast to bedtime in the same dumb state that had taken them through adolescence. A fair number had grown up quite simply dimwits, and stubbornly remained so even in their dotage. He wanted to venerate them, for with their lined faces and dignified bearing they reminded him of august men of state. But then they spoke.

On the neighborhood black market he was known to have sold purloined bottles of liquor, a dog-eared copy of *The Joy of Sex*, Super Plus size tampons (a novelty item that inspired great speculation among the local boys), brassieres, and once

a Polaroid of Adam Scheinhorn's naked sister. Her eyes were small as currants in a bleached-white face but the rest of her was so clear that fingers trembled as they held the photo, pinching the frame along the very edge. Oh yes: he knew where value lay.

Although he learned to put the lion's share in the bank, throughout high school he also kept a small safe in his room. And on occasions when he felt rebuffed, when he perceived an insult or failed at something he had desperately tried, he would retire there and carefully remove the portion of his stash he always kept nearby. With hands in latex gloves he soothed himself by counting out rare dollar bills—the two, for instance—and old coins that were prized by collectors, including many dark and brittle rounds dating from Roman times. These he would remove from his safe in ritualized style and lay out on a sheet of newspaper spread across his desk, in strict order from least value to most.

And it was not only the ritual, not merely the repetitious and the pious act of counting that afforded him comfort. He liked to hold and see the legal tender and then bend his head and close his eyes, the metal or the paper in his hands. He would order himself to concentrate until his jaw was aching from clenched teeth and his eyes beneath his eyelids almost hurt; in the still room both his ears would ring and he would feel himself reeling, as though in one position, bowed over his desk, he hurtled through a static night. He reeled, he reeled: he might disintegrate: his mind was pulsing like a heart.

After such effort he was spent.

•

One of his lowest moments in high school came at the hands of a friend's mother. The friend was Perry, short for Pericles, who was not a first-order friend but one of the less fortunate (prominent teeth, flood pants) to whom he granted favors in exchange for services rendered. They were playing Donkey Kong when Perry's mother entered the bedroom.

At first she made small talk, distracting them from Donkey Kong but failing to penetrate; finally she dropped the pretense and called T. away for what she called a "private chat." Perry rolled his eyes and seemed ashamed, but did not have the upper hand. His mother ushered T. hastily out the door, whereon a large poster of Captain James T. Kirk was boldly tacked, and into the nearby laundry room. There she shut the door behind them, began to fold towels with agitated precision, and asked him in a whisper where he got off, as she put it, "taking" Perry's allowance money.

T. nipped this in the bud with a quick denial, but she persisted. Though Perry said he was giving the twenty dollars weekly to T. in exchange for protection from various jocks who had it in for him, she did not think it was "fair" for T. to "extort money on that basis."

"It's more than fair," said T. "Before I stepped in, Perry got beat up like twice a month. One time they broke a tooth. He had to get new braces and a crown. You don't remember that? I mean how much did that run you?"

"The point is, if you're friends he shouldn't be paying you

for helping him. It's something you do for your friends for free. Friends help each other, T."

"I'd like to do it at no charge to Perry," said T. firmly. "I really would. Believe you me. And in a perfect world I could. But here's the situation: I'm not the problem. I'm the middleman here. Those dollars go straight to the guys who were doing the beatings. In return, they keep their hands off your son."

"But T. —"

"Mrs. G., we were lucky they took the deal at all. I mean, they really like beating on him, Mrs. G. It's basically all they've got to live for. They didn't want to take the bribe at first, but I convinced them. So now they target other kids instead. But if we stop paying them—especially now we've had this gentlemen's agreement and everything was going smoothly—they'll boomerang on him. They have this thing they do with locker doors? He could lose the use of his pinkies."

"If it's that serious, T., Perry's father and I should just take it up with the school administration, or maybe the parents of those reprobates who like to hurt innocent little boys."

"Sure you could. But I would advise against that, Mrs. G. It would be like killing Perry. I mean socially. It would get out that you had to go in there for him and everyone would be saying one word to him: *L, O, S, E, R. Loser,* Mrs. G."

"I can spell too."

"He might not take as many physical beatings, that's true, but the psychological scars would be lasting."

She stared at him, annoyed, gaping slightly, one hand on a stack of towels. He looked her in the eye, affecting an earnest concern for Perry's well-being. In fact the jocks in question had been easy to convince and now received a mere five a week.

"You're a slick little bastard," she said finally, picking up

the towels and turning her back on him. She walked out of the laundry room and slammed the door behind her.

He waited for a few seconds after her leave-taking, drawing deep breaths. Then he summoned his pride, squared his shoulders, and followed.

In the main there was seldom a reckoning, seldom any conflict. In his early adolescence what impressed him most often was the willingness of people to be fleeced — the ease, almost the gratitude with which they surrendered their assets. On his block, at least, where the housewives had expensive hair and his mother was the sole Catholic, his many good works appeared to offer a welcome relief from the mall and the salon. Almost monthly he collected for the United Way, the Boy Scouts of America, the YMCA or sometimes a church group conducting out-reach to the poor and unfortunate. He always dedicated a percentage of the take to the cause at hand: so his efforts, if not entirely selfless, yielded what he liked to call a "pos-itive net effect."

And this was the language he used in the confessional, which he visited at intervals to keep his mother happy. His father, once he recovered from a brief but intense bout of spirituality around the time of the wedding, had declined to set foot in the church. This seemed to sadden his mother, and T. felt it was his duty to take up the slack. He was not hesitant to disclose all his activities; for after all, he reasoned, the priest was bound to observe the sanctity of the con-fessional and must be quite a sound businessman himself, for the local diocese alone had assets in the hundreds of millions. Indeed he was surprised when the priest did not laud him for his strategies.

"I can't believe you're penalizing me. My economic

activities have a positive net effect on the community as a whole," he repeated staunchly, when he was set the heavy penance of ten Our Fathers and ten Hail Marys.

"They would have a greater 'net effect' if you refrained from lying and stealing, Thomas," said the priest gently.

T. shook his head. "That's what we call looking at the glass half empty."

When he recalled those years it was in brief flashes; there was no continuous line but only a few vivid moments. His mother back then was different from the mother he left when he went to college. When he got home after school she was always in the house, a steady glowing fixture. She smiled and was interested in him; she had soft pictures of the Virgin on the wall, some of them holding a baby Jesus T. believed might be a stand-in for him.

She wore a large crucifix beneath the hollow of her throat, which T.'s friends from school decried as "weird" and "foreign." Their own churches and mothers were unadorned and in their living rooms there were few pictures of anything but water lilies and fall leaves, flocks of geese flying over farmhouses in rolling country.

But they liked his mother and afforded her a certain respect, for she was pretty and kind and discreet. She welcomed the boys into the kitchen with sodas and lemonade in spring and hot drinks in the winter, and there she drew them into peaceful conversation but never kept them too long. All in all she seemed mainly concerned with her son's happiness.

His father commuted into the city for work and returned quite late at night on weekdays; he was dense and silent in the house on weekends, rarely seeking out others to speak to them. He watched sports and worked in the

yard and the garage; he always seemed to be turning away to what occupied him. Later T. remembered mainly the sight of his back.

As he grew up his love became sophisticated. He no longer needed to touch coins or bills; he found his satisfaction in surges of energy, in the stream of contact between machines that processed binary. He learned to like abstract money better than its physical body. The solid house that money built sheltered him and he felt keenly that money was both everything and nothing, at once infinite, open potential and an end in itself.

Money was commerce and the movement of broad arms. It was how, in the great halls of trade and public service, the walls were so thick that sound could not penetrate and the foundations so strong an earthquake could barely move them. There was the honor and austerity of money as he walked through art galleries, as he saw around him the collections of oil paintings by dead men, lit so carefully that warmth seemed to emanate from within—and not because their art was loved or understood but because it could be sold and bought for handsome sums. He gazed upon the paintings steadily and for a moment thought he knew their private beauty as his own, as though it had only ever meant the same thing once, to him and him alone: and as he turned away he felt a hush of air rise in the corridors.

There was the noble trace of money in the half-imagined bodies of the dinosaurs, looming with arched necks in the shadowed halls of natural history museums, the back-lit shapes of toothy deep-sea fish brought up from dark fathoms below; money in the shining link between the Treasury Building and the aircraft that flew across the continent, the trains that ran through mountain towns, the cabins perched

among the pines. There was money in the grandeur of the
ranks of the imperial armies as they might march across the
deserts underneath the skies, in the great thick cables that
ran beneath the surging Atlantic, the intricate and freezing
satellites that whirred a thousand miles above the surface of
the earth, displaying all the ingenuity and subtlety of human-
kind as their metal veins ran silver in the moon's reflected
light. It was the alchemy of money then, the shivering power
of its quiet numerals, the wish of money that was such a
clear command.

Currency infused all things, from the small to the mono-
lithic. And to be a statesman the first thing needed was not
morals, public service, or the power of rhetoric; the first
thing needed was money. Because finally there was always a
single answer. As there was only one intelligence residing in
a self, as trees grew upward toward the sun, as women lived
outward and men walked in insulation to the end of their
lives: when all was said and done, from place to place and
country to country, forget the subtleties of right and wrong,
the struggle toward affinity. In the lurch and flux, in all the
variation and the same, it was only money that could set a
person free.

•

Of having private gluts of feeling, holding his secrets close,
and seeming all the while the whitest of white bread; of being
perfectly opaque and seeming transparent; of being merely
well-informed and shrewd while seeming like a prodigy—he
was guilty of all of these and in all of them excelled.

By the time he left home to attend college in a small town

in North Carolina he had amassed sufficient funds for an account with a discount brokerage firm. He attended classes in deference to the wishes of his parents but all the while his real work was day trading. He was always discreet, and few knew of his enterprise; when he had losses he did not reveal them and of course his wins went unheralded also, which gave him on some days an air of quiet satisfaction.

The stiff discipline of discretion was part of his training. It was crucial, he believed, to learn which aspects of his character to make available to sight and which to keep hidden. Honesty was seldom the best policy in social intercourse; and when it was invoked as an ideal, he felt, it merely reflected a childish desire for pure simplicity in matters of personal trade. Those who claimed shriekingly that honesty was a sovereign virtue were in fact merely fearful of the complex.

No, honesty was useful chiefly within the confines of the self, where careful scrutiny of successes, failures, victories and losses was necessary for progress.

He joined his father's old fraternity—less out of enthusiasm than to be respectful of his father and ensure his continued goodwill—and there became treasurer and then vice president. He lost no time in making himself well-liked with the fraternity brothers, and while he did not reveal his dealings in the stock market to them he did include them now and then in other less significant undertakings. Quite soon they came to know him as a skillful card counter who graced the black-jack tables of Atlantic City and Foxwoods when he could find time to drive north for the weekend. Typically he invited a few brothers to accompany him, and they told tales of his acumen back at the frat house.

Both men and women tended to admire him, for he practiced a kindly reserve that invited affection but discouraged any more intimate advance. Men were comfortable with this,

relieved by how little he asked, and women deemed him enigmatic and sought out his favors. But he did not want a girlfriend, nor was he willing to engage in the forced aggression and later awkwardness of one-night stands. Instead he held himself apart.

On evenings when his peers partook too liberally of spirits he alone remained sober, a reassuring presence on the edge of the revels. He was never too close for comfort nor too far away to spring into action, and so could always be looked to for the rapid solution of problems ranging from the merely distasteful (Ian Van Heysen's dramatic episode of incontinence in the Kappa house dining room) to the outright felonious (Ian Van Heysen's exuberant vandalism of townie cars during Pledge Week). It was T. who quietly confiscated the keys of brothers unfit to drive, who deftly staunched the flow of blood from flesh wounds caused by gleeful unrestraint; it was he who politicked behind the scenes to dissuade frivolous accusations of date rape, negotiated truces with disgruntled neighbors and bored campus police. It was he who took in hand forlorn and suddenly shameful users of Lysergic Acid Diethylamide who skulked in basement corners, scraping at their sturdy wrists with plastic knives from the dining room and posturing self-murder.

On one occasion Van Heysen, whose father was a tobacco mogul and major donor to the cancer ward of the university hospital, became fleetingly convinced of his own lack of worth and threatened to dispatch himself by jumping off the roof of the university's observatory. This was in the small hours of a mild spring morning, following a laser light show set to music. During the show—chiefly intersecting colored lines projected onto the dome of the observatory, which at other times displayed the constellations of the northern night sky—Ian had drunk a fifth of whiskey and chased it

with unspecified pills. T. sat with him on the edge of the roof as he mulled over the decision, keeping a firm hand on his shoulder. Even the fact that the roof of the observatory was a mere twenty feet off the ground, above an oleander hedge, did not completely dispel the urgency of the situation.

After the worst had passed Ian dried his eyes and spoke of philosophy.

"It's like, the world is awesome? And also it sucks."

"I know exactly what you mean," said T., nodding and consulting his watch. The Tokyo markets were already closing.

"Sometimes I wish I was like a peasant or a farmer. Like in Guatemala."

"Trust me, Ian. You don't wish that."

"But it's like, things would be way easier. You just get up and eat beans and then you work all day, like, hoeing shit. Whatever. Then at the end of the day you're all tired and sweaty and you just take a hot shower and crash."

"I'm not sure you'd like the part in the middle there, Ian."

"I'm just like so tired of, I don't know. Everything."

"It's tough sometimes. Isn't it."

"I have this one dream where my father is a gigantic building? It doesn't look like him but it is. It's all gray and gigantic. He's like a skyscraper in Manhattan. And in the corner of the dream, where no one ever sees it, is this tiny, like, shining mouse. And the mouse, T., get this. The mouse is actually Jesus Christ."

"Whoa. Slow down there, Mr. Deep."

"I wrote a song about it. It's called 'Jesus Squeaks.' "

When they left the roof they were applauded by brothers in the parking lot below. Ian went drinking with them and T. went to sleep.

He was useful to his small society, and few fraternity

brothers who had benefited from his clear thinking could
forget it quickly. Sorority girls whose soft, still-shaking
hands he had held gently as he persuaded them not to file
charges remembered him not with resentment but with
tender respect, and Ian Van Heysen, Sr. had been known to
show his gratitude to T. with gifts of cognac and Cubans
sent by courier.

That he was mature beyond his years was obvious; and
while they placed their trust in him they also knew he stood
apart from them, too rigidly controlled to mix his solemn
molecules with theirs. He was a father their own age, claiming
the loyalty of all and the passion of none.

But while others looked to the present for their pleasures —
holding these four years to be both their first and their last gasp
of freedom — he looked to the life beyond, past the confines of
the fraternity house with its dusty oak wainscoting, the campus
buildings with their wide lawns and white porticos, and the
small college town with its crowded hilly streets and dog-
woods that bloomed so cloudily in spring.

He saw beyond what there was, and in the not-yet-existent
imagined a great acceleration.

His parents visited one weekend in October and once in
April, always at the same time. His father liked to attend an
annual old boys' fundraiser for the fraternity and his mother
liked to pick up an iced tea at the cafeteria and then wander
at a leisurely pace through the campus's Botanical Gardens,
holding her purse and gazing at the magnolia trees. She
would point at the small, old-fashioned signs on their tidy
stakes in the earth, which bore in careful lettering the names
of tropical and subtropical plants — *Ricinus communis*
(Christ's Palm), *Alonsoa incisifolia* (Devil's Rattle) — and say
how gracious were the stalks, how beautiful the leaves and

languid the flowers. As she said this she would bend her head and a wishful tone would come into her voice. Watching her he saw how she envied the plants, so peaceful in the shade, so smooth and green and cool. They grew there and they died there.

And while his father, as he aged, grew stiffer and more pointed, almost an exaggeration of his younger self, his mother quietly faded. Her warmth rose like vapor and left a still surface; and later, when she had forgotten everyone she knew and even her own name, he would think back to these college gardens and how she had loved them. "I could live here," she would say, as he walked beside her in the dappled shade and they looked down at irises and lazily floating wasps. "Here, right here, in the waterfalls and the ferns." She had grown up in a southern climate and the winters were long in Connecticut.

He endured the visits only to see her, to know how she was faring and to try to elicit from her some spark of vigor. For her sake he would stand awkwardly by while his father toured the fraternity, always with a jocular handshake for the sons of old peers, always with what seemed to T. like a desperate and transparent need to be one of the boys again. But the chill of his mother's absence was steadily deepening. Stepping out of the rental car after the drive from the airport she had a measure of distraction in her gaze, as though her true allegiance was elsewhere while she kept this trivial but mandatory appointment.

And yet she had nothing else; she had no other appointments.

Whenever his mother was visiting he took her to the town's only Catholic church for Sunday Mass, and for her devotions every evening when the church was empty. She went to church more now that he was gone, she told him.

Once they sat in a pew near the front, and he watched her face as she looked up at the stained glass, where Jesus was pictured in a triptych. On one side he was an infant in the arms of his mother; on the other he was greeting Mary again in his thirty-fourth year, on the way to Golgotha bowed down under the weight of the cross.

In the tall, central window he was crucified and dying. His crown of thorns had been jauntily fashioned, thought T., bored and ruminating. His knees bled in perfect symmetry.

"Look at the Blessed Virgin," whispered his mother. "Look at her eyes. Her face is sad even when he's a baby. You see? It's just as sad as it is in the fourth station, when she meets him going to be crucified. She's always sad, sad and wise. The sadness on the Via Dolorosa is the part I've never believed."

"You don't believe she was sad?"

"A mother wouldn't be sad if she saw her son in the street like that. On the way to his death at the hands of tyrants, and suffering? With blood running down his face from the terrible thorns? Even if she knew it was for the glory of God and for the salvation of every soul the heavens could ever hold. A mother would never be sad, T. A mother would be screaming."

"But she wasn't any mother. She was the mother of God. Wasn't she?"

"Even the mother of God. There's only one explanation, dear. The Blessed Mother was serene because she was gone. The second she saw him like that she was gone forever."

The next morning his parents left for the airport, his mother clutching her purse close to her side. She kissed him quickly on both cheeks before she got into the rental car, her lips cool.

When he was a toddler, a young boy, even an adolescent

she had fastened to his every act: how urgent her love had been, how full. There had been no difference between them, his mother and a refuge.

But in the past few years her interest had diminished until it seemed almost to equal her interest in other persons, until he was merely another among them. In ceasing to be a child, he thought, he had disappointed her so fully that she came to believe he was someone else entirely. With this new person she could have civil conversations; with this person she could walk, eat, or drive. But he was no longer hers and due to that she was no longer his either.

Falling asleep at night or walking down a deserted street, craning his neck to look up at the dizzying stars, he made his mind busy by leaving the present behind and situating himself in a moment that was yet to be. As a child he had lived in the present; now he lived in the future; soon, how soon he would live in the past, an older man nostalgic and nodding.

And yet each was its own delight, each relation to time. In the first long moment of life nothing was recognized beyond the present; there was no past to look back to and no idea of the future yet. In the second moment the present was shed in favor of a future that hovered but never arrived, the promise of a realized self; and then that moment passed too. In the third moment, as life declined, the future disappeared, the present was diminished, and all that remained was the past. He was now in the lucky moment of forwardness—this time now—where seeing the future dawn was how he was sustained.

Step forward, he told himself, step, step, step, daily into the night, nightly into the day! The unknown shimmers there. There was a paradise still to come.

He might wonder how much velocity should guide him

and how much calculation; he might wonder this with deli-
beration, a delicious mulling. It was part of the reward to
dwell on strategy. Then, for a moment, it would strike him
that the future was sad.

He had already lost something, and in any future it would
still be missing—if not his mother's love, then the fierceness
of it. It could not be called back.

But by the square light of day he did not dwell on this or
even recall it. Fleetingly it would come to him, as he did
something else: not all things could be perfectly arranged;
not all things were correctible.

This gave him a start of recognition. Then it passed.

•

During his four years in college—his only vices coffee, a stiff
scotch and soda some evenings before dinner, and the occa-
sional cigar—he produced the results he desired, and was
gratified to see how effort and control could yield steady
returns. This was no myth; it was a law of nature.

He studied the words of Adam Smith and William
Jennings Bryan and even J. Paul Getty, the parent of such
phrases as "The meek shall inherit the Earth, but not its
mineral rights." He read old texts with great pleasure,
particularly those written by certain stalwart Puritans whose
parsimony seemed born of a voluptuous and secret greed.
He combed through the texts for signs of this sinful
covetousness—a pornography of spirit, for nothing was more
of a guilty pleasure than the greed of those who believed
themselves righteous. He enjoyed the sermons of clergymen
like John Wesley, whom he understood to have advised his

flock it was by definition quite impossible to serve their God and mammon both—much as no color could be at once pure black and white—and thus no qualms of ethics should stand in the way of a good Christian man who wished to amass great wealth.

Surely little remained of the Puritan legacy of prudish rectitude, he thought: surely this was now a country of excess, gluttony, lust, and sloth; surely this had grown into a land where obesity reigned and even the poor moved ponderously down the street on big thighs that rubbed fatly together. What had become of the pilgrims' gaunt and stingy oversight? He knew in part it was the visionary genius of enterprising men, but such entrepreneurs were only the tools of a hungry culture. For the descendants of those gray, upright pioneers had cherished cravings for beef patties with ketchup, deep-fried chicken and vats of ice cream, chemically scented and dyed all the colors of the rainbow, and billions upon billions of gallons of soda. Their thirst had never been quite slaked and so they never finished drinking; and this was the market in all its streamlined functionality—which, precisely where the supply and the demand curves crossed, had swiftly produced a nation of paralyzed giants, fallen across their couches much as soldiers on the field of battle, their arteries hard, their softened hearts failing.

The market made a fool of you by giving you what you wanted. But this did not make him resent it; it merely earned his respect. From the day you were born you were called upon to discern what to choose.

If Ian Van Heysen and the other brothers did not often show him that capacity he had so treasured a mere ten years before—namely the tending of all people toward the enigmatic greatness suggested by a dollar bill—they could

not be blamed for it. There were times when he stooped to irritation; that he should be the steward of such a wayward flock was occasionally a burden.

But they were children with handicaps, though these handicaps were not always visible: ease, abundance, over-stimulation. He thought of their tendencies toward indolence and abuse as a temporary run through the gauntlet of privilege; they would grow out of their puckishness all too soon. For they were correct in believing this was their last hurrah, and most of them would age fast once the halls of the university pulled away behind them. He himself was disposed to a persistent cheerfulness that flew in the face of his rationality; he knew how fortunate he was. He had always been purposeful. But he could see in the faces of others how many were not so disposed, and likely never would be.

Before the rest of life there were hijinks, the joys of brash ignorance and selfishness. But he did not begrudge them their entertainment. It was increasingly clear to him that the company of straight men was seldom a pleasure for other straight men. What the fraternities offered was a last gasp of boyhood before the assumption of a purely adult identity, one that for most would bring loneliness. To each other, men were useful mostly for business: and it was through their ranks that he must move on his forward trajectory, for they held the reins. But most of them lacked important social skills beyond the manipulation of power; most were unable to muster even the pretense of intimacy with others of their gender. This was particularly true among the wealthier classes, where, absent a clear oppressor, there was little need for solidarity.

Moreover most men, he suspected, agreed with him, though they seldom admitted it. Their peers were largely competitors; their wives became all they knew, socially. This was why after they married they rarely looked beyond their

houses again, unless it was for the purpose of changing wives. Meanwhile, at their sides but otherwise occupied, the wives maintained a wide array of friends.

And it became clear to him that his early mentors—the founders, the dead sages of the judiciary—did not have modern counterparts in government. The great roofs that had sheltered them were raised now not over heads of state but over the motile geniuses of corporate novelty; these men now wore the mantles formerly worn by the fathers of the nation-state. They held up economies and reshaped them at will. After the robber barons had come the technophile visionaries, the practical philosophers of earning, and they, not the government men, were the new kingmakers.

He read their bestsellers.

Meanwhile the discipline of watching stocks, keeping up with his classes and managing the welfare of his peers kept him busy, and he was seldom melancholy. And if, when he was roasted along with his fellow fraternity officers shortly before graduation, he felt slightly needled by the remarks about his stodginess, the allusions to Fred MacMurray in *My Three Sons*, the denigration of his manhood implied by such terms as *monk* and *eunuch* in reference to his lack of prurient interest in the fairer sex, he gave no evidence of such. He laughed at every boyish jab and raised his tumbler of Glemorangie from his seat at the head table, and when the fraternity president dealt him a manly clap on the shoulder during the applause he only smiled and shook his head with good humor, to say: How cleanly have the arrows met their mark.

•

Five months after he left the fraternity and the small green town he made his first six-figure profit, not in fact by trading—which he would subsequently give up as a job, though not as an avocation—but by brokering the sale of a derelict apartment building.

It was a building on a beach in south Florida, owned by an aging heiress whose long-dead father had made his fortune growing sugarcane in the Everglades; T. had met the heiress at school through his father, who had pledged with her son Brad. He visited her after graduation, out of politeness, and she offered him the commission. In this way all the hours of his indentured servitude, his careful stewardship of the brothers and many small defenses of their honor were repaid instantly.

Shortly before the sale Brad took him on a tour of the old sugarcane plantation, where they stepped over piles of crumbling yellow brick that had once been the walls of a manor house and looked out over a soggy field of cattails. By way of explaining the recent repossession of his BMW—it had left him driving a cheap rental car for which he felt the need to apologize—Brad gestured to the canefields and said, smirking, "Big Sugar belong to Big Mama."

On behalf of the mother, and for a modest percentage, T. sold the building to a hotel chain at a price far beyond her original asking.

Several weeks later the gentle old lady sank into a coma, leaving Brad crowing with glee at his suddenly liquid assets and believing firmly that T.—whom he called "this serious, intense guy," because T. did not laugh at his jokes—had been

his salvation. His patronage, and the praise he repeated in various old-boy circles, would prove vital to T.'s fledgling enterprise.

Around the same time the nightly news was prone to show millions succumbing to famine, far away in a sandy country. More popular than the news was a sit-com about an arrogant bartender and a frigid waitress, which T. watched every week with a female neighbor. He was living near Wall Street in a bare suite of rooms in a high rise; the neighbor was an emaciated model who got into the habit of dropping by with a bottle of bad wine and a packet of good cocaine exactly five minutes before the program began. The cocaine was for her; he partook of the wine; and there was a tacit agreement for sex when the program ended. The model, doe-eyed, quiet, and with low self-esteem, made no demands on him beyond their weekly appointment. When they passed in the hallway in the days between, she slouched past him with her head down and her doe eyes averted.

"Hey," he said once, for an experiment. She nodded almost imperceptibly and shrank back against the wall.

He regarded the arrangement cautiously, grateful for her favors but reluctant to take them for granted, and his caution proved well-founded. After an episode in which the bartender proposed to the waitress and was refused, and before an episode in which the waitress spied on the bartender's date with another woman, his neighbor was found in her kitchen with open veins. The man who discovered her was apparently her boyfriend. She was carted off to rehab and would never return to the building.

For a week or two T. watched the program alone; then he stopped. He thought of the model with remorse and slight wonder: but there was no place for him in any of it.

He called his parents' house a few days after she left.

His mother could barely muster the energy to speak to him, preferring only to listen. This had become common-place between them. She claimed that she liked him to call, that she wanted to hear what he was doing: but when he did call the conversation was purely one-sided. He recited a litany of his activities into the receiver, falling into a rhythm defined by her silences; for when he asked what was new in her own life he would invariably hear, "Oh, you know, dear. Nothing much." This he would counter with a further inquiry—"Well, then, what have you been *doing*?"—but this would meet with the same answer, until he gave up asking. It was as though nothing much stretched through her days, nothing much united and guided them: in the whole of her experience there was never event.

His father was always busy or sleeping or engrossed in a television show, and did not come to the phone at all.

Soon he decided he needed a change. It would have to be New York or Los Angeles, since these were where both life and business happened; and so he moved to southern California, where he incorporated for the purpose of buying and selling real estate.

He liked the curving drive up the rocky coast from the angels to the Franciscans, sweeping past on his left the wide-open Pacific, on his right the rolling hills of chaparral that cost a thousand dollars per square foot. He liked the fact that specu-lators tended to ignore the foreshortened future of the hills, their promise of imminent collapse by mudslide, quake or fire.

And when he struck out east across the inland empire to the desert of Palm Springs, the air-conditioning in his S-Class raising goose bumps on his skin, he felt a legion of tycoons riding shotgun. He could almost detect their quaint presence in gas stations along the barest stretches of the freeway. There

behind the counter, where sparkles in the white formica leant an air of yesteryear, sat a disheveled Howard Hughes bent over a bottle of milk; or there beside the newspaper rack stood William Randolph Hearst, paging though a tabloid. He grew to see greatness in open space, which fostered the illusion of a last frontier; for out West, where there were few monuments to the founders of the Republic, there was instead a breathless intuition of novelty.

At twenty-two he had an office in Santa Monica and two assistants much older than he, one in her mid-thirties, the other fifty-three. What might have seemed an awkward age discrepancy to someone of different character made no impression on him; he knew only that all the job applicants in their twenties had been incompetent. Various could not spell, add, or type, two did not remember his name after he shook their hands, and one came into the room wearing earphones, which she did not take off until several minutes after he began speaking to her; a dumpy woman with large, frizzy hair told him she enjoyed Primal Scream Therapy. If he had even briefly thought to find himself the proud employer of a secretary young, smart, coy and possibly wearing bright lipstick, this vanished when the interviews began.

Finally he was satisfied with his choice of amanuensis; that she was almost his mother's age was to him unworthy of note, since she was smart and came to respect his own efficiency, first in planning, then in making money. He knew that when she took the job she believed it might not last, but within weeks she trusted him and was even somewhat deferential. She hired for him a second woman, also competent, who handled contracts and bookkeeping.

The two were quiet and kept to themselves, though on occasions such as holidays or his birthday they would step forward with small tokens. Further they sent a rare orchid on

his behalf for Mother's Day, without needing to ask; on Angela's birthday and Christmas they delivered Bonsai trees and shiitake mushroom logs. This seemed to please her and made T. feel, for his part, that he was treating her well. He kept Susan's and Julie's birthdays and anniversaries of hire on record and made sure never to overlook them. He knew Susan was married and had a daughter who was in a wheelchair; he knew Julie had an old and incontinent cat named Bookchin and shunned Christmas in favor of a holiday called Kwanzaa. He had never heard of this holiday before he met her.

"It's a Swahili word. It celebrates the African-American community," she told him.

"I see," he nodded, though he was confused since Julie was a Caucasian Protestant from Milwaukee.

"I personally observe it as a gesture of solidarity."

"Very thoughtful," he said. "Are there, uh, certain special days? Rituals?"

"Basically it's a harvest festival. To celebrate the crops."

"African-American harvest," he said, nodding.

She and Susan were his only intimates in the city; he trusted them, in part for their capable hands and in part for the puzzle of their willingness to labor indefinitely in menial positions, which linked them to him in a pact of loyalty.

What wings lifted him then, what banks shored him up along the river of work? Not the mechanics of the deal: rather it was the faces and the words of those he moved through and past and with in seeking his object, the nuance of his own approach in knowing and predicting the impulses and calculations behind them, that captured his interest. In pitching his company's plans or services it fell to him to read the tics and quirks of investors as he sat across from them in restaurants, county commissioners as he rode the elevator beside them, urban planners across tables in well-lit rooms.

He caught the small tells that accompanied a lie, the fluster and the cover-up that followed an inadvertent truth, the way these varied among persons: but he was most astute in that he gave the appearance of being caught up in his own velocity when in fact his mind was carefully fixed on the other.

Although always watchful, always wedded to the close observation of detail, he pretended otherwise. He projected a confident nonchalance, an air of serene neutrality, and with this attitude would casually make reference to vast sums. The rules for his own comportment were few and simple, and first among them was, always speak as though unimpressed by large figures; always convey the impression that the grandiose is commonplace.

And so it will be.

In time he planned to leave development and begin to forge a path elsewhere. It wasn't that he needed to be well-known — he would be happy to be the gray eminence behind a publicly traded logo — more that he wanted to have a hand in the revolutions of the market itself, in the ebb and the flow. But he needed to make connections. That other people found a community easily struck him as mysterious; the city was a wide network of generic streets and buildings, among which small figures were suspended in casual segregation. The space between them was air and metal. Mainly it was air, though also concrete and sheetrock and glass.

How was this air to be bridged?

Finally he joined an exclusive racquet club whose monthly membership dues would have paid the rent on a small mansion; a dully middle-class clientele would be no use to him. He hired a racquetball instructor and went to the courts four or five times a week; when he was competent he wrote his name down on lists. His games were played with

older men mostly, who shook his hand with a too-firm grip beforehand and afterward wore their white towels around their necks and talked to him at their lockers while they sprayed their armpits for too long with powerful deodorants. He averted his eyes from their stocky and hairy bodies as they changed, the deep tans that looked like plum-colored bruises in the hollows of their sagging chests. He walked with them out to the parking lot. One showed him a motorcycle; another tried to interest him in sex. Most had wives and girlfriends and business cards, and some of them had capital to invest.

One of the younger players, name of Fulton, was blustering and arrogant and tried hard to impress. He spoke in jocular terms of his wife's intimacies and wanted T. to be aware of the dimensions of his new power yacht, anchored over in the Marina, which had platinum bathroom fixtures; he made sure that T. knew the cost of his redwood cabin in Tahoe.

"What the hell do you do for fun, man?" asked Fulton, after a game T. had played neatly but without much vigor. "All work and no play."

"I'm a dull boy," said T. "Granted. But if you've got cash sitting around you're not doing much with, I can make you more than a ten percent return on your money. Far more."

"Color me hooked," said Fulton. "Wanna pick up a beer?"

Over the beers T. pulled out a copy of his business plan and prospectus, at which Fulton barely glanced. He pitched the current project steadily—the purchase and renovation of an industrial park on a Superfund site—and Fulton nodded generously, though in fact, T. suspected, he understood almost nothing. But he liked to use words that implied he was in the know, and to be treated as though he was not faking it.

Still, T. assumed it was a waste of time until three beers in.

"Get your lawyer to write up the whole deal and fax it to my guy," said Fulton. "But we gotta go in slow till I see what you're made of. Few hundred K to start."

They stayed at the bar for some hours. T. had the nagging suspicion there was still something to be secured, details to hammer out. It had been so easy it seemed impossible. Likely the man had no money, finally, and was playing him.

At last the drinks trailed off and it was time to go, and it dawned on T., as they walked along the sidewalk back to the parking lot, that though Fulton had almost nothing to say, what he chiefly wanted was someone to listen.

When they reached a white Cadillac, one of a fleet of personal vehicles Fulton apparently owned, he turned the key in the ignition to show T. the dashboard in the dark, a vast expanse of red and indigo lights. Rap music blared: it turned out that Fulton, despite several racist remarks at the bar, enjoyed gangsta rap. "When I'm called off, I got a sawed off. Squeeze the trigger, and bodies are hauled off," he recited loudly, tapping the steering wheel.

T. tried to take his leave with a handshake, but Fulton insisted on a high-five.

He spent his evenings and his sleep alone and was satisfied: what he loved was to ride in after these quiet nights, these black nights of deaf and solitary thought, into the world of day, where sound enfolded him and he could scramble over chaos to order again. He liked to be away from people and then suddenly face-to-face: all in a rush they would converge, burning with self-interest like pillars of fire. He listened to them and learned to know the difference between what was said and what was meant, and—save with men like Fulton, who had no interest in concealing themselves—this was the key to all lesser insights. What

people valued and professed to value were quite different objects, and he made constant note of this, always refining his study.

There was variation, of course, but there were many common replacements. When they said they wanted passion, they meant the feeling of novelty; instead of what was beautiful, they wanted what affirmed; instead of a challenge, an easy victory that others believed to be hard-won. Instead of God, a father who showed his love; instead of Jesus, a friend who proved his love; instead of faith, a mother who loved them with a love that never changed.

2

He killed her driving to Las Vegas, after a truck stop and a few bites of a turkey club served by a waitress with lurid curling fingernails; after a dingy restroom whose yellow urinal mints made him turn away in disgust. He was still in a state of repulsion when he emerged from the diner into twilight. Then the feeling fled: there was a dusky earthshadow in the east, a dim violet light that made even the asphalt look soft.

Driving up the freeway on-ramp he turned the radio on and knew the smoothness of his buttery seat leather against the backs of his thighs. He was satisfied; he was easing in. Then a shape, blurred and fast from the right, and he hit it. The car bumped over it and veered off the road onto the shoulder. He jammed the brake pedal to the floor and sat shaking.

Dust rose behind and beside him, and his two right wheels were off the shoulder pavement. He looked out the window behind him to see if there were other cars coming. What was that on the road? What was hit?

He could see a mound on its side, legs outstretched. His own legs shook with delayed fear but there was already a stream of headlights behind the animal. No time. He pushed his door open and ran back toward it, stomach weak and face hot. He tasted dust and iron on his tongue.

A coyote. People said they were pests. They took pets out of yards in the suburbs, ran off with children's kittens.

He was briefly relieved: no one to be angry at him, no owner. But everything was too fast. The cars were closer, the headlights brighter, and the whine of a horn made him lurch sideways in alarm. A truck swerved around him. He closed his eyes and slowed his breath. Its back legs were pulp. Jesus! He winced looking at them. But he had to move it. It could not stay in the road. It could cause another accident.

He leaned down and put his arms around the front, picked up the body with its head lolling against his chest, the rear half sagging. It was curiously light for its size and left a sweep of blood on the blacktop when he dragged it.

He let it go as quickly as he could, safely out of traffic. He stood there gazing down, his chest clutching. But then he saw its flank moving. It breathed. It was still alive. It could have bitten him. Did coyotes bite people? They were always shrinking away; they slunk along the roadside and veered off into brush as the headlights swept over them. He looked into its face, the muzzle sharp at the nose like a fox but somehow humble-mouthed like a dog; the light eyes, which were open and seemed to see him.

"Oh," he said, and knelt down. It would not bite. It was dying. And if it did, he thought, that meant it was planning to live.

It made a sound from its throat—a growl, maybe. If he had a gun he could shoot it. Because Jesus: the legs! Nothing should have to bear that.

"Good boy. Quiet there, boy," he said uncertainly. It probably did not want him near; he should back off. Better to die alone if you were an animal like this one, a loner that avoided any contact with humans. He looked past the flank to the underbelly; nothing there. The poor thing was a bitch. "Steady, girl," he said. "It's OK."

He stood creakily and stepped back, but somehow he could not leave. He went to sit in his car. He waited, listening to a country music station.

But he was restless and anxious and soon he got out again to see if she was dead yet. He had an idea he should move her, once she was gone; he should carry her into the brush, where she could go to ground.

He willed himself not to look at her legs, to try to ignore what was back there bleeding, the cracked bone tapering into nothing. He looked only at her face and her side to see if she was still breathing. But despite the fact that he was not looking, as he sat beside her, he imagined the shock from the ruined legs coursing though her body, what must be the blind surge of the pain as the end closed in. A loud end—the rush of cars still distant punctuated by the searing noise and glare of those approaching, bearing down viciously and then fading again. She was dying in the smells of asphalt, exhaust, and gasoline, no doubt also the smell of her own blood, and him, and other smells he could not know himself.

The fullness, the terrible sympathy!

Had he felt this before, he wondered? Maybe when he was a boy? Animals died by the road and you saw that all the time, everyone did. You saw them lying there, so obvious in their deadness, sad lumps of dirty meat; you saw their limp furry masses thrown up like flowers along the yellow stripes, the tumbly asphalt edges. You saw the red insides all exposed. You thought: that is the difference between them and me. My insides are firmly contained.

And were *I* to lie on the side of the road dying, it would be nothing like that. No one would drive around *me*: the cars would stop, tens upon hundreds of them; there would be lines of stopped traffic for miles as they removed my body, flashing their red and blue lights of crisis and competence.

Presently he realized her flank had ceased to rise and fall. He was relieved but oddly disoriented. Where was the ambulance? No: he was all that she had. All her lights, all her rescue workers.

It was just a coyote. No one would fault him for leaving.

And yet he felt confused.

"Good girl," he whispered.

•

Back in Los Angeles he traded in the S-Class, chose a modest 190 to replace it and drove off the lot quickly. Irrational, but he had to get rid of it.

We all kill sooner or later, he said to himself, fine. Was she maybe half-blind? Maybe when they got old they went blind and could not hunt anymore, as birds died by starving. Maybe she had been feeble and exhausted and thought, trotting onto the blacktop for the last time: welcome, friend. All the times she must have seen the cars fly by, in their hundreds and hundreds of thousands.

But no. A coyote might want relief from suffering, but to plan for her own end seemed human.

Still a particular moment recurred within him, the sense of a rising pity he could not repress, in which he sank like a stone and could not get to the surface again. He saw the coyote's face as she lay in the dirt of the road, eyes half-closed,

the long humble line of her mouth. He thought of the crushed legs. He asked the pain if it was sharp or dull and throbbing; he asked pain, he asked the coyote, he was left in silence.

Any animal could be gentle while it was busy dying, he told himself. That was hardly a mark of distinction. But the sorrow persisted, as though he was worrying an open cut.

In his house growing up there had never been pets. He had wanted one, of course. But his mother said dogs and cats left their hair on the furniture and smelled, so he tried asking for gerbils, guinea pigs, and then hamsters; his mother said rodents in cages reproduced and smelled, birds squawked and smelled, reptiles had scales and smelled, and even butterflies—which he had once been given in the form of a caterpillar kit in a colorful jar his mother would not let him open—seemed pretty at first but would soon die and smell too. The only pets that were smell-proof were fish, due to their immersion in water.

These, however, she also rejected, on the grounds that they defecated. He recalled the conversation well even now. He had asked for goldfish, his last resort; he figured he could breed and sell them, be they ever so boring. His mother had shuddered and said, "They go right in their bowls with them, and then they breathe it in. They *poop* in the *water!*" To which T. replied—quite wittily, he thought—"Well, you do too." Then she had called him disgusting and sent him to his room. Lingering around the corner on the way upstairs he heard his father say, "Kid's got a point, Angie."

And while his mother was tolerant of animals, even curious about them as long as they stayed firmly where they belonged—that is, in paintings, stories, even stained-glass windows, but far from her living room—his father was simply indifferent. His father had little interest in anything that moved, beyond athletes on the small screen or the college

friends that called occasionally asking for contributions to the alumni fund. Pets seemed at best an unnecessary burden, at worst a lingering nuisance.

Yet a few weeks after the accident he found himself walking past the kennels at the Humane Society, thinking this was how caution got thrown to the winds. He chose a thin, middle-aged dog, white with tan markings, a homely but intelligent face and a tendency to back away, frightened, whenever he made a sudden movement. At first he was not sure what to do, glancing at her speculatively from his armchair as she lay on the floor beside him. An animal was with him, an animal *companion*. Arbitrary, he thought, arbitrary. The dog seemed superfluous, a being without purpose. He gazed at her muzzle resting on her front paws and wondered if she suspected his coldness.

But as the days passed he found himself growing fonder, almost as though their positions reversed: he was faithful now and she was ambivalent. Still she learned to trust him and he began to feel, as he watched her eat and grow stronger, various anxieties allayed.

And finally he looked forward, at the end of the workday, to going home. If he had business engagements in the evening he drove to the apartment first, snapped the leash to her collar and walked her along the path on the beach, listening to the waves and watching her tail wag as she trotted ahead of him. Outside she was far less fearful than indoors, as though a weight lifted when the ceiling above her disappeared. This puzzled him till he realized that whoever had beaten her had not done so in public.

He was on the telephone discussing the details of a condominium conversion in Laguna Beach when Susan knocked on his office door and pushed it open, flustered. Behind her

stood his mother, who sat down heavily in the chair on the other side of his desk.

As he hastily cradled the receiver he saw his mother's makeup was smeared; around her eyes the mascara had streaked and the eyeliner run. She was bedraggled and for the first time in his life he could see gray at the roots of her blond hair.

"What are you *doing* here?" he asked. She had never visited him in Los Angeles.

"Your father's gone," she said, and began to cry noisily, pulling a clump of wrinkled pink tissues from her purse.

He felt a wave of shock. He forced himself to get up.

"Gone? What do you mean, gone?" he asked, and came from behind the desk to kneel beside her with an awkward palm on her shoulder. He wondered if he should embrace her, but she did not turn to face him.

"I don't know. Gone!" she wailed, and hunched over sobbing.

I don't know, he thought. So not dead.

He stood and rubbed her back lightly with the heel of his hand, in circles, waiting with what he hoped seem like patience; he shook his head at Susan when she opened the door and mouthed *Can I do anything?*

Finally his mother finished crying and blew her nose.

"Here," he said, and guided her to the sofa against the wall. "It's more comfortable here."

She sat down and instantly looked wretched and pathetic, so he sat down beside her. Wiping at her eyes with one of the balled-up tissues she only succeeded in spreading the black smears.

"Now take a deep breath and tell me what happened," he said. "OK?"

"I just woke up and he was gone," she said. "And he didn't leave a note and he never called me."

"And when was this?" asked T.

"Three weeks ago," she said quietly.

"Three weeks? It's been *three weeks* and you haven't told me before this?"

"I went to the police but they just looked at me like . . . this one policeman looked at me meanly. It was very mean the way he looked at me."

"No doubt he failed sensitivity training."

"Your father took exactly half the money from our joint accounts. I think he's, you know. *Left* me."

"I can't believe it," said T., shaking his head dully. "Did you—I mean—"

"We weren't fighting," she said. "We never fought."

"So everything was—"

"It was fine," said his mother. "It was the same as it's always been."

"So you were—he was—happy?"

"Apparently not," she snapped.

"I meant—"

"We weren't having relations, if that's what you mean."

T. turned away from her and examined a potted plant, one Susan and Julie had given him called an asparagus fern. He closed his eyes for a second and opened them again on the fern. It had not moved, of course.

Meanwhile his mother was rummaging around in her purse, pulling out a purple rosary, a wallet with a checkbook, a pair of tweezers, a lipstick, a comb, keys, mints, and spreading them on the sofa on her other side.

"That's none of my business," he said softly.

"Not for years," she went on, "many, many years," shaking her head, and T. got up abruptly, experiencing minor palpitations. He wanted to block his ears.

"He hasn't been in touch with you?"

"Nothing. He did use the credit card a few times. Once he got gas in Michigan. It was a Texaco. Or no, it was Exxon. No, Texaco."

There was silence in the office for a few long seconds, broken only by the faint blare of a horn out the window. His mother found a compact in the spillings from her purse and snapped it open.

"Oh! Lord!" she said, and rubbed vigorously at the mascara. "Why didn't you say something, T.? This is a time in her life when a woman has to look decent. Where's my cold cream?"

"Here," he said, and lifted a small blue pot from between the sofa cushions. "Is this it?"

She grabbed the pot and opened it, and while she spread the white cream around her eyes kept up a rapid patter.

"Mary Louise called from the K of C office and asked if we were going to come for the meningitis evening. I was so humiliated. You can't go to those things by yourself. They have kids up on the stage that have bravely survived. But then they go deaf or retarded. Water on the brain. It's always this overcooked salmon. Two hundred a plate. I don't know where he is! He could be anywhere! What should I say? What if I tell everyone and then he decides to come back and it turns out I never had to tell them at all?"

"Is that what you're worried about? Is that your main worry?"

"It's time for my car's thirty-thousand-mile service, I got a notice from the dealership. He always takes it in. The lights give me migraines. The fluorescents. What if it just breaks down on me and I have to walk miles in the dark to a pay-phone to call triple-A and I get raped on the way? That would be his fault then!"

"No one's being ravished, OK? Here. Do me a favor. Can you just slow down a minute? Sit back and relax. Close your eyes and breathe deeply. Would you do that?"

"Don't talk to me like I'm crazy! I am your *mother*, T.!"

"Of course you are. And I'm your son and I'm worried about you."

She looked at him blinking, and he thought she was considering his words until he noticed she was not looking at him but over his shoulder.

"And what is *that*?"

He turned and followed her gaze. It was a pencil sketch by a famous expressionist. He had bought it at a Sotheby's auction.

"It's art, Mother."

"Don't be ridiculous."

But she seemed mollified, and began to pack her personal items back into her purse.

"Let me take you to my place, OK? I'll make you dinner."

"I'm not hungry."

"Then maybe just a cup of tea."

"I'm not an invalid, you know. I'm just a woman whose husband walked out the door. For all I know he's doing it with his secretary."

"He took early retirement. He doesn't have a secretary."

"You know what I mean. Some random floozy."

"Let's just go, OK? Let's talk about this when you're rested."

"And I don't need to stay with you. I made my own arrangements. I have a room in a four-star hotel."

"Well, *I* need you to stay. Come on. Come home with me."

Weeks later she was still in his guest bedroom. He did not always mind and was even glad, at times, that she was there, but in terms of progress her presence threatened to reduce him. She was a liability.

He liked to present himself as solitary and free, an argument for potential; he moved and spoke with the official neutrality of a man sprung fully formed from the background of commerce. But now suddenly he carried personal freight, which threatened to hold him back. He cringed at the thought of business associates encountering his mother, whether by design or accident. He did not want his investors, for instance, to think of him beholden to a mother, childlike. And she was bad for his image, far too frail and specific to reflect the broadness of his interests and his command of prospects.

The most austere among his investors, in fact, the ones who had wide ocean views out their office windows, gave the impression of never having been born at all. They would die, admittedly, that much was tacitly conceded; but this was understood to be almost a polite gesture on their part, part of a genteel tradition whereby the old bowed out into the wings to make room for the young.

So they would die, when their race was run, but they had never been born: they had not been children. They had not ever been anything but what they were now. And he would not make the concession either.

Still his mother was pathetic, hurt and lonely. He could not bring himself to hurt her further.

When he was at the office she walked the dog three times a day; arriving home he found his laundry washed and folded, shirts hung in the closet by color, mail carefully sorted. She busied herself with the housework usually done by the cleaning woman, and when for the first time since his mother's arrival the cleaning woman arrived and let herself in she found a screaming middle-aged blonde in a kaftan and every surface spotless.

His mother rearranged dry goods and crockery and occupied herself changing drawer liners and purchasing items for

which he had no use, such as fondue forks and silver napkin rings. In corners of his apartment things sprang up that bore no relation to him. On the toilet tank, a china shepherdess with rouged cheeks and a crook and a curly-haired lamb at her feet; on a wall in the foyer, a framed picture of angels accompanied by a homily; on the arms of a leather sofa, elaborate lace sleeves.

"I don't remember," he mused over dinner on the day the shepherdess appeared, "you decorating our house this way when I was growing up."

"What way?" asked his mother.

She insisted on cooking for him every night; the meals were low-fat and almost completely devoid of flavor. He had taken to eating a fast-food hamburger on his way home from the office.

"You know—the thing you put in the bathroom, the Little Bo Peep thing."

"You don't like it?" asked his mother, her spoon suspended halfway to her lips, trembling.

He heard something in her tone and noticed her eyes were brimming.

"It's not that," he said hastily. "I wouldn't have picked it out myself, per se, is all I meant."

"You needed somewhere to put the guest soaps," she said, and resumed eating. "You can't expect guests to use the same soap you use. It's not hygienic."

"What the hell good is soap if it's not hygienic?"

"You get your germs on it. Or from shaving. A hair could stick to it."

"I appreciate all your efforts," he said. "I love having you here, and I know the dog does too. But maybe you should focus on yourself, for once. You know? There are good day spas in walking distance. Susan made up a list for you. Or

you could take one of those weekend cruises to the Catalinas."

"When will you stop treating me like the walking wounded, T.? I'm fine. I like to keep busy."

"I realize. But I think you've been looking after someone, two people, right?—for the last twenty years of your life . . ."

"Twenty-three. Thirty-three if you count from when we got married, which you probably should. That man hasn't ironed his own shirts since 1963."

". . . and maybe you need to stop looking after other people and look after yourself. Concentrate on what you want, what you need. Because my guest soap is, let's face it, not yet at the level of a national emergency."

"You don't like it, do you? It's an antique. It is *Dresden china*, T. From Dresden, Germany."

"Mother? I'm not entirely sure you're listening to me."

"They're famous for their china. Wonderful workmanship. Little blue marks . . . I may be alone, my husband may have left me, but I know how lucky I am, T. At least I know that."

"I'm sure—"

"You know what we did to Dresden in 1945? Your father had friends who were pilots in the air war. And some of them—we're talking about boys who were eighteen years old here, T., barely out of puberty who still had facial acne—they talked about trying them as war criminals. Their superiors told them they had to bomb Dresden, so they did. Some of them were shot down. They still had *facial acne*."

She gazed at him balefully.

"You know what happened with the carpet bombing? There were fires that burned at fifteen hundred degrees. The cold air rushed in from outside and all the people got sucked into the flames and burned to death in terrible agony. Those

were someone's friends, T. Their friends and their families. They had friends and someone was friends with them. Someone lost their friends then."

"Uh . . ."

"Hundreds of thousands of someone's friends burned to death then, screaming."

He tried to catch her eye but she picked up a salt shaker.

"They were someone's friends and they saw right out of their eyes, like you do. They watched things pass, there was nothing they could do about the world. Nothing they could ever do."

"Are you—"

"And what did they get for wanting? They wanted the world to be different, T. You can be sure of that. They *wanted* the world to be a good place, full of holiness and wonder. We all do."

"It—"

"But what did they get? They got burning to death."

"Lis—"

"They got watching their children burn. Their children and their babies. *Babies*, T. Little children, toddlers holding their toys, babies with those wide eyes . . . mothers had to watch their children die right in front of them, trapped in the burning buildings. Children die faster than adults. And their mothers had to watch it. Choking from smoke inhalation while they burned to death. Hundreds and thousands of babies. Watching them cry that sweet baby cry as their little faces burned away to a crisp."

She spooned up her soup, shaking her head. His own utensils lay untouched on the placemat.

"And you don't like that poor china girl holding the cute baby sheep? Talk about looking a gift horse in the mouth."

There was a tinge of hysteria, certainly.

She paused to reach for the salad tongs and he leaned forward and laid a hand on her arm.

"Mother. Listen," he said gently. "Isn't it sort of a stretch? The firebombing of Dresden and my opinion of a toilet ornament?"

She shook her head, frustrated.

"Your generation thinks that wanting means getting. But most of the people in the whole world . . . for them what they want has nothing to do with their life, with what their life actually is."

"I realize that."

"Here people want something, they get it, and they say that's, you know, happiness. Or success. And those other people, those poor people everywhere . . . I mean there's nothing to envy, they live in terrible privation and I pray for them every day, but one thing they have you and your friends will never have."

"What's that?"

"Longing, dear. Longing makes the soul. Without it . . ."

She gazed at him sadly.

". . . the soul has nothing. It just gets forgotten."

What rose in him was tenderness—he was sorry. He wanted to comfort her.

•

His father called him one day at work. He stepped out of a meeting in his conference room to take the call at his desk.

"Hey, kid."

A forced tone of good cheer.

"Where the hell are you?"

"I'm just driving. Stopped for a cup of coffee. Wanted to let you know I'm doing A-OK."

"You need to call my mother. You've been together thirty years, you can't tell her you're taking off?"

There was a dull buzz on the other end of the line.

"Dad? You hang up?"

"You know, there comes a time . . ."

His father's voice trailed off.

"She's staying at my house. Call her on the phone there. She's the one you need to talk to."

"Easier said than done, my boy."

"I'm not saying it's easy. I'm saying it's your duty."

There was silence on the line again.

"It's not a mid-life crisis, you know."

"You already had one of those. When you got the hair plugs."

"This is not a mid-life crisis."

"I need for you to call *her* now. This is between the two of you. Seriously, you don't think you owe it to her? A few words?"

"Did you ever have a dream so real it felt like you were awake?"

"Uh, yeah. I guess."

"What if one day you woke up and you realized your whole life had been a dream like that? Your whole life, from some point where you fell asleep, was only a dream. The kind that tricks you into thinking you're wide awake."

T. was quiet, waiting. He looked around his office, the receiver pressed against his ear, and thought he saw a shade descend on it, roll dimness down the walls. A cloud had moved in front of the sun: his office had a weather all its own, and here he was, suddenly old. With the night coming on.

"My whole life was like that," went on his father, over the static. "From when I left college, from something I did then. I mean I never chose a single thing, when I look back on it. When I married your mother I wasn't really awake. I wasn't awake when she had you. I never woke up once for all these years. It was just not real to me. You know who you were looking at, the whole time you grew up? I was a ghost. I wasn't really there. It was all, I don't know, some other guy's life I stepped into by mistake."

T. felt drunken, his legs heavy beneath the desk. He swiveled in his chair and sadness closed his throat. There they were in his bedroom, when he was a little boy. His father sat on the side of his bed; it was bedtime, and here was his father to read him a story. Usually his mother read the stories, but this time his father had left the television and come upstairs. He almost smelled the new fresh paper of the picture book; he saw his father's large hands turning the pages with deftness, with authority. In the book there was a family of beavers, and they lived in a dam. Inside the dam it was warm and golden, and the beavers ate their dinner at a round wooden table. He remembered the softness of his father's voice.

Not real to his father; a life lived by a stranger. Sitting there on the side of his bed, reading the book about the beavers who were warm in their dam, had been no one.

"Until a month ago. That's when I woke up. It was sudden, like an alarm clock or something. Now I'm awake. It's too bad, but your mother is an innocent bystander. She's a casualty."

T. found he could not speak.

"I'll drop her a line, on down the road."

He barely heard the rest.

As soon as he got home his mother asked, as was her daily custom, whether his father had contacted him. He had fully intended to keep it from her—his father's callousness could hardly fail to do her an injury—but as he crossed the threshold into his apartment he saw, first, all the contents of his kitchen cabinets and drawers spread over the counters around her as she organized them, listening to golden oldies on a tinny clock-radio; and, second, the lettering on her apron, which pictured a slice of bright-red tomato and the words RIPE AND READY.

Exhaustion settled over him. He could not answer swiftly when she asked, and she was onto him.

"What? When? What did he say? Where is he?"

"I don't know," he said wearily.

"Did he say anything? What did he say?"

He moved past her to the refrigerator, whence he removed a bottle of water. Uncapping it, tipping it up and drinking thirstily, he closed his eyes: this moment by itself must restore him. He opened the back of his throat into a wide hollow and felt the water in it, cool and flowing.

When he lowered the bottle again she was staring at him, fever spots on her cheekbones. Her hands shook, clutching a baking sheet.

"He didn't tell me much. I told him he could call you here," he said, and instantly regretted it. He had asked, but his father had not called. And now he made it worse by telling.

"Is there another woman?"

"I don't think so."

"He didn't mention anyone? He's claiming that he's all alone? He didn't say where he was going?"

"No. He only said he was traveling," said T. faintly, and reluctantly pulled a stool up to the kitchen island. The dog rose from the floor and licked his hand.

"Traveling where?"

"He didn't say."

"So why did he call you, if he didn't want to tell you anything?"

"He wanted to tell me he was on a journey of self-discovery. He wanted to let me know he was alive."

His mother turned away, put down the baking sheet and picked up a shining triangular implement he did not recognize. No doubt she had purchased it for him. A cake knife, possibly.

"How nice for him," she said softly, and tipped the cake knife from one side to the next, watching the glint shifting.

While he was showering she went out without leaving a note; he waited for a while and then got into bed. At two in the morning a bartender called him. She had polished off a bottle of champagne, passed out in a bougainvillea, and was waiting to be picked up near Venice Beach.

"I must be allergic," she said to him, as he drove her home. She was still slurring her words.

He patted her knee.

"Drunk, we call it."

She gazed out the window until they pulled into the parking lot beneath his building. Then she stayed sitting, her eyes glassy. He walked around the car and opened her door for her.

"You're a good boy," she said fondly, and stumbled over the door lip. He caught her before she fell.

Finally he persuaded her to take a vacation. He loaded her suitcases into his car; he bought her a yellow rose, which she pinned to her lapel. Then he drove her to a cruise ship docked in San Diego, bound for Puerto Vallarta, Mazatlan, and Cabo. She wore a wide-brimmed hat and a white dress as

she walked up the gangplank; she waved at him from the rails smiling madly, as though there were streamers descending around her and theme music playing.

That night he took his dog onto the bed with him, a gesture his mother roundly condemned as unsanitary. In the deepest part of the night he woke up and listened to the dog breathe, the regular pace of the breathing. There was no moon, and through the thick drapes his mother had hung on his windows even the light of the city did not penetrate. He lay with his arms and legs frozen, imagining paralysis: he tried to feel the gradual freezing, the numbness that crept up into him. As a child he had done this.

Back then he had liked to play for a short time that he was something else. In the water he was a dead man, in the grass of the yard he was a fallen log. Then he forgot childish things.

The silence of the apartment was unaccustomed now, since his mother had often paced at night, washing and ironing, watching cable television and drinking instant decaffeinated coffee. Always if he woke there was the faint hum of activity beneath him. Before her, what? Now he barely remembered how his nights had been. Before his mother, the dog; before the dog, nothing. But now he was used to company.

He pushed back the covers and moved to the foot of the bed, where he lay next to the dog, along her warm back. His arms were pulled in close to his body and the dog's head was a few inches from his face. Could he sleep here, or would he be distracted?

For a while he was: he smelled the skin of the dog, the hair of the dog: he felt the dog's warmth. But patiently he waited for all this to pass, and tried to match their breathing.

And near morning, waking with goose bumps raised along his arms, he pulled the covers down around both of them.

•

Then his first golden egg, a swath of empty desert would be converted to subdivisions for retirees, with golf courses and Olympic-size swimming pools and luxury spas and a phalanx of nurses to monitor cardiac rhythms and tend to recovering hip and knee surgeries. Down the road, thanks to economies of scale and various state and federal subsidies, it might become a great citadel—light rail systems, a solar-powered mall. But in California nothing ambitious came without an array of planning difficulties and lawsuits from the liberal fringe, and soon enough there were cases in district court; he excused himself from conference calls with his public-relations consultants, which droned on and ate into his time on other undertakings.

The project stalled.

Meanwhile he got regular postcards from his mother, who claimed to have met "wonderful people" on the cruise and decided to fly from Yucatan to Guaymas with a claims adjuster from Toledo.

Dear T., read a postcard featuring a sombrero, *The weather is beautiful hear. You would not recognize me with my brown sun tan I look just like a native!! My espanol is muy better too.*

The court's opinion could easily go against his enterprise—he did not watch the details but this much was quite clear—so it was imperative to develop fall-back strategies. He must multiply his options, not wait for the court to decide his future—for when had he ever made of institutions his own enemy? They were his bulwarks, his cathedrals. It was for

him only to move on steadily on the assumption that the case and the development were already lost. Plainly nothing could be forfeited through such anticipation, everything gained. He instigated an aggressive search for high-margin properties and stocks and while immersed in the search let other matters gratefully fall away: his mother weeping on the toilet seat abjectly as she stroked the porcelain tresses of the shepherdess, his father who took no pains to hide his lack of conscience.

Setting himself to research he also ignored small matters at the office, failing to notice when Julie the paralegal, absent several days, returned from her sick leave with red-rimmed eyes and a white mark where her engagement ring had been; failing to return a call on his answering machine until the caller called again—his mother's next-door neighbor at the house she had vacated in Darien. A squirrel had become trapped inside and gnawed on the wooden window grilles until it died of starvation.

When his father left a stiff message on the machine, stating that he had completed a mandatory period of residency in Reno, Nevada, and subsequently secured a divorce, he erased the message impatiently.

Some mornings he woke with a nervous premonition of imminence: an event lay in wait. On the day his case was finally decided he had been up half the night researching a stock and even considered cocaine, increasingly popular with the upwardly mobile and visible everywhere. But he was not fully tempted. And then he heard. He had won. The project could move ahead.

That night, exhausted but jubilant after drinks at a bar, he lay back and watched a news segment featuring politicians. The faces on the small screen were interchangeable, not only with each other but with his own: quite possibly they were

not only his representatives but his representations. What was a face on television but a code, and what was the difference between these electronic faces but the realignment of line and color to shift among symbols? If he grasped deeply this language of symbols, grasped it beneath the surface, he would course through the currents of authority as they coursed through him like heat or the tremble of cold. That near! He moved in impulse and in fret; shot through with glowing nerves he willed himself on to the rest of what was. The tides shifted beneath him but he was holding fast.

That was what they didn't have, those men of state and industry, he thought before he fell asleep in the flickering blue light. They were hard vectors of self, undisturbed by the vestigial presence of others who were less powerful and therefore eternally unlike them. They did not have what those others had, the softness and the whimsy, the coasting— the others far outside their sphere who imagined and felt and enjoyed everything and ended up going nowhere because they needed nothing more than to be.

Fortunately he was not one of them.

•

She came with an investor to a cocktail-hour meeting one Friday and in minutes he was converted. Like all conversions his own was sudden. The lights of the restaurant bar bathed them in browns and reds and he watched her laugh. Where there should have been the awkwardness of strangers there was fluency. The investor went home to his wife after a short while, leaving the two of them at the counter, where they stayed and stayed on.

Beth, she had said. She was the investor's assistant. She did not give him her last name. She had erect posture, an effortless dignity and perfect light-brown skin. It was her self-possession that got him, though her features were also lovely. They drank too much as the evening wore on, became lightheaded and carefree: life was an arc in the air, ascending. Everything smaller was treated with a deft and glancing humor, and from the tops of the stools the skin of their knees touched briefly.

In the privacy of the bathroom, where he removed himself for a pause, he felt giddy, liberated and captive both. The bathroom was a confined space but he was hardly confined; nothing was tawdry around him, nothing filthy despite its superficial patina of dirt—or rather he forgave it for its tawdriness. The peeling stickers on the wall, graffiti, wet floors with patches of wet toilet paper adhering—surprising for an upscale establishment but then bathrooms were the main tell when it came to restaurant management, not what came out of the kitchen. All these elements were part of the story, the grounded earth before the flight. This was the instant of exulting, and even the grimy walls could not dull his exhilaration.

The room was a holding pen, a split moment. Outside the room was the rest of his existence. For years he had been detached and now in a stroke of time he was not. He would move, he would touch—no one would think to impede him, they would see him go and be glad—he could be anything. Do not embarrass yourself, he told himself strictly, but could not help smiling. There she was at the bar: their faces met before he got there.

This was how he lost his autonomy—he had moved along at a steady pace and then he was flung.

Around midnight she agreed to let him drive her home in her car. She had a low tolerance for alcohol and was slurring her words despite the fact that all she had drunk was watery Mexican beer with slices of lime. But his building was nearer than hers, and once in her car they decided to go there instead. He drove with one hand on the wheel and the other along the back of her seat; she curled in her seat to watch him as he drove. Music coursed through the car and both of them, he was sure, felt the uplift of the new. A bright panic filled him.

But when they pulled into the parking garage there was his mother—sitting, her suitcases around her, at the base of the stairs that led up to the lobby. She was darkly tanned and smoking a thin cigarette. A few feet away stood a man in a white suit, also tanned and smoking.

"I can't believe this," said T., and turned to Beth, who dipped her head to look past him out his window. "I'm sorry," he said.

"I'm back!" sang out his mother gaily, and stubbed out her cigarette on the concrete step. She stood up and spread her arms. She had lightened her hair. "And this is?"

"Beth. Our first date," said T. "So don't say anything I'm going to regret. Beth? My mother. She's been on a cruise."

His mother was down the steps and flinging her arms around him in a wild embrace.

"Not just a cruise. I took *buses*. I stayed in these fleabag hotels. Chichén Itzá! Where they sacrificed the virgins? Hello, dear. Pleased to meet you. And T.! Do you even recognize your old mother?"

"You look great," he said dutifully.

"This is Terry," she said. "A friend. Terry is Lebanese!"

"Pleased to meet you," said T., and they shook.

"I tell you what," said his mother, "why don't you just let us in and you kids can retire, or do whatever. We just flew in. We need to crash."

He did not recall the word *crash* in her vocabulary, nor had she called him a "kid" in recent memory.

"I can't believe you're smoking," he said, as they lugged her cases into the elevators and through his front door.

"I picked up the habit," she said. "Filthy, I know. So, have you heard from your father?"

Less than a minute.

"I haven't talked to him," he answered, evasive.

"A letter? Anything?"

"He hasn't written to me. Let's wait another day to discuss him."

He drove Beth to her apartment, since the mood was shot. He walked her in and called a cab and kissed her until it came.

Waiting to fall asleep afterward, his mother and Terry installed awkwardly in the next room, his thoughts of her attained a certain plateau. He thought of how she might walk down a future of clean avenues beside him, how she would confer her elegance on any landscape. He saw that this was selfish, or worse was self-aggrandizing, as though she was an accessory, but he felt more than that selfish impulse, felt something more exalted, frankly, and the thought of her beauty extended throughout his life was nothing short of captivating. It was not only that he would benefit from having her at his side, it was the shock of how the world glowed with it—how she lent her surroundings the style of her presence, its effortless assertion of grace.

In the desert subdivisions would spread, life radiate outward from the sand as the tone of her flesh shone on the planes of her face, through buildings and cables and gas mains and

roads. He thought of the cool of night descending over the settlement—were those coyotes howling out there in the dark, beyond the warm lights from thousands of standardized windows? Coyotes. He thought of them rarely but when he did he felt a pulse of identification and regret, curious and painful . . . In the distance homeowners in the settlement would be able to make out in the night sky the hulking shape of the Panamint mountains, the lights of the naval base winking beneath.

And in the morning, as the sun rose to the east over the national monument, automated sprinklers would come on and begin their twitching rotations, misting the putting greens and the fairways and the sculpted oases of red-and-yellow birds of paradise and palm, bringing songbirds out of nowhere to perch in the mesquite and palo verde trees lining the courses.

Hundreds of units were already presold.

The place would not disappoint; it would be almost heaven for the buyers, whose profiles were already known to him. Aging golfers whose children lived far away and avoided contact, whose fixed pensions were supplemented by a moderate annual influx of dividend and interest income from conservatively managed accounts, whose idea of leisure involved little more than a sunny clime, eighteen holes minimum and a view of pastel-colored fake adobe; these golfers and their wives, most of whom would outlive them, watching the sunset as they sat in the dry air, gentle, quiet, sipping their gin-and-tonics, smelling the barbeque from a few doors down and watching the colors in the western sky deepen. Was it not a decent way for life to end, in the peace of all that slowness? That he would not wish for an end like that himself was irrelevant. The buyers were not him.

Never pretend to know better, had been the first lesson of real estate. His own preferences were only a private luxury.

He would drive down the softly curving streets when they were built, he would survey the burg in all its idle readiness before the people moved in, when it was waiting, an infant of a city, clean and unmarked. She would be with him then, with her consent. The shining hair that hung down her back, the quick smile, the set of her shoulders and deep curve at the small of her back. He found it satisfying to imagine the completion of this, the village in the middle of nowhere and the contours of her person.

He knew it was her—was not surprised he had held himself aloof from others till now, knowing the perfection of this new sentiment.

•

In the morning his mother called down from the landing. "Have you been keeping my mail for me?"

She held a toothbrush and wore a black lace robe. In the past she had favored white cotton nightgowns that buttoned to the neck and were patterned with sprigs of flowers.

"In the desk," he said, inclining his head in the right direction.

But he had noticed, among her letters, one with a Reno postmark. Fear took hold of him. He had to go.

He glanced outside and saw that the taxi that would take him to his car was already waiting at the curb. Hastily he left the buttered toast waiting for him on the counter, the poured juice; hastily he left his dog for the day with a last pat on the head; hastily he grabbed his keys from a bowl on a side table. He left.

All day he worked hard and took very few calls, and it was past seven when he finally finished. He was the last to leave

the office, something he liked because he could survey it at his leisure, walking around, shuffling his nearly noiseless feet across the carpet. He stood and stared out various windows that offered views past other buildings and onto pieces of the ocean. He saw the blurs of ships like cities in the distance, unmoving on the gray surface. They were large ships, dark ships, solid and far across the waves. Often he saw them through these office windows and the next day they were gone.

When he got home his mother sat red-eyed in a lawn chair on the balcony, Terry in another chair beside her, an ashtray balanced on his mother's chair arm. He felt a pang of need—Beth should be here, she would be better at this than he was.

Of course after one evening they were not at that point. It would be far from appropriate.

He knelt in front of his mother and took her hand.

"Are you OK?"

She nodded slowly, vaguely. Her face was clean of makeup.

"Do you need to talk about it?"

She shook her head.

"I'll get us something to eat."

"She broke things," said Terry, catching up to him in the kitchen.

"She *broke* things?"

"She threw the dishes down on the floor. See? No plates," and he opened the cabinet door above his head to display its emptiness. "She threw out all her shoes. And the—what—vacuum cleaner."

"She was just, what was she? Angry? Crying?"

"I gave her a tranquilizer. I have them for the airplanes? And so she is better."

When they brought the food out his mother decided she wanted to be inside, but she also wanted to smoke. T. opened the windows and the three of them sat at the table. His mother stared down at her soup with a lit cigarette in her hand; Terry slathered butter onto a piece of bread.

"You shouldn't be able to do that," said his mother finally, in a voice so soft he could barely hear it.

"Do what?" he asked.

"Get a divorce without telling the other person."

He watched her long ash fall onto the table.

"I was thinking," he said softly. "When you were staying here before you went traveling, you were going to Mass at St. Anne's, right?"

His mother nodded.

"Maybe we should go in together tomorrow. You can talk to the priest."

"I hardly know him."

"Then let's call home. Let's call Father Stevens. OK? He'll be able to help with this."

"I didn't tell him I was leaving," mused his mother. "But I did send a postcard. From Cabo."

"Let's call him."

He left his hand on her shoulder. In the morning, he was telling himself, she would talk to her old parish priest, kindly and soft-spoken. She trusted him implicitly.

He would marvel later at how a mind could slip into otherness without you even noticing it. Slip away right beside you, motionless.

After dinner Terry turned on the television in the living room, where he settled down with a beer to watch a game, pretending intense concentration. Angela said weakly that she was going to wash her hair, which T. seized upon as evidence

of a restored normalcy. He said his own goodnights to both of them and retired to his room with the portable telephone, relieved.

While she ran her bath in the room next to his he called Beth and spoke to her, told her in low tones about the crisis. She was sympathetic and sounded sincerely worried; she offered to help but he did not want to give an impression of neediness. After he hung up he lay in bed letting his mind roam to business, legs splayed on the bed, one hand idly scratching the hair on his groin; while his mother picked up and inspected Terry's orange vial of tranquilizers he patted the bed and watched his dog jump up to curl at his feet. He closed his eyes and considered the wind farms of Palm Springs, the cost of the turbines, the megawattage that powered Coachella Valley. His own development would be powered thus one day, if he could swing it; and he was considering a contract with the wind-farm company when his mother removed her woven sandals and dark blue skirt.

As she stepped into the bath and opened a bottle of baby shampoo, he was already falling asleep. For a while they floated side by side like that, only a thin wall between them—she with her hair lathered, a towel rolled beneath her neck to soften the bathtub edge, he in an undershirt and boxer shorts on the bare sheets, the blankets pushed down hastily to the foot of the bed. As he fell asleep he was seeing the turbines that stretched along the San Gorgonio Pass, rows and rows of long, white windmill blades that whirred against the sky.

He had once spotted dinosaurs off the freeway there, a brontosaurus and a tyrannosaurus rex, their massive heads held high.

Stumbling out his bedroom door to the bathroom in the middle of the night he peed staring at the china shepherdess: and as he turned from the toilet to the sink to wash up he saw his mother.

He dropped to his knees and despite the shock of her nudity grabbed her out of the water and tried to breathe into her mouth and pump on her chest. He called out in panic between breaths, called out to Terry downstairs; and Terry was behind him fast. They kneeled over her together and did what they thought they were supposed to do, did what they could again and again until the ambulance pulled up wailing outside and the attendants were rushing up the stairs and bending down around him. He welcomed them as he had welcomed no one before; with gratitude he relinquished her to them, a towel thrown across her stomach.

The paramedics took her over and made him stand up, urged him back from her a few steps so that they could work. He stood useless and spare in the corner, breathing hard, his T-shirt soaked in soap-smelling water, his underwear dripping down his bare legs.

When one of them said she had a pulse the strength went out of him and he sat down hard on the toilet seat.

Later he learned it had been a stroke caused by an overdose of Terry's tranquilizers. Later, sitting beside her bed and barely seeing her face for the tubes and the paleness of the skin, he would recall that—after all this panic, all this dread and this commotion—she had never seemed to notice his father much at all, around the house, back in the olden days. His father's absence, he realized, meant more to her than his presence ever had.

Even furniture could be an object of nostalgia . . . in recalling her life with his father, as she lay there in the soft

bathwater, he imagined her dulled by the weight but then, as if recalling an old armchair with fraying arms, stricken by homesickness. He imagined the life she had led, her weekly route to the grocery store where she had shopped throughout his childhood. He saw her holding the steering wheel and turning right and then left and then right again, watching the wipers shunt back and forth in the rain. She had grown up, as he had, and found the same thing: the warmth of other bodies dissipated as you pulled further and further away, and in the space between people the air became cool.

On the small television in her hospital room, which was on all the time, families sat in a row of chairs and argued. Women hurled recriminations at their stolid husbands and sons and then, meeting with indifference, broke down in a torrent of weeping. A Kleenex box on her nightstand was printed with brown flowers.

He had requested a private room but there was a waiting list, so she shared with another prone woman who was always snoring. During the first week of the coma he took Beth once to visit her, which should have been too intimate for an early date but felt natural. In fact Beth reminded him, standing over his mother's bed with a compassionate expression, of a nurse — not the nurses who actually worked in the hospital but an ideal nurse, capable, courteous, modest. He wondered how she came to have this capacity for appropriateness wherever she went.

But mostly he went alone, not wishing to overwhelm her.

They sent in orderlies to bathe the patients, and on the day his mother came out of her coma the orderly had secured her hair to the sides of her head with a pair of pink barrettes. He went to the bathroom in her room, wondering idly why there were plastic butterflies affixed to his mother's

temples, and when he came out her eyes were open. She blinked several times.

"Mother?" he asked, and fumbled to press the call button. "Can you hear me?"

Her face still did not move and he picked up one of her hands, pressed it gently.

"It's me," he said, "T. You're in the hospital."

Finally her mouth worked dryly and he put down her hand. He ran to the bathroom and filled a paper cup with water.

"Here," he said. "Here, drink this."

He spilled the water over her chin and down the sides of her face, trying to tip it into her mouth.

"Can you talk? Do you know me?"

"Tell me your name," said a nurse, cutting in beside him.

"Angela," said his mother.

"And can you tell me what year it is?"

"1990," said his mother.

"OK," said the nurse. "Just lay back there, honey."

"I died," rasped his mother, after a long pause. "I died."

He leaned in and clasped her wrist.

"You almost died," he said. "You had a stroke. But here you are."

"Thirsty," she whispered, and he poured more water into her mouth. He could hear her gulping, and the nurse raised the head of the bed so that his mother sat up.

"You don't need to talk," said the nurse. "Just relax. You're doing great."

"I died and went to another place," whispered his mother, straining to lift her head off the pillow. "But it was nothing like what I expected, T. It was nothing *like* it."

"You can tell us all about that later," said the nurse. "OK? Right now we need you to just lay back and relax."

"You believe me, don't you," whispered his mother, reaching for his face. "You believe me."

"Of course I do," he whispered back.

"I was surprised. I thought it would be heaven, T. But it was bad, very bad," said his mother, and moved her feet suddenly beneath the sheet. "It was the International House of Pancakes."

"I'm surprised too," said T.

"I thought it would be more expensive than that."

He studied her face to see if he could detect humor but there was nothing, only a vague and yet urgent concern.

"We're just glad to have you here with us," he said, and leaned down to kiss her cheek.

"I don't want to go back there again," she said, and closed her eyes. "I must have done something wrong, T. Something very wrong to go there."

"I'm going to get the doctor now," said the nurse. "And you best be letting her get some rest. Visiting hour's almost done anyways."

"Sure," he said.

Before he left he reached over and removed the barrettes.

He found her a small apartment, on the first floor of a yellow-brick building a block away from him. She would convalesce there and T. could check in on her easily. It was pleasant and airy, modest and clean; the windows of the large living room gave onto a common garden whose grass was a deep green, with white plastic lawn chairs and a kidney-shaped pool. The doors were wide enough for a wheelchair and the inside smelled of lemon.

He and Beth furnished the apartment on the day his mother was to be released, drinking coffee and watching as men from a furniture rental company rolled in the chairs and

sofas on dollies. They brought over her few belongings from T.'s apartment and Beth put daisies in the window.

"Oh T.? I think we forgot something," she called from his bathroom when they were getting ready to leave for the hospital. She came out holding the Bo Peep figurine.

He was struck by the sight of this—how the statuette, which he had previously viewed as ridiculous, did not appear so the way she held it, how the fluidity of her gestures seemed to steady and ground its frivolity. In her hand it was almost acceptable.

"No," he said softly. "I don't think so."

"Are you sure? It doesn't remind me of you," she said, and put it down on a shelf as they walked together through his front hall, keeping pace, both their key chains jangling.

"She bought it for me," he said, and pulled the door closed behind them. "She believed in guest soap."

•

He never found out whether the overdose had been an accident. Angela was changed, shifted sideways from her previous self; it was not quite that she was absent, merely that she seemed dislocated. The patterns of her speech had altered and frequently her sentences wasted into nothing; but then some days she seemed to rise from the fog, sharp-tongued and beady-eyed, and would lecture her son on his selfishness or his lack of religion.

Her time in the coma had persuaded her into an angle of devotion more stringent and bizarre than her old way of worship. She had always assumed that when she died the Blessed Mother would shelter her; instead she had been

relegated to a dingy House of Pancakes, and the shock was considerable. Whether her banishment had been to hell, purgatory, or as she first implied a disappointing version of heaven remained unclear to him. But she seemed to be certain of what the experience signified; she had found herself in a place of disillusionment where fluorescents had threatened to bring on a migraine and the other patrons, fat, pasty-faced, and dressed in loud prints, had studied her resentfully. None of them were Catholics.

It had been a stern warning, and one she would heed— for the House of Pancakes outcome could be averted, she told T., by renewed attention to matters of the spirit. She had fallen away from attention to faith in recent months, she said, with her self-absorption and her self-pity. Of course the divorce itself, being a violation of doctrine, might also have brought on her punishment despite the fact that she had not had a hand in it personally: it was no coincidence that she ended up in the Pancake House the very day she was notified of the legal severing of her conjugal bond. Starting now she would devote more of her time to charity, attend church daily and curb her language.

But her concern that he might end up in an IHOP was greater than her worry for herself. Her admonitions to him were constant, and on her sharper days he sometimes caught himself wishing she would return to dimness. If an elderly lady with a walker was preparing to cross the road a half a block away, she would wave wildly with both arms to stun her into halting her progress; then grab T. firmly, pinching, to hustle him over to the woman's side so he could support her for the brief traverse. And as he and his current ward made their way through the crosswalk she would often leap around wildly beside them, fending off cars with a fierce and mobile series of facial expressions despite the fact that all of them

were already at a standstill. Recipients of her largesse were
not always grateful for the interruption but she ignored this;
and several times, hands flapping on T.'s back to hurry him
along, she pressed him into the service of perfectly hale and
hearty men in their early forties.

She also urged him toward charitable contributions —
here five thousand dollars for a local chapter of Mothers
Against Drunk Driving, there five hundred for the Roman
Catholic Anti-Defamation League of Newfoundland. When
T. resisted her tithing demands she would finger-wag and
remind him of the flicker of long tubes over his head, the
blue-white light, and the laminated menus with close-up
pictures of heavy foods.

Behind the wheel of her car she carefully avoided not
only the various Los Angeles locations of the International
House of Pancakes but all breakfast-oriented restaurants that
were national chains. And if she was struck as she drove with
the sight of a Denny's or Waffle House, unexpected, she
closed her eyes tightly until it was past.

•

He rarely saw the men he knew from college days. But early that
spring there was a call from a fraternity brother reporting that Ian
Van Heysen, Jr. had relocated to the Hollywood Hills and was
hosting a housewarming gala. The new home had a pool with a
view of the city, a whirlpool and sauna and steam room; it had
previously been owned by a B-list actress with famously bee-
stung lips. This, and not the independent features of the property,
was what had attracted Van Heysen and inspired him to cajole
from his father a purchase price in the mid-seven figures.

"You gotta come, man," said the fraternity brother, now a pharmaceutical rep. "You being right there in the city and shit. I mean guys are flying in from Singapore for this thing. And you'd give it that real old-time flavor, you know? I mean shit, we haven't seen you since eighty-fucking-six. It's gonna be a hell of a shindig."

"I'll do my best," said T.

He took Beth with him and they headed up the front path through the garden, which was crowded with exotic plants. Near the front porch they found two men holding beer cans, ties loosened.

"Ron, how are you," said T., and they clapped each other on the back. "This is Beth."

"Pleased to meetcha," said Ron. "Wow. You got a keeper there, T. She a model or something? Whoo-hoo!"

"See you later," said T., and they left him standing with the other man, who leaned over a birdbath and retched.

"My," said Beth.

"Ron was never one of our very brightest stars."

"Reassuring."

Inside the house was palatial, with a spiral staircase and a massive window giving a view out over the light-dotted hills in the dark. Caterers moved among the crowds, and in the corner of the main room a tubby man in late-model Elvis sang karaoke.

"T. holy fucking shit! My man!"

Down the stairs came Van Heysen, red hair mussed, his round and florid face shining.

"Ian," said T.

"My man! I can't believe it!"

He found himself clasped to Ian's chest, and when he was released a blast of whiskey breath almost floored him.

"What the hell you been doing? I hear something like real estate?"

"Something like. This is Beth," said T., and Ian looked her up and down.

"Hot," he said, and stuck out his hand.

"Nice to meet you too."

"So are you like Asian or black or something?"

"You grill everyone about their ethnic background, Ian?"

"Hey. If she wasn't so foxy I wouldn't give a shit. So step on up to my garden of earthly delights. We got coke, we got weed, we got speed, we got X."

"No, thanks," said T. "You remember who you're talking to, right, Ian? Straight as a pin."

"Does a Pope shit in the woods? Is a bear Catholic?"

"What can I say."

"Thought you might have eased up, is all. Mellowed out. But hey! No harm no foul."

"I'd like a vodka tonic, if you have one," said T.

"Sure thing. You?"

"White wine, please," said Beth.

"Stay right there."

"Triple T.!" said a man with a beard, stepping back from the table. White dusted his mustache.

"Stewart," said T. "How are you."

"Great, great, great," said Stewart, and clapped him in a bear hug.

"So I see."

"Hey? You know what? Coincidence for ya. I was at this old-boy thing in Atlanta, right? A month ago or something. Mostly fossils. We're talking Class of 1940 and shit."

"Uh huh."

"It was all ear hair and prosthetic legs and boring Okinawa stories. I went there for business, looking for investors for my new record label."

"Record label. Huh."

"It's completely fucking brilliant, T.T.T. Talk about niches no one's thought of grabbing. Get this: Aryan rap. More on that one later. But so guess who the fuck I fucking ran into there?"

"I have no idea," said T., and held out his hand to accept a drink from Ian.

"Your old man! Your fucking dear old dad. I mean fuck me!"

T. stared wordlessly. Finally he lifted his tumbler and sipped.

"He was looking good," said Stewart earnestly. "Real deep tan and shit. I didn't remember him being so buff. Has he had any work done?"

"Work?" asked T., still stunned.

"Stew! Come here!" someone yelled from outside.

"Hold your fucking horses!" called Stew, and turned back to T. "And he had this kid with him, your brother I guess?"

"I was an only child," said T.

"Oh. Some young guy, then," said Stewart. "I don't know why I thought he was family. Maybe the age difference."

"Did my father happen to mention where he was living?" asked T.

Stewart stared at him until the French doors banged open.

"Stew! I'm serious!" said a woman in pigtails. "Laney's having a bad trip or something! She's like saying she's gonna slide down the cliff on a wine crate! Like, *now*!"

"My stupid wife," said Stewart, "she always does this stupid shit," and followed the pigtails out the door, shaking his head.

Later, before they left, he went looking for Stewart but could not find him.

Presently his father sent a postcard from Key West. Several days later he had a lunch meeting with Brad, a native of the Keys, whose mother's building he had sold four years before and who now had a large stake in the Mojave project.

"You run into my father around town?" he asked Brad casually, when business was winding down.

"I guess he works in this one bar these days," said Brad, signing the air for the check.

"A *bar*?" said T.

"This one is, you know . . . you know."

"I know what?"

"You know. For queers."

T. found his mouth working without producing words. He saw his father putting an umbrella in a margarita glass, wearing a bright pink shirt festooned with sunsets and palm trees.

"T.? You with me there, man?"

"Sure. Yes. I'm just surprised. I always thought he was narrow-minded."

"Yeah. Hey! I'll get this one." And Brad slapped down his card.

T. flew into the Keys on a propeller plane, the thin seat beneath him vibrating. Beneath him the blue was vast, and then he saw the gray precise line of a highway cutting its way across the ocean, between the thin islands. A man sitting next to him told him the road over the sea had been built on a bedrock of dead corals for a railway itself long since destroyed by a storm. One bridge alone was seven miles long, the man said.

From the small airport he took a taxi to a condo Brad owned on the beach, which was pink and had tiers like a wedding cake. He hung his spare shirt in the closet, showered and lay

naked on his back on the bed with the sliding door open to the terrace, waves crashing outside and the sea blowing salt wind across his body. The smell of crisp sheets was tinged with the smell of coconut and a breeze came in off the ocean and lifted the white drapes; it grazed the light hairs on his stomach, raising goose bumps and giving him an erection. He thought of Beth, cotton and skin. He should have asked her to come with him. But even with her this would not have passed for a pleasure trip. This was a gesture, but it rankled, it was awkward, even confining. She would not have thanked him.

And it was still not too late to avoid a meeting. He did not have to go any further than this; he could stay where he was, lie low. The prospect was beckoning.

But glancing through the open door to the bathroom he saw white tiles and was briefly touched by the body of his mother, naked and slack—there she was, and there the towel he had tossed across the darkness of her lap for the benefit of the paramedics, because he was ashamed.

By night the bar was crowded and hot. A muscular black man in a net T-shirt handed beers over the counter and there behind him, though it took a few seconds to be sure, was his father.

Newly blond, darkly tanned, his father wore a polo shirt and smiled whitely to a patron waving money at him as he shot soda into a highball glass with the bar gun. Both his father and mother, it struck him, had made themselves blonder: both of them had lightened their hair and darkened their skin—possibly, he thought, to attract attention through contrast, birds with bright plumage. They had turned themselves into summer people, as though they could stave off the winter ahead.

Maybe, he thought hopefully, he had imagined his father's coldness. Maybe his father was only reluctant to face him. He stepped toward the counter, waiting for a hole to clear between other patrons; he stood facing the bartender in the mesh, who nodded at him impatiently.

"Actually, if I could talk to *him*," he said, and pointed to the other end of the bar, where his father stood, back turned, punching buttons on a cash register.

"Davy!" called the bartender.

As his father turned he felt his stomach flip—carnival rides from way back, the roller coaster that went upside down or the fixed platform that seemed to drop in free fall and then swooped up again. His father's face remained blank for some time. Then he came around the end of the bar, unsmiling, and the first thing that T. noticed, looking for him as he pressed toward him through the close crowd, was his feet. At the bottom of his cream-colored slacks his father, who had always worn plain black leather lace-ups, battered sneakers or a pair of Redwing work boots, wore a snow-white pair of espadrilles.

When they met the next morning for breakfast his father was late—five minutes, ten, then twenty. As he came in he offered a brief, reflexive smile, quickly dropped, and barely glanced at how T. waited for him: ramrod straight in his chair, holding his *Wall Street Journal* rolled up in his hand as though he might have to deploy it in the swatting of flies.

As he approached T. understood in a rush that he was not the same man. His bearing was different, his movement, everything: a dog, for example, would not recognize him. Strange as this altered man was to T., the new self suited him,

that was clear. At the same time this new parent was closed to T. Not even the awkward intimacy of confession lay between them anymore; his face was shut like a door. He had simply moved on.

He waved at someone behind T.'s shoulder. Then he sat down and adjusted the chair several times, back and forth, tucking himself beneath the table edge.

"You order yet?" he asked, and opened up a menu, signaling to a waiter. "Could I get a cappuccino here?"

"Of course not. I was waiting for you," said T.

"Oh, you didn't need to do that," said his father distractedly. He did not look at him, tracing a finger down the list of menu items. "I'll have the eggs Florentine."

"Huevos rancheros," said T. "So. I ran into Stewart Albin a couple of months ago and he said he saw you in Atlanta."

"I always go to the reunions," said his father, nodding. He seemed bored.

"I know that. He said you were with some kid. He thought it was my brother."

"Stewart, Stewart. Oh yes. He was the one hitting us up for investments in a record or something."

"Aryan rap."

"No one had any idea what he was talking about. I think he's insane."

"So then I got your postcard and then I was talking to Brad Deering and here I am. First off I want to tell you. My mother had a stroke."

"Oh dear," said his father faintly, and clucked his tongue. He reached out and adjusted a daffodil.

"We thought she was dead at first. It was an overdose and the stroke happened while she was unconscious. It happened in my bathtub."

"Oh dear," repeated his father, still not meeting his eyes. "But she's doing fine now?"

"It depends what you mean. She's all right physically," said T. "As far as the tests go. But she's not what she used to be."

"We're not so young anymore, are we?" said his father comfortably. "I've had these tension headaches lately."

"Headaches," repeated T.

"Aspirin does nothing for me. Ibuprofen either. The only thing that does anything is Tylenol with codeine. That stuff is sheer magic."

T. stared at him, but he played with his fork and smiled vaguely.

"I'm sorry about the headaches," said T. slowly, "but I'd really like to think you felt some concern about my mother. That when I tell you she almost died, that you—you know—actually care."

"Sure, sure I do," said his father lightly, but was looking past him again, smiling and waving.

A woman in a straw hat descended on them.

"Davy! Darling!" she said.

She was nut-brown, like his father, and wore shimmering peach-colored lipstick. She was draped in scarves.

"I haven't seen you for *weeks* it seems like," she said, and kissed his father on the top of his head. "I'm over there with Boolie. He can barely keep down his coffee. He overdid it last night."

"This is Carol," said his father. "A friend. Carol, my son T."

"Well hi!" squealed Carol, as though she'd won the lottery.

T. nodded curtly. Clearly his father wanted her there.

"When did you start going by Davy?" he asked. "It was always Dave or David, my whole life."

"That was the old me," said his father.

"The new you is more jaunty," said Carol.

"Well, Carol," said T., "it's been nice meeting you."

"Join us!" said his father, and put his hand out to grab the back of a chair.

"Are you kidding?" asked T., incredulous.

"Not at all. Here, take a load off," said his father, and patted the chair.

"Just for a minute, while Boolie's in the little boys' room."

"I was telling my father how my mother had a stroke recently," said T. resolutely. He would not be diverted. "But he doesn't seem to be interested."

"Florentine?" inquired the waiter, plate-lifting.

"That was so speedy!" enthused his father. "Right here."

The waiter tried to put the other plate down in front of Carol.

"No, I'm the huevos," said T.

"I'll say," said Carol.

"What?"

"It's important, when you're starting fresh, to let go," said Carol with a therapeutic lilt. She reached out and patted the back of T.'s hand.

"I don't know what you're talking about," said T.

"Your father is like a beautiful butterfly," said Carol. "For him to spread his wings he had to leave the dusty old cocoon behind."

T. stared at her and she stared back, smiling and blinking. Her two front teeth were different shades of white.

His mother had no knowledge of any of this, yet he felt hurt for her.

"You've got to be kidding," he repeated finally, and turned back to his father. Who seemed not to be listening; he was carving into his mound of spinach and egg with a fork as though he had been starving for days. "Are you there? This

was a person who spent thirty years with you. This is your wife. My *mother*."

Carol played with her rhinestone-studded watchband and his father continued to eat, patting neatly at his mouth with his still-folded napkin.

"Your son is an angry person," she whispered finally, and his father shook his head ambiguously as she turned back to T. "You know, honey, that resentment is just like a poison. It will just eat away at you. You should work on it."

"Carol? This is a family conversation. Give us a minute, if you would," said T. "Please."

She looked at his father and got up reluctantly. T. watched as she flowed over to a table in the corner, where a fat man in a baseball cap sat sucking a bright red drink from a straw.

"That was very rude," said his father.

His father waved at the waiter and made a check-signing gesture in the air.

"I have to admit, I really feel like hitting you," said T.

"I'm used to homophobia," said his father, and patted his mouth with his napkin again. "I've been exposed to it all my life."

"Jesus Christ," said T. wearily.

He gazed down at his refried beans congealing beneath a dollop of sour cream. He felt disinclined to touch them.

"I have to protect myself from people who are full of hate," said his father.

"Dad, listen to me," said T. "So you're gay? Great. What-ever feels right. You look good, you look healthy. But do you have to be cruel to her?"

"I don't have to listen to this, Thomas."

He felt a buzz in his ears, a wall of deafness rising within him. He was hot; he had to get out of the restaurant. He took

a card out of his wallet and laid it down. "Her new telephone number. Please at least call her. Please at least tell her why you left. That you're not coming back. Do her that small favor."

He rose, his father half-swiveled away from him in his chair, and tossed down a twenty; passed Carol and the morbidly obese man named Boolie, who glared at him with bulging eyes. He felt tamped down into fury, the tension of his rage making him want to burst into a run. As soon as he was away from the restaurant, enough distance behind him, he turned off the road down to the beach again and took off his shoes.

He did run then, along the cool tidal sand: he pounded the wet grit with the tender soles of his feet, a shoe clutched in each hand, until the bottoms of his feet were raw and he was winded and gasping. Then he slowed to a stop.

By nightfall he was on the West Coast again, curled warmly around Beth's smooth back and listening to the whir of his own ceiling fan. There he drifted back to the sand, the beach beside the pink stucco building.

The sand was full of fathers in bathing suits, sleeping; he was the only one awake, with fathers all around him. He did not wear a bathing suit but a body cast, and none of the sun or the sand reached his skin. In the cast he was cool. He felt no need for movement.

The tide was so far out that the low white line of the waves breaking was barely visible on the horizon. Between him and the sea the sand was hilly with dunes, and yet past it he could still see the wide flat ocean. Everywhere fathers were dreaming in the warm sun, the fathers who

had once been little boys, running; the sun that made them gleam. Crabs sidled up to them and wasps landed on their lax bodies.

No, wait. Were the fathers asleep?

Their eyes were wide open. They were there, gold and massive, but they saw nothing.

The fathers lay still, their faces toward the sky: until the wind passed a hand over all of their eyes, closing them.

3

His first houses went up almost overnight—slab, frame, roof, electrical and plumbing, drywall, finish and landscaping—fast and cheap, designed not to last but to become obsolete. Retired people moved in, gathering in the desert from cold northern suburbs. In his downtime he presided.

He strolled alongside the tennis courts, watching the vigorous play of sweating players through the green mesh and idly calculating the probability of atrial fibrillation. When she did not have other obligations Beth accompanied him, and together they sat in the Mercedes and purred along the newly minted neighborhoods as the sun rose, observing the early risers—a gawky racewalker in headphones, dog-owners with scoops and bags, brightly dressed matrons walking in twos as they chatted nasally. Beth liked to ride with him, either because she was captured, as he was, by the completion of this beginning, this forecast of greater growth, or because she was content to be in his company. She gazed out her rolled-down window, idly drumming her French-manicured

fingers on the shining wood panel of the car door, the breeze slightly moving stray tendrils of her black hair. Pulling around the bottom of a cul-de-sac he admired the smooth action of garage doors rolling upward to disgorge shining sedans; he cast his eyes over sculpted xeriscape bushes in the rock gardens, the well-hidden spigots that watered them. There was no better way to behold this neatly emerging landscape than from behind the clean windshield of the 190, which framed external scenes and kept them at a perfect distance.

There was a tidiness to his circuit, and satisfaction filled him from bottom to top like liquid. His profit was projected and beyond even that profit—the perfect and curtained margin that made liberty—here was a good settlement; here was a small country, planned step by step and now filled with citizens. It was a modest piece in a patchwork, stitched into the vast fabric by roads and cables and aqueducts, by cheap gasoline and abundant rubber and lumber from the northwest, by the dominance of car companies, the willingness to drain lakes and dam rivers, the invention of Freon and computers and urea formaldehyde. This was the apogee of civilization.

And he was, in part, a designer of the lives that would wind down and likely end here—strange position, insignificant he knew to anyone but him. But out of his intention had sprung the last rooms, the final gardens.

If he was harried he liked to force a pause in his day and sit down in the dimness of the community center weight room, seldom used, where he could look through the glass wall at the older women in their water aerobics class. The angle of their swim-capped heads above the water's surface brought him a sense of calm. He thought how the world would feel if it were populated solely by elderly women—a

world of forbearance, where all touches were careful. Once they had given birth, raised children, worked, but now all of that was behind them. Now they swam. Their heads cocked, they waited patiently for instructions.

His father never called and finally it was Beth who took his mother aside. He was not there but he heard about it later: the two of them walked together on the cliffs over the beach, on the emerald-green grass that grew under the palms. Beth held his mother's arm, as she often did when they walked, and spoke clearly and carefully. Did she want to sit down? Here was a bench, and it was clean. Sit down. There. Now. This was going to be difficult; this was not easy.

His mother looked at Beth, searching her face for something, then turned away and nodded absently. She came to acceptance slowly: the worst had already passed. In the ensuing months the only sign that she knew the facts of the case was the occasional vague reference, in her speech, to *your father's new lifestyle*, his *new identity*.

His father's defection was more forgivable now, in fact, for now his mother was no longer a failed wife and therefore a failed woman but merely a woman who had once been married to a failed man.

At the office, over coffee and donuts, Julie announced she was leaving to work on a worm farm in Guatemala. She had been accepted by the Peace Corps.

"Congratulations," said T.

"Good for you!" said Susan.

"I didn't know you had an interest in worms," said T.

"It's more the people," said Julie. "They're underprivileged. It's about helping them to realize their full development potential."

"Will you actually be touching them?" asked Susan.

"The people?" asked Julie.

"The worms," said Susan.

"I think you wear rubber gloves," said Julie. "And a dust mask. There can be airborne illnesses, like Legionnaires' disease."

"Isn't that the one where you cough up blood and die?" asked Susan.

"Hardly ever," said Julie.

"Still," said Susan.

T. handed her a coffee made the way she liked it, almost white with cream. "Better you than me."

And yet he thought of her, after she left his employ, recalled her with an impulse that was almost paternal.

•

Beth took his mother out shopping on a Saturday afternoon. He watched them leave from the steps of his building's lobby. Beth led the older woman carefully to her car—his mother, for some reason, walking unsteadily. He felt grateful, felt pulled toward them, but stayed where he was.

At the time his mother was freshly withdrawn from the driving economy. Upon receiving a citation for weaving across the median—applying lipstick, as it turned out, while gazing into the rearview mirror—she had been forced to attend traffic school, where a drill-sergeant type showed videotapes of the gruesome aftermath of high-speed collisions.

He looked at Beth steadily across the lawn and the light around them was nearly solid, the air immaculate: he felt his arms rising toward her, although he was not moving.

After they pulled away from the curb he realized Angela had forgotten her crucifix. It was a small wooden crucifix that usually hung from his own rearview mirror; she had affixed it there over his protest, because she often rode with him and insisted on having it with her when she did. He did not like his car decorated with such talismans; a car interior should be smooth and well-ordered, not festooned with hopeful signals of the driver's personality. Because then the two went to war, car and driver, and the car always won, with its seamless factory complexion. The driver looked like a child trying desperately to adorn.

He plucked a beer from the refrigerator, uncapped it and tipped it up; when he recalled this afterward it was as though he was still frozen there, fingertips poised against the cool condensation on the bottle's shoulder. The afternoon unfurled before him in an air-conditioned calm. He had research laid out on his coffee table: a small jungle island off the Central American coast. It was a short boat trip from one of the longest coral reefs in the ocean, where lemon sharks cruised in the shallows to the delight of tourists. The water off the beach was warm, clear and shallow for hundreds of feet, and on the mainland nearby were lagoons and rainforests, ancient ruins and a burgeoning service industry.

This perusal, this moment of early planning in serenity when a project was unrealized, had always been delightful to him.

Then the ring of the telephone interrupted his speculation and he heard his mother's voice, faint and shaky. The tone of it made his stomach cramp as he ran out to the lobby and slammed down the stairs to the parking garage, fumbled with the car door. He drove with pins pricking behind his eyelids and his palms slipping against the steering wheel cover, sweating. When he got to the hospital he ran across the

parking lot, and out of breath and coughing said their names to a clerk. Finally someone led him to a room, or maybe he got there alone.

His mother sat up in a bed, a bandage on her forehead, one of her arms in a sling. She said a word he could not distinguish and he saw she was fine; he reached out a hand for her, stopped and dazzled by the white light from the window. He was unable to make out her facial expression then and he let his hand drop.

"But you're OK, but how about her?" he asked, turning to the nurse who had led him in. "Where is she?"

The nurse took his arm and led him out again and he forgot everything as he walked behind her: as he followed her back it felt dutiful, though at the same time he was enslaved. He grabbed his hands together and felt their clammy pressure. Nothing was true except the white back with the vertical seam down the middle and the wall beside him. Was she in traction, her eyes bruised and fearing in a bandaged face?

It was not Beth he saw, however: it was a fat-stomached doctor who came at him from the side, seeming to materialize out of the blur of a door. The doctor took him by the shoulder and steered him into an alcove. There a plaster statue of Mary looked down on them with almond-shaped eyes; this was a Catholic hospital, he realized, a feature he had not noticed before despite the name of it, which was the name of a saint.

"I am very sorry to have to tell you," said the doctor, a man with glasses and a receding chin, "that your wife did not make it. We did our best to resuscitate her but it was simply too late."

He heard the doctor's mistake: your wife. He did not correct it. His ears were ringing. He was choking and his knees buckled. His head was squeezed, itched and stung. The

doctor and the nurse had him; they led him to a cot in a room and sat him on it, his head bent between his bent legs. There was a rush of sound, dense walls around him but no support for his arms; then his bowels loosened and he had to find a toilet. He was not sure he could make it.

When he came out of the bathroom, hands wet and teeth chattering, they were both still waiting. The teeth chattered out of control; his jaw was not his own. He thought his eyeballs might be jarred loose. It was comical, probably; it was idiotic. He could not prevent it. They took him back to his mother's room, where the nurse pulled up a chair beside her bed for him. But he could not sit down again. He stood holding the metal end of his mother's bed, dizzy but insistent. He waited for his jaw to stop its manic trembling.

"Accident?" he heard himself say finally, part of him.

He saw his mother shake her head.

"She collapsed," said his mother, and began to cry again. "At the wheel. We ran up on the curb and we stopped . . ."

"We are not one-hundred percent certain yet," said the doctor gently, a hand on his arm again, patting, "and we will have more to tell you later, but I believe the cardiac event may have been caused by a condition called arrhythmogenic right ventricular dysplasia."

"But she's healthy," said T. faintly, without force. His mother nodded eagerly, as though together they could persuade the doctor to change his mind. "She goes to the gym."

"This is a condition that sometimes afflicts young athletes, for instance," said the doctor. "It causes fibrosis of the heart muscle and a susceptibility to fatal cardiac arrhythmias and is rarely diagnosed. Often the first sign we have of a patient's condition, with ARVD, is sudden cardiac death."

He was not sure where to keep his body. Where was it supposed to go? His arms felt very long, but with no hands: where were all the fingers? His cheeks tingled.

At the window was a tree and a wall, he saw, staring. They were several floors off the ground; it could be six, he thought, or two. He noticed the tree. That should be a clue . . . or maybe not. He imagined the tree floating.

"It's instantaneous. She would not have been aware of what was happening," went on the doctor. "It's very, very rapid. You don't have to worry about suffering. She was already gone by the time the paramedics got there. Probably by the time the car stopped. Would you like to see her? You can see her if you want to."

"Oh," said T. He shook his head, or maybe by accident he was nodding. He felt a chill spike through him, up from the soles of his feet. His face was hot but the middle of him felt icy. He shivered.

"Come with me," said the nurse, and the doctor separated from them at the door.

He followed her white back again and thought he would never not be following it; almost hoped. It would guide him. Keep in line, he thought, stay in line . . . it was all he could do, all he would ever do.

They turned a corner and another one. People were shapeless as they passed him, wretched. The dreadful home-liness of the race. A laugh, another door opened, and there on the table was a covered woman, paper blanket all the way up to her neck. He moved closer without trying.

He was directly above the face now and something was unnatural about it—the skin was sallow, the full cheek-bones too sharp. He had never seen them so sharp. And the jaw looked weak, as though it had collapsed toward the chest. Unhinged. The certainty came to him, almost as a

relief, that the face was shaped wrong, so it could not be her.

He leaned over and touched the cheek, which was not cool but tepid. Lukewarm. Then he felt squeezing and fluttering in his chest, and caved in.

•

He got home by himself, he never knew how, and lay there in the sheets. After the first night his mother came in, on the edge of his vision like a hair trembling at the corner of a projected screen. She had a broken arm and scraped face, but he barely saw them. Time was foreign for many days, the texture of time and all things alien in their existence, at once strange and dull. He was flattened, pinned on his bed.

He heard his mother explain her condition to him. Once or twice she described the minor accident that had occurred when Beth had lost consciousness. He could not stand to listen.

She sat on the bed and felt concerned—he knew this, though he closed his eyes and could not bring himself to say anything—and twice a day she made him food and brought it in to him on a tray. It rested on the nightstand beside the Mass cards that piled up there, which she also brought to him: apparently Masses were being said for Beth. Then the food was cold and limp and she took it away again. He drank water from time to time, finding a glass in his hand with ice cubes that clicked against it thinly, but nothing else entered him. He had the suspicion that cogs were spinning, the universe beyond his walls was functioning and he was not, but he had no choice. His dog lay on the bed alongside, jumping down periodically to eat from her bowl or when his mother offered to walk her.

His mother filled and refilled the dog's bowl; it had been moved from the kitchen to the bedroom and sat dirtily in the corner, brown pebbles of food scattered on newspaper on the floor around it. He stared at the grimy bowl as he stared at all of it.

Presently the cleaning woman came and his mother talked to her softly in a faraway room. Was she even using words? It was as though the women were speaking in hums, tonal variations with no alphabet.

When he broke from the weight that held him down, rarely, he was conscious of resentment. Anger rose through him and was trapped at his throat, unable to exit. Once he thought: It should have been her! and pulsed irritation in his mother's direction, silently. She was older. She had lived more and anyway now she was mostly a shadow; in a bathtub she had forfeited all her rights, all her rights with that stupid gesture. He did not tell her this only because his tongue would not move in his mouth. But sometimes he wished to lash out. She had forgotten the crucifix, she had brought it on them. She might as well have killed her.

Then the coldness of this and its meanness struck him and pressed him even further down, now in a well of shame as well as self-pity. *Sorry sorry sorry*, he thought pathetically to his mother in a cracked-open beg of a thought. He forgave her for everything and wished that she would forgive him.

He sank and he struggled, felt his body lighten when the tear ducts were empty. Then he grew heavy again and collapsed into the mattress, a sinking gray heft. He slept and slept on and learned to despise the surfaces of his room, the walls and the ceiling and the curtains: and his room was only a substitute for the rest of it, which he loathed even more.

Finally his mother brought in a doctor and the doctor forced him to eat. The doctor gave him a shot, a pill. He

shook his head when the doctor first sat with him but gave in when his stomach began to ache with a new ferocity. At first he could not get the food down his throat but with repetition he was able to swallow it. He had to sit up against the pillows to eat, and sitting up he saw his legs and feet extending below his torso and his underwear and barely recognized them. They had lost muscle, he thought, they were pale.

When the doctor had left, and his mother after, he scanned his room languidly and noticed his wallet on the nightstand. He opened it with a dull lassitude, removed a single and traced his fingers over its minuscule ridges. The lines on Washington's brow impressed him particularly, the curved precision of their alignment. Washington was well presented— better, surely, than he had been in life, with greater authority. T. felt a wash of nostalgia.

He did not possess a lithograph of Beth, of course. But this was what he needed, a dollar bill that preserved a particular aspect, that enshrined a moment of bearing . . . photographs would present a problem. He could not control them, her expressions in them—how casual they had been, flippant almost, his quick shots, few and far between. All he had was these thoughtless snapshots now, when what he needed was a definitive image, an image that spoke to posterity. An image that embodied acceptance, contentment. If he looked through the photographs for such a representation he would be at the gravest risk. What if the expression was unsure, frightened? This could not be allowed. He could not stand to see that. He had to see her one way and one way only: smiling ruefully and shaking her head.

Because this attitude, her smiling and shaking her head— almost shrugging—was a powerful reassurance. In a lithograph, of course, the motion of the headshake could not be conveyed, and he would have to settle for a knowing smile, a

smile at once wise and playful. It would serve to project her contentment over time, her self-containment, not unlike, for example, the Mona Lisa's.

Thinking of her as she shook her head, smiling ruefully, he saw that she accepted and even embraced the great levelness of all things.

One morning his mother told him the burial had already taken place. Beth's mother had flown in and flown out again; she had taken her daughter's body back to the desert, where the family came from, and had a funeral there. He would never attend the funeral. He had missed it.

"It was just a few people," she said. "Very simple, very brief. The mother was heavily sedated."

He thought he would snap. He had the sense of a white snap above his head, the air cracking. He tilted, then was steady again. She was gone. He would have to get up.

He asked his mother to leave so that he could get dressed. She smiled brightly, her face infused with relief. He was surprised that he noticed it. When she closed the bedroom door behind her he could not move at first, but then he remembered the shoulders and the arms and the hands and saw Beth put her hand on her hip and shake her head ruefully, resigned but temperate. She let all of it pass, the wide well of grief was subsumed in her rueful acceptance.

She even laughed!—.

He stood unsteadily, dizzy, beside the bed. He tottered to the bathroom on wavering knees. The dog stood at the bathroom door, head cocked quizzically. He was sorry the dog had been so neglected. He put out a hand to pet her but she did not move quite near enough for him to reach without stretching. Later, he thought. He dropped his shirt and bent to peel off his pants. Hot water fell on his head.

Even the clean clothing was heavy when he dressed—he could not choose the elements, only put on what was nearest. He opened a drawer and found the topmost shirt where it lay, and the first pair of pants beside it. Walking too was a slog through thickness. Still he persisted, down the stairs to face his mother in the living room, who smiled uncertainly.

"Well," she said. "Be safe and come right home. I'll make you a sandwich."

All sandwiches everywhere were absurd; the very idea of a sandwich was ludicrous. How was it that people did not laugh at them?

But he did not mention this.

"It's OK," he said with difficulty, pushing the words forward. "I'm OK. You don't need to wait here. You can go home and rest. I will eat."

"You promise?"

"I promise."

He waited till she left to go out of the apartment himself. He closed the door on the dog's expectant face.

"And I'll walk you later," he said, when the door was already closed.

He was overcome by inertia. He turned away from the door without locking it; let anyone steal anything they wanted. If he walked in on the thieves he would only stare at them.

In the elevator he gazed at the floor buttons, SB B L 2 3 4. Where his car was he did not know. Was his car even here? Tentatively he reached a finger out and touched B.

A small nudge with the pad of his finger, that was all, but Beth could not do it.

He sobbed once and then caught it. Someone was getting on, an alert little girl with a backpack slung over one shoulder.

"Hi," she said, and he nodded. "Lobby, please."

He raised his hand to hit L but the arm, crooked and immobile, would not move fast enough. It was almost frozen.

The elevator began to descend, down through 2, and the girl, impatient, reached out beneath his hand and tapped the button herself.

"Are you physically handicapped?" she asked.

He shook his head.

"Oh," said the girl, and nodded wisely. "Retarded."

He almost smiled but his face would not obey. The girl looked at him with sympathy, then quickly reached out and took his hand. She had a light, sweaty touch.

"It's OK," she said. "My cousin's a retard too."

Then the doors opened and she let go and got off.

He was giddy for a second as the doors closed after her. He could almost take the sensation for happiness. He kept his eyes on the fine horizontal score marks along the stainless steel surface. Out of his sight behind the elevator doors the little girl walked across the lobby; she went out the front door.

She would have loved you, he thought. Would she have loved you?

First she was here, then it could never be known.

At the office a well-dressed young man with wavy hair stood in front of him. He considered turning away again, but even that was too hard. Susan was out of sight. He walked past the young man at the front desk without speaking.

"Excuse me," said the man. "Excuse me. You can't go in there!"

"My office."

"What? Sir, you can't just go *in* there."

The young man got up and hovered beside him. He wore a strong aftershave.

"Mine. My office."

"Oh. Oh, I—sorry."

He could not wait; he passed by. He opened his door and closed it in the young man's face. The young man was doglike. For some reason neither people nor dogs expected you to close doors in their faces.

He did not intend rudeness, but it was crucial to raise the barrier speedily. With utmost speed.

"I'm very sorry for your loss," said the young man from the other side. The muffled voice trailed off.

Blinds were down on the windows. He walked over and raised one. Ocean in front, desk behind. Sturdy. The last time he had sat in the chair, behind the flat expanse of wood, she was living. He had not known the future; now he did. He was different in the full knowledge. He was different but the desk was the same.

Susan was there. She stood looking at him, her eyes filling.

"T.," she said, and came and put her arms around him.

He stood woodenly.

"I'm sorry," she said. "It must make it worse when people do this," and she wiped her eyes with the back of her hand. "Are you actually here to work? Or are you just checking in?"

"In," he said, and nodded.

"OK. Everything's fine. I needed help, so I hired Robert for Julie's position."

"OK," he said, nodding again.

He went toward the door again.

"You already leaving? You want me to walk with you?"

He shrugged but she took his arm anyway and gently led him.

•

He went back to work, faded and listless but with the rudi-
ments of function. His mother's psychiatrist had prescribed
him antidepressants, which he was directed not to combine
with alcohol. The pills took effect slowly and as a result the
days stayed thick for too long, his limbs hard to move.

But he worked in order to keep up the pace and the focus,
worked hard and steadily, and gradually the usual texture of
rooms crept back—rooms, buildings, streets and the sky. In
the office he watched as elements of the lobby lost their alien
particularity. Turning to background again were the file
cabinet, the phone, the television with ticker tape running
across the bottom. In his own office was a relief map of the
Mojave project; he put his hands on the hollow ridges of the
mountains and felt the plastic peaks digging into his palms.
He closed his eyes and pretended he had a bird's-eye view.
There was no longer excitement in it, it was a dull extension
of the already dull routine, but of course he would continue.

A few weeks later her mother left a message. There were
still some of his possessions in her daughter's apartment and
the lease would run out at the end of the month. He did not
wish to go—whatever remained there of his he would gladly
forget—but he had to, because the mother asked.

He went over at nighttime, because though night was
more difficult than daytime it was also, if he could fall asleep
early, more quickly done. In the dark the hardwood floor
shone from a streetlamp outside the window; standing in the
doorway he flipped a switch and saw there was nothing there
but a pile of white cardboard boxes, neatly stacked.

He was flattened; he did not want to do anything. He stood waiting for the inertia to pass. He waited to be changed but nothing arrived to change him. He felt only restlessness, increasing. Finally he went inside, because time was slow without movement. There was nothing else to be done.

At the back of an empty closet shelf in her bedroom, his fingers scrabbling in the film of dust over the cracked wood, he found something. He pulled it out to look at it: a white tennis sock, half-tucked into itself. It had the shape of being peeled off in haste, tossed aside. He sniffed it—a very slight smell, maybe worn for a single hour, for one run on the beach. She ran beside the water, where the sand was damp. He breathed in the scent. This was what he had left.

He held it close to his chest as he left the bedroom. He placed his key with deliberate care on the kitchen counter; he laid the sock gently atop a box and lifted them up.

His mother liked to walk the narrow residential streets to her new church, the streets with their small overgrown gardens. Sometimes when it was late she asked him to go with her. Once she asked on a mild night; as soon as he stepped out his door he could smell the ocean.

Both of them were silent as they walked. His mother let her hands trail along the trumpet-shaped flowers that grew on vines along so many picket fences, so many gates. She said in a low voice how she loved the flowers here, the flowers and the trees. Los Angeles was a paradise of exotics, wild with succulents and shrubs and flowers, cornucopias. She gazed down into a bed of twisted aloe and it occurred to him that she had been close to Beth too, yet he had never acknowledged this.

"You took care of me," he said. "But no one took care of you."

"Of course they did, dear," said his mother, and reached up to touch the cross at her neck.

He slung his arm around her shoulders as they walked.

"But T., when I'm gone you'll be all alone," she said, and looked up at him from the crook of his arm.

"What are you talking about?"

"When I'm gone."

"You think I'll never meet another woman, huh?" he asked lightly, and jerked his arm minutely as though threatening a headlock. "Thanks for the vote of confidence."

"It's not that, honey. You're very good-looking. The girls have always run after you, even if you didn't notice. I'm talking about your soul, T. I'm afraid you'll always be lonely in your soul. In the core of your being."

"Isn't everyone?"

"T.! Of course not. That's why we have Our Lady."

"I'm glad you have the Lady."

"But I want to know, T., when I go, that you're under her protection too. That you're not outside. In the cold."

"You don't need to worry."

"I don't think it's enough to be confirmed. I think you have to stay close to the Lady. You have to love her, T."

"You want me to go to confession?"

"I'm not talking about tonight. I'm talking about eternity."

"You worried about the IHOP again?"

She stopped and looked at him, her face very small. Behind her was a window into a brightly lit kitchen, ducks and chicks in a porcelain row.

"I want you to be with the angels, T. I want you to be with the saints."

He studied her face, the furrowed brow. Without him, he thought—the thought hurt—she had nothing.

"When I can't be here anymore, honey . . . it worries me.
I mean I lie awake about this. I want you to be with the Holy
Family."

"OK. OK. I'll do my best. You don't need to worry about
me. Please, OK?"

She consented to turn and resume walking. They moved
out of the window light.

At the church he released her as they went in; she genu-
flected and he followed suit. He could see no one else save a
teenager seated at the far end of a rear pew reading something.
His mother lit a votive candle and prayed; T. sat down near
the front and leaned forward, his arms on the back of the
pew in front of him, resting his forehead. He was tired; he
almost dozed, and when he raised his head again another
woman had come out of the confessional and walked past
him and was speaking sharply to the teenage boy. They
left with him gazing idly at them, the boy trailing behind
sulkily.

As a child he had rarely been able to think of sins to confess;
in his own view he had committed none. Often he had made
up a sin, knowing it was expected of him. And penance was
a fairly easy punishment, a good bargain.

The church felt Latino, he reflected, whereas Angela's
home church back east had a certain Anglo-Saxon reserve, a
certain genteel repression. Here the walls were crowded with
paintings of the saints, flowers strewn at their feet; deep colors
surrounded them, animals and children, and the blood of the
martyrs flowed crimson. He rose from the pew and walked
the perimeter, gazing at them. The Virgin of Guadalupe, in
green and red; St. Francis, preaching to the birds; St.
Michael, St. Elena, St. Jude. On the windows, again and
again, the Madonna and child and in the background the
light of God, rays emanating from the disk of the sun.

This was what made it what it was, made it clutch the hearts of women and ennobled their silent men in armchairs. This was what made it the first world religion, with its two billion adherents, and rendered dull by comparison the merits of the too-serene Buddhists, the Moslems without graven images, the secularists like him. Of all the stories it alone offered a drama morbid and luscious and sentimental— wounding that suffered in silence, cuckolds and miracles and sadism and murder, forgiving spirits who rose from the tomb and shimmered on through the years. It was a bestselling love story, beautiful sad mother and perfect child, and in the background the absent father, pure energy, who was apparently benevolent despite appearances to the contrary, who was present despite his apparent absence, good despite his apparent cruelty, right despite his apparent wrongness, and beyond that all-knowing.

What a vast permission.

His mother emerged from the confessional, walked in front of the altar and came toward him, her face lightened. From the beginning so little had been asked of his father, he thought, so little asked and even less given.

•

Beth had wished to be wrapped in a simple cotton shroud. She had not wanted a coffin. He knew this from a conversation they once had in passing, whose relevance he had dismissed out of hand—a conversation that had seemed at the time like a morbid fancy. Her family, he assumed, would not have known of this preference; no doubt she lay embalmed in cherry and velvet.

In the early morning he ushered his dog through his mother's front door and woke her up by mistake; she was sleeping on the living room couch, having taken a sudden dislike to her bed. He apologized for waking her and whispered to her bleary, sleep-dug face that he was leaving on a road trip. He did not say where.

He drove and slept and drove; he reached the desert city shortly before sunset. Even at dusk the air was hot, and to the east he could already see an orange moon rising over the mountains. The cemetery was a flat field with rows of gaudy flowers dotting the brown grass under palm trees and eucalyptus. It took him a long time to find her, and there was no grass or stone yet. Hers was one in a row of new mounds, each with a small nametag on a stake at one end.

Someone had left a bunch of plastic roses near the stake that bore her nametag, bright magenta with a dull green stem protruding, and beside them a small plastic Jesus on a cross. It was a garish Jesus with huge imploring eyes and light-blue tears flowing from them like prison tattoos. Roughly he grabbed the plastic Jesus and the roses and clamped them under his arm. All around him were corpses with plastic flowers: would the people buried here want these ugly tokens? Fake flowers defeated the purpose of remembering—fake flowers that lasted forever, making the effort of further visits unnecessary. The field of thousands of them

On the other hand, plastic was eternal.

Most of these people had died of old age; they might not mind the shorthand of plastic. But she had not been old and so she was not the same as the old, who more deserved to be dead.

He looked around him once, swiftly. There was no one, only a man with a lawnmower in the far distance and the rush of traffic along the road beside him. He strode with the

Jesus and roses toward a chain-link fence that marked the sides of a ditch. He hurled them both into it, toward the cavernous mouth of a pipe.

"There," he said aloud.

Now the Jesus lay at the edge of the pipe, face down.

He was about to turn but could not. The sight of the Jesus face-down was abject; it was wrong. He had to get it back.

He would have climbed the fence, but it was too high to step over and too weak to hold his weight if he climbed. Instead he ran along the fence, seeking an opening. There was a desperate urgency to him: every second the Jesus lay in the mud was pressing on him unbearably. He found a tear in the fence and stepped through into the ditch, where his feet went over candy wrappers and bottles until he could lean down and grab the Jesus out of the pipe. Saved! A save.

He held the Jesus tightly. Despite its garishness, or possibly because of it, he was terribly sorry. He would keep the Jesus close, where nothing bad could happen to it.

He was breathing hard and felt afraid of being caught there, someone emerging from the darkness of the pipe and seizing him.

He walked back to the grave and looked at the plastic stake, looked at the ground, barely believing her body was there. He was stepping on it . . . he would pretend she was not here at all. He could not think of her decomposing. He wished she was thin air. That was what she should be.

The base of the Jesus said MADE IN CHINA.

He took it back to the car with him.

Later at the motel he read a newspaper in bed, the same sentence four or five times before he realized he was failing to read it. What would she say, watching him here? She would see his newspaper open to the business pages; she

would think he had already forgotten her; but even as he had this nagging thought he also registered, in the long small-print columns, a P/E ratio of 45. He had been holding the stock far too long and it was grossly overvalued. Her death had diverted his attention from its meteoric rise—fortunate, since he would have already sold elsewise, having guessed it was peaking long before this.

She would be so injured!—to follow this train of thought. As consolation you thought of the dead and liked to assume them with you in some sense, present in the ether or the fiber of the mind. But then you had to admit that if they were in fact present, abstractly present as you wished to believe, if they were there in the molecules, their spirit in everything . . . what fresh horrors would they find? If the dead could be spirit must they also read minds?

They must be revered, must be felt in the air; at the same time they could not be let in.

He still relied on the vision of her—shaking her head rue-fully, dismissing with her competent assurance the suggestion of a grief that might be inconsolable. Only she could consign her own death to the tumult and natural flurry of event. He could not do it alone. It was crucial to the maintenance of his steadiness. All things were reconcilable, she said; all things had been accounted for.

Each day for the next week he rose at the same time and drove to a nearby diner; ate eggs and toast; then drove back to the hotel, as the heat of the day oppressed, and closeted himself with his television to watch the market, the tele-phone at his elbow. If he could not work his current projects while he was here at least he could speculate.

In the hour before sunset he always headed back to the cemetery. It was only then, at the close of day, that the desert

air settled into gentleness; it was then that a warm wind blew over the sand lots and the baked pavement began to cool, paper and dust skittering in swirls along the roadsides. The sky turned sweet, fleshy colors of orange and pink and the moon rose over the dark line of trees and hills, vaster than it had ever seemed before. He could see the craters in fine detail, the gray hollow rounds where the eyes seemed to be. By the time the sun was finally sinking behind the mountains he was usually pulling slowly along the cemetery road, dun-colored, half-visible birds swooping up from the dirt, flapping beside the front wheels of his car before they disappeared.

The desert had hard days but soft nights, he was learning. Nighttime was when it came into its own.

The third night he went to the grave he began to feel he had to bring something. Yet nothing came to mind, or what came to mind was wrong for her, wrong as the plastic Jesus. The fourth night he placed a small twig on the dirt, a twig with a living leaf, snapped off a hedge at the cemetery's perimeter. The fifth night he moved the twig and then added others, making a nest of them on the mound; the sixth night he dragged a broken branch across the dried grass to add to the clot of brush that was already there.

The seventh night he woke up at three a.m. It had struck him as he slept that her grave was surmounted by a pyre now, with tinder and kindling.

He pulled on his clothes and drove; he parked his car in an empty lot down the street, for they locked the cemetery gates soon after dark. Clouds crossed the moon, silver and streaming.

At the grave he knelt down with a match. It blew out and he lit another, stooped over the wood. He had never built a fire in the woods, never even built a fire in a fireplace since his parents always had a fake log. The tinder burned low

without lighting the main fuel, and the sparks died. He gathered a few more twigs and found a bag of lawn litter beside a shed; with this extra kindling the fire crawled till it took.

He was pleased to see what a tall blaze the small pyre made. As it burned higher he breathed in the smell of the smoke and watched cinders rising and floating; after a while he dropped to the dirt and sat down, gazing into the fluid shift of the flames. It was lovely, he thought. He could almost think it was something she had said once, unloosed.

Personally he would choose cremation; he would have chosen it for her, if it had been up to him, for if you were burned then you could go anywhere. On the smoke your particles would be dispersed over foreign countries, the poles and the tropics; who knew where you might end?

He watched with orange searing his eyes and when the fire was embers he stood and stretched his cramped legs. He blinked up at the darkness until the fiery imprints faded; he bent to touch the ashes and lifted his fingers to his mouth.

On the way to his car he heard sirens in the distance but he was unalarmed. He did not hurry, did not change his pace. At the street the coast was still clear. No cars, only traffic lights in a long line into the distance, shifting silently from red to green.

That he had stood for some time beside the fire and no one had approached him while it burned, that he walked away at his leisure and got into his car, had an effect: he could not say what it was but suddenly he had room around him, as though he could move with lightness.

Authority was not all.

Was it she who had a new freedom, or him? He thought they might have burned off together.

But his hotel room was airless. He sat upright on the bed, alert between the four walls. Why should this city have been the place that produced her, dry and lusterless place? Wide streets and strip malls, flat shining acres of trucks for sale beneath the grueling sun . . . but he would not see her mother, though she lived nearby and might have told him something. His was an inquiry into which no other persons could safely be admitted, because once others were let in there was always the risk of distortion. There would be no whole and single unity of remembrance if he went outside for knowledge; he wanted his own Beth to remain, the pillar of what she was.

He could see the dismal afternoon elapsing already, he and the mother seated gawkily on a couch, awkward in the knowledge that they might have been family but now would remain strangers. And her pathetic apartment—it would have to be so now, even if it had once been otherwise—would leave an impression on him that detracted from his other memories of her daughter. Instead he and the mother, in remote locations, would live on in complete separation. In time one would die and the other would never know the difference.

4

Soon grief ceased to order his time and his old demeanor returned intact. But while the pace of his life was restored the tone of it had altered, though the precise nature of this alteration at first escaped him. In keeping up his routine in business he was now almost dutiful—almost as if the accumulation of capital was nothing more than an obligation kept up for the sake of honor. Still the obligation was strong, and he held onto it.

First among his new tasks was the purchase of the jungle island in Belize. So inexpensive was this pristine land with its surrounding reefs and atolls that he considered himself well-advised to focus his acquisition program in the tropics, assuming he could gain enough expertise in transnational business and tax practices. There in the sunny lands lay the leisure fantasy of all northern peoples; there despots fell, borders opened, and wealthy tourists streamed. Or in some cases, his contacts informed him, despots did not fall but would cooperate for minimal subsidy; borders still opened; and younger but still wealthy tourists streamed, in disregard of despots.

He went to the island twice a month to meet with local contractors, taking investors with him. His property was a twist of mangrove and deciduous forest in the midst of sea with no fresh water or roads; on the small strip of open shore sand fleas bit relentlessly and pelicans splattered white on the rocks. He stayed a short boat trip away, in a luxurious beachside resort on the mainland.

Once a guide took them out to scuba-dive from a small motorboat, to gauge the asset value of the reefs; he instructed them on the basic functions of valves, how to sink and rise again. Fulton, his investor, declined to enter the water, remaining on the boat with his wetsuit peeled open down to the waist and a cooler of beer at hand. He sat fishing off the bow with a rented pole, catching nothing but refusing to budge from his post.

So T. dove by himself, over the guide's objection. He had not dived before or even snorkeled but it was not hard, beyond the awkwardness of the heavy tank as he rolled backward over the boat's side. He swam peacefully thirty feet below, moving his fins languidly among conch and sea cucumbers, and was glad to be alone there. He found he luxuriated in the perfect seal of his mask, the muted quality of sound.

On the veranda of the hotel restaurant he watched wet-haired children run around the pool, laughing as the sun glanced off the water behind them, chasing each other on the slippery tiles until they cannonballed into the deep end shrieking. At his own resort he planned docks for boats and for swimming, and on the end of the swim docks would be circular decks with palm-thatch roofs, white hammocks beneath them suspended around a floating bar. Guests could drink their cocktails standing in the shallows; fish would gather around their legs to feed on the scraps, bits of lemon

and maraschino cherry and olive. Sand as blindingly white as snow, which made the shallow water above it look deep turquoise for the brochure photographs, would soon be shipped in and dumped over the native sand, which was colored a natural and dull brown.

But first the shoreline would have to be scraped of vegetation, so he went out to the island to supervise the clearing of the first beachhead. From a small yacht anchored in the shallows he drank coffee and watched workers with power saws cut down and bundle the bushy trees along the waterline. As the limbs fell their small glossy leaves rained down onto the water and the boat captain, seated behind T. with a hand on the tiller, smiled gently and described them to him: red mangrove, black mangrove, white. Buttonwood.

He thought of her then, watching flotillas of leaves drifting and bobbing on the surface, and it was less difficult than before—as though the shock, once absorbed, had spread so thin and wide that it was only the skin of the world.

As he regained strength his mother's mental health seemed to falter again, as though, watching him be restored, she deemed herself released at long last; as though she could resign her duties and retire once more into premature senescence.

He saw her almost daily when he walked his dog. Invariably she was seated at her dining room table, face bent low over a jigsaw puzzle as her reading glasses slid down her nose. She worked on one puzzle after the next with no rest between them, keeping a stockpile at the ready, and when she finished placed each one atop its predecessor in a stack in the closet. Because she made her selections on the advice of a young clerk who worked at a nearby toy store, and content was irrelevant, puzzles featuring water lilies, moon landings

and civil war battlefields all came within her purview and passed out of it equally. Because she did not like interruptions to break her concentration, talk was often stilted, and T. would soon leave again, his dog straining at the leash to continue their walk.

He had barely noticed while Beth was living but he had no friends outside business: he had spent all his free time with her and now was left with no one. He took up the habit of playing racquetball thrice weekly with Fulton, who slammed the ball so hard against the walls and the ceiling of the court that a former partner, omitting to don safety goggles, had lost the use of an eye.

He played only partly for the exercise and expedience and partly for entertainment. Fulton, who specialized in mutual funds when he was not investing his wife's family fortune in T.'s projects, could go from zero to screaming fury in ten seconds flat. He delivered angry monologues as he played, expletives often drowned in the deafening ricochet; and his phrases were punctuated with vicious swipes from his powerful but imprecise forehand.

"That—piece—of—shit—had—the—goddamn— sweaty— little—balls," he might scream, running and leaping to slash downward with his racquet, "to—say—that—*we*— could—not—upzone!"

In racquetball no response was needed for Fulton to proceed with his soliloquy, and this rendered the sport relaxing. When Fulton suffered a setback or personal loss—his son was sidelined on the soccer team, his daughter's orthodontist indicted for tax evasion—his rage stayed bottled only long enough to reach the courts, where it was funneled easily. There was no subtlety to Fulton, who was always most alive when fulminating. At Fulton's sure-footed advance, complexity took flight: what did not surrender to his simple will to

dominate was plowed under forthwith, and wrongs were crudely and rapidly redressed. The sheer effectiveness of a brute had never been so clear to T.

Observing the investor's unfettered path through life T. felt his distaste tempered by incredulousness. But though he patronized Fulton, often speaking to him as others might to children or the feeble-minded, he also had to stand back and cede his position when confronted by the stampeding bull. Stupid rage commanded the obedience of more even-tempered men in a way impossible to deny or moderate; a Fulton cured of his instinct toward wrath would be a pitiful creature.

Beth had only met Fulton once, over dinner, on a night when Fulton had chosen to adopt a curiously meek stance. It was as though he had known by instinct when to retreat; for his quiet deference to Beth, which T. thought bordered on toadying, had marked him forever in her eyes as a gentle, self-effacing presence. Later that night, as she and T. prepared for bed, she had remarked innocently that she really liked Fulton. "Does he have just a little bit of a lisp?" she had asked with the lilt of sympathy in her voice, raising the coverlet and sliding beneath. "Poor guy. That must be very hard for him in his job. Face-to-face with so many new people all day."

At the time he was vaguely puzzled by the remark but forgot it in the pleasure of bed; but later it dawned on him that on their way into the restaurant, briefing her on the backgrounds of those she was soon to meet, he had referred to Fulton as a banker. By *banker*, in this case, he had meant an individual who—on the strength of a Harvard MBA, family connections and very little in the way of native intelligence—made investment decisions for tens if not hundreds of thousands of retired nurses and welders, whose future pensions he placed in the hands of such corporate luminaries as Royal Dutch Shell and Monsanto.

But she had assumed he meant Fulton was a teller.

Fulton did not have a lisp; if Fulton were ever to meet a man with a lisp he would surely ridicule him, most likely with reference to words not contained in a standard dictionary. When it came to details such as social identity and stereotype Fulton was nothing if not a blunt instrument. Indeed Fulton suffered from no articulation disorder save rudeness; at one point during the dinner T. had noticed him talking about his daughter's pony with his mouth full of beef stroganoff. Possibly this was what had given Beth the impression of a speech impediment.

Since the two of them had not met again the illusion of Fulton's harmlessness had never been dispelled. Certainly, if he dwelled on it, he would be forced to concede that Beth's positive impression of Fulton could not have been sustained through multiple encounters: but as such encounters had never occurred he did not have to make the admission to himself openly.

Was it the man's brutishness itself, his triumphant profanity, that was so intriguing? Fulton's awareness of the independent existence of others was vestigial at best. T. had the feeling, in fact, that for Fulton the presence of other people in the world was purely hypothetical. Like the philosopher Bishop Berkeley, whom T. had read with considerable interest in college, Fulton was certain only of his own existence; all others were most likely figments.

On his mother's birthday he took her yellow roses. Once they had been her favorite but she barely looked at them, nodding at his entrance as she fitted a jigsaw piece. Leaning over her shoulder he saw the work in question was titled "The Ages of Man," a vintage puzzle depicting the stages of human evolution from Australopithecus to Homo sapiens. An

illustration in full color, it pictured many different hominids, historically separated by millions of years, performing daily activities concurrently in what appeared to be a vaguely Native American encampment. Some among their number wore papooses on their backs and squatted in front of teepees.

Putting his face closer he saw an apelike figure labeled CRO MAGNON standing beside a small pile of sticks, thumb and index finger posed lightly on his chin as though lost in thought. Possibly he was discovering fire. Female apes milled uselessly in the background, their hairy breasts hidden behind interposed branches, and in a far corner a Homo erectus raised his cudgel over a frightened rabbit.

He smiled as he looked at it. It was primitive in depicting the primitive. That was it.

As a child he had thought man advanced.

He stood still now, back from his mother, frozen.

As a child he had thought man advanced.

Moving into the kitchen he found a pair of scissors in a disordered drawer; he cut the stems and stuck the roses into a vase. In former days his mother would have leapt to the task, but now she demonstrated no interest. Thorny stems in his grip he popped the lid of the trashcan, which was overflowing; he barely registered the smell of rancid food as he stood there, thorns digging into his thumbs.

That was what had changed, he thought. To love posterity and the great institutions you had to believe in the wisdom of men. You had to love them as a child might, gazing upward.

He recalled himself presently; a thin string of blood crawled down his wrist, tickling, and his nostrils were compressed. Atop the trash lay a limp piece of uncooked

chicken, blueish. He coughed briefly, nauseated, and let the garbage lid fall shut again. He dropped the rose stems in the sink; he washed the blood off his hands. Two small punctures, was all.

He turned and pulled out the full bag, tied it and carried it, bulging with sharp angles, out the back door. His mother had fallen from her attention to cleanliness, fallen far and quickly.

Glancing around for her outdoor garbage bin he saw a small shrine on a stucco wall and moved closer. The centerpiece was a photograph of Beth that must have come from one of his own packets of loose snapshots; around it, stuck to the stucco with pushpins, were snatches of poetry, rosaries draped ornamentally, prayer cards and lace and dried flowers. He saw sacred hearts, haloed angels and melancholy Marys, faded and curling and made porous by rain.

Sorrow.

The evidence was everywhere: he could not avoid it. At first he had believed only a few men were childish, and raised himself above them. Arrogant, because all men were childish, including him.

They still had their institutions and those institutions still had their beauty—less grandiose, however, than ruined. He loved them nonetheless, revered them even as they declined. But the beauty they had, did it mean something? Or was it artful like the scrawls of preschoolers—chiefly by accident?

•

In his relationship to Fulton he knew he had found a pastime that allowed him the twin guilty pleasures of judgment and observation: his passivity under the onslaught was that of a voyeur.

When Fulton committed infidelity, for instance, he did so as a paying customer, every Tuesday and Thursday at three. This kept him, he claimed, safe from the fear of detection and perfectly blame-free. When T. inquired as to the workings of this absolution Fulton gaped at him openly, as though T. was the world's first moron. For he, Fulton, was committing no act of betrayal; he did not love the prostitute; theirs was a business arrangement.

T. asked him then if, in fact, he actually loved his wife. He could easily believe that Fulton did *not* love, prostitute or wife equally. In fact the proposition that he *did* love had a tinge of absurdity.

"I married her," said Fulton. "Same fucking thing."

Possibly, T. reflected now and then in the wake of some particularly egregious revelation, Fulton trusted him with the confidences simply because he knew that he, Fulton, represented a primary capital stream to T., one that T. would not dare to put at risk through disloyalty. Or possibly, he suspected at other times, Fulton actually liked him.

But Fulton barely knew him. As a rule T. revealed little in the way of personal information, since Fulton did not seem to require it. For Fulton communication was a one-way street. And when, on occasion, T. chose to contribute to the conversation with a brief disclosure of his own, Fulton became bored and changed the subject.

"So my father," said T. on the way to the racquet club one Wednesday, reclining in the leather passenger seat of Fulton's Land Cruiser, "used to be an ad executive in Manhattan, but now he mixes drinks at a transvestite bar in Key West."

"He turned gay?"

"I guess so."

"Huh," said Fulton, hunching down and squinting into the side-view mirror. "Did you see that? Asian woman in the Hyundai almost rear-ended me."

"No. Didn't see."

"Asians can't drive for shit."

"Might want to keep that insight to yourself."

"It's not exactly a secret, T. Damn, you're a rube. Disoriented Orientals. Ring a bell?"

"If the poor woman had rear-ended this car she would have been killed instantly."

"You gotta watch out, T.," said Fulton, shaking his head. "That stuff's in the genes. You could turn homo too."

"You think so?"

"Watch out for it. If you feel the urge, rent a copy of *Anal Alley* and have a jerkoff marathon."

"That's very helpful."

"What am I saying? That's like offering smack to a guy on methadone. Better stay around the front side, T. Avoid the ass region completely."

"Good tip."

"Janet's sister's church has this deal where they deprogram them. I don't think it works though."

"No? Doesn't work?"

"It's a boot camp. They tell them man-boy love is the work of Satan. They bring in straight guys to teach them how to act straight. Like you're not allowed to smoke, it's faggy. Then

they lock them up in small rooms and yell their heads off at them. 'Repent, sinners! For the sake of Jesus Christ Our Lord, cast out the homo devil from your butt!' It's kind of like hardcore bondage and domination. It's supposed to scare them straight but I think it actually makes them horny. Some Christian faggots actually hook up there. Serious. It's basically a dating service for Christian homos."

"What does Janet's sister think of that?"

"She put her son in it and he came out of there with a brand-new assfriend. That's how she found out the real deal. I have a faggot nephew."

"I didn't know."

"No blood relation though. Janet's side of the family only. My genes are pure hetero. I had a great-grandfather who was a rapist."

"Excuse me?"

"Yeah. The guy raped. Rapists are basically superheteros. A rapist is a hetero on steroids."

"That's quite a theory you've got there."

"I forgot to tell you, you gotta use the shit racquet today. The titanium's being restrung."

Over time, as T. had suspected he would, Fulton delivered an education.

The change came suddenly, when the two of them went back to T.'s apartment for beer once after a game. Fulton claimed he wanted to see the place. As soon as they pulled up stools to the kitchen island and sat down, lifting freshly uncapped bottles to their lips, the dog came trotting over. She stood on her rear legs and put her forepaws on Fulton's stool, tail wagging, with the slavish affection she sometimes bestowed on strangers who seemed welcome.

Fulton surprised T. by pushing her away roughly with an elbow to her face and the side of his shoe to her flank. Grimacing, he wiped his arm on his gym shorts.

"Dog spit. Disgusting."

"Spit? What spit? This dog doesn't slobber at all. Come here, girl."

The dog retreated to T.'s side, where he put a protective hand between her ears and stroked her head. He was irritated.

"I don't touch dogs."

"Why? Are you allergic?"

"I don't like to touch the things, OK? They lick their anuses. You got any chips? Crackers or something?"

T. stared at him as he tipped his head back and took a deep swallow.

"No chips," he answered. "No crackers."

"I'm starving."

Fulton jumped up and opened the refrigerator door, scouting. T. followed him with his gaze and felt a tide of revulsion rising in his bones, in his blood and muscles. Fulton's back was a wall of hostile blankness; Fulton's neck was no neck.

He got off his own stool abruptly, a cursory glance at his watch.

"Know what? Forgot. Got a meeting. Escrow thing."

"Take the brew with me, then," said Fulton without missing a beat, and turned toward the door of the kitchen with his beer bottle still in hand.

T. watched him leave without saying a word.

That night he kicked his legs in and out of the sheets, turned and punched his pillow into different shapes against his cheek. The cheek felt slack, distracting as he tried to sleep. There was no good position for the side of his face. The scissoring of his legs and pulling and twisting of the

blankets kept the dog awake too, circling and circling and rearranging herself head to feet into her curved moon of sleep.

Finally he got up and went toward the bathroom, dog rising once more on the bed behind him. He leaned over the toilet with his eyes closed and saw pricks of light on the surface of his eyelids. Nothing happened beyond a head rush.

He had let him kick her. Almost a kick. His dog—but it was not whose she was that mattered, only how devoted she was, how she followed without questioning. Would follow on and on forever.

He stood. He was taking Fulton's money, certainly. He would take it as long as he could. But to bring him home? To seek him out?

His dog should not forgive him.

•

From a garrulous surveyor who worked for him in the desert, a man with psoriatic arms and perpetual mint covering the whiskey on his breath, he discovered that a group of small rodents called kangaroo rats had been displaced by the paving for his subdivision. This had been part of the lawsuit that had held up the project; the rats were the last of their kind, on the brink of disappearing.

He met with state and federal biologists and offered a parcel of land in what the bureaucrats called mitigation; after the agreement was signed he acquired the habit of walking there, on a few acres of gravelly dirt studded with patches of grass and backed up to a low hill on a far edge of the project. Here, one of the biologists told him, the rats could settle the

abandoned burrows of pocket gophers and build their nests; they could nibble on buckwheat and brome and filaree. He was gratified to find a use for the parcel, for it was a desolate, stark piece of ground, flat earth and old mine tailings in a bright, bland slope. Here and there an anthill. The weight of ants, a biologist told him, was equal to fifteen percent of the weight of all land animals; ants roiled beneath the surface in untold billions.

Biologists had captured some of the rats before paving began and were breeding them, planning to move them to the site when the numbers were sufficient. One afternoon, at the invitation of the biologist, he toured the biological field station, which smelled of bleach and cedar shavings. She showed him a cage of baby rats called pinkies, squirming alongside their mother. The mother was sleek and looked less like the rats he had seen—gray, oily subway vermin with hairless tails and sharp faces—than a chipmunk, with a head too large for her body and bright dark eyes.

"They're technically not rats, actually," said the biologist eagerly. "They're in the heteromyid family. They've evolved to extract all the water they need from seeds."

He looked closely at the pinkies, their miniature bodies with finely articulated feet, their closed eyes as they struggled to feed. In the softness of the impression the room glowed amber at the edges. What was this? He felt receptive; he had an inner buoyancy.

But the sense of well-being fled when he left, and in the course of the relocation the baby rats died. The biologist mentioned it weeks after it happened.

"The mortality wasn't complete," she told him. "But this was a delicate situation, because the numbers were already so low. So, and I mean this is best-case scenario, there's a question, with the reduced numbers, of population viability."

"I'm so sorry," he said.

"With so few individuals in a population there would be problems of genetic drift and inbreeding depression. Resilience to disturbance drops. The gene pool is too small for long-term survival."

"I'm very sorry," he said again.

"Worst case, and what we're probably looking at here, is extinction. The remaining adults aren't thriving. They're losing weight, starting to die off. Haven't identified the cause. But we can't re-release them like this."

The biologist was not emotional; she was matter-of-fact. But oddly he found his own throat closing.

Was it something else from his life? It must be, something else glancing across from the side as he stood here. Still always Beth, possibly; he could not be choked up over the kangaroo rats. But he felt tentative, suspicious—as though someone had slyly robbed him and only now was he suspecting it. Cities were being built, built up into the sky, battlements of convenience and utopias of consumption—the momentum of empire he had always cherished. But under their foundations the crust of the earth seemed to be shifting and loosening, falling away and curving under itself.

He found he was barely breathing. He let out his breath and filled his lungs again.

When he slept that night it was the ants abandoning ship. They left in their billions, all of them, and as they went away holes opened up in the earth, yawning sinkholes into which oceans and mountains poured.

•

In subsequent weeks he was often irritated by the Mojave
project's denizens. The racewalker, for one. As he walked
along the road one morning—a cul-de-sac called Elysian
Fields—the racewalker bore down on him with ferocious
intensity. The racewalker's lips were pinched together and he
wore a mesh singlet bearing a single word: WIN!

 The racewalker, he saw, was a rigid man clamped together
in barely suppressed resentment. As they passed each other
T. waved and nodded politely; the racewalker looked straight
at him but made no acknowledgment. When T. turned to
watch his retreating back he noticed the racewalker's defiant
gluts, moving up and down with vigorous emphasis.

 He wondered what the racewalker had been doing when
he took refuge here; he was barely in his fifties, surely, and
must still be working, but here he was in a retirement com-
munity. The racewalker had a wife, if he recalled correctly, a
potato-like lump of a woman who stared sullenly and rarely
spoke: most likely the racewalker perambulated their house
with barely a nod at her lumpen presence.

 Leaving the racewalker behind he proceeded to the house
at the base of the cul-de-sac, recently purchased by a couple
from Texas he had not yet welcomed. He rang the doorbell
and waited, and when the woman opened the door he smiled
at her pleasantly. Yet he found himself dwelling on the car
parked in their driveway, on a political bumper sticker of
obnoxious intent. When the husband emerged from behind
his wife he took an instant dislike to the man, who wore a
loud flag-pattern T-shirt and a cowboy hat. He could barely

stand the pressure of the Texan's outstretched hand. When the Texan announced a plan to replace his desert-landscaped front yard with asphalt, T. struggled to remain civil.

"Sorry, but the bylaws won't allow that particular kind of modification," he said. "Visual quality, for the benefit of the neighborhood as a whole. I'm sure you appreciate that."

"With the turning you gotta do to park here, you know, if we had a bigger driveway we could just drive right onto it straight. You know, not have to turn at all, first left and then right, when we come down the street to the end right out there."

"Labor-saving," said T., nodding and tapping his foot softly.

"You know, we could just keep going straight and park right in front of the door here."

"You'll get used to turning the steering wheel, I'm sure," said T. "I mean that's what they're made for, right?"

"Huh," said the Texan.

"I think you'll find the nice look of the trees and flowers in your yard will be worth it. The extra effort of wheel-turning, that is."

"Plus which," said the wife, "we wouldn't have to back out. We could just turn a little and go out frontward again."

"It sounds like what you want is a crescent drive," said T. "You know what? We're building some homes on the other side of La Terrazza that are going to have crescent drives. They're even larger. Maybe you can trade up when they're finished. I can put you on the waiting list, if you're interested."

"This little hideaway already drained me dry," said the Texan. "Are you fuckin' kidding?"

"Just a suggestion," said T. mildly. "How's the rest of the move going? Got your bearings yet?"

"She was the one wanted us to move here," said the Texan. "I'm strictly an Amarillo man. SoCal's not my bagga shit."

T. turned to the wife. "And how are you liking it?"

"When are they gonna have the full schedule for step aerobics?" scolded the wife. "The brochure said step aerobics! Five days a week!"

When he finally left them his neck was itching against his collar. He stopped at the pool, but the pool was empty. The elderly ladies were not there, not swimming. This place, he thought vengefully, had probably killed them off too. The Texan in his monster truck.

He pulled out of the parking lot for the drive back to the city and found himself turning right instead of left, toward the set-aside. He parked and walked across it up the slope, stepping around the bunchgrasses and peering into the holes that had been meant for the last individuals of the rat species, the ones with the babies.

The rats were gone now, the biologist had told him. They had been extinguished.

He looked up from the sandy ground to the red tile roofs across the arroyo, arrayed in military precision. He could hear crickets somewhere in the dry grass; in the stasis of the morning all he heard was this chirping and the faint rush of traffic on the Interstate, over two miles away. He stood without moving and stared at the roofs, the low adobe wall that ran along the wash. They had built it to stave off erosion but it also served to separate the built environment from the desert; here the brush was not clipped or manicured and the rare tall cacti, when they aged and fell, could be left to rot on the ground. At dusk black beetles crawled faltering over small rocks, as though the pebbles were boulders, and coyotes ran lightly down the wash.

Coyotes could live anywhere. They were not like the rats, who lived only on one small patch of land. They could live

anywhere and die anywhere too. Like him. They were oppor-
tunists. And the Texans with their path of least resistance, the
racewalker . . . they would give up nothing they were not
required to, they would insist on their right to all that they had
and more, unyielding. The pinky rats had been struggling to
feed: then they died, and took their parents with them.

How was it he could have changed like this? Before it
had been a triumph; then it soured. He resented the people
he had sold to, but he was worse than they were. The race-
walker, the Texan were familiar aspects . . . he saw it like
diamond, like a flash on metal.

He felt the sun on his head and a wave of nausea.

Win, win; oh, not to have to turn the wheel. To not turn
wheels at all: to stay in one position. Pave it over, make it a
smooth and continuous surface, flat and gray on the world,
speed and ease.

And yet the seedeaters. Infants.

But it was not sentiment, not at the base of this—he felt
for them, but it was not empathy. It was fear. It was the knowl-
edge of the ants beneath them, the ants pouring away and
taking with them the very foundations. Everything.

He was cold.

The foundations would be gone. Once the ants left, first the
rats and finally even the ants, there would be nothing left of them.

He got back in the car, dazed. It took him a few minutes
to turn the key for home.

•

He kept going back to the set-aside. He was permeable there,
oddly inseparate from the dirt and the dry golden grass. He

liked to park the car and leave it, walking up the slope with its tumbled rock, his feet slipping, till he crested the hill and went down the back side. Then he could no longer see the pavement or the road, and would sit on the flat top of a boulder. Sometimes at dusk he would sit there for hours, listening to what he once would have thought was silence.

He had never before sat anywhere for hours, unless he was working. He had never, he realized one night, been away from a road before, never in his whole life been out of sight of pavement. Unless he was in an airplane or building. Or out near his island.

What place would that be, a whole world without roads? It was a panicking thought. A world without roads! He would go nowhere in such a place. He would be trapped where he was, he would have lived out his life only where he was born.

And the world outside the roads was not straight or smooth. It was not shored up like those roads and the buildings, metal and cement and right angles. It was whirlpools and washes of soil and the mass of the clouds, dispersing into each other and leveling distinctions. It was trying to invade him and he should be alarmed. He was in danger. What you needed more than anything, for the purposes of ambition, was certainty, was a belief that the rest of being, the entirety of the cosmos, should not be allowed to penetrate and divert you from the cause—the chief and primary cause, which was, clearly, yourself.

Yet he was laid out to receive it. He was laid out by the force of gravity itself, by elemental physics. Sediment accumulated on him, buried him gradually, and more and more he was silted in.

5

The zoo was on the edge of a wide desert valley, with a view of cactus-dotted hills above and, in the flats spread out beneath, flocks of small white houses. He went there after a meeting in Scottsdale, to fill an empty afternoon. He was restless in his hotel and had seen the zoo in a tourist brochure, with a picture of a wolf.

In a series of arid gardens connected by pathways there was a hummingbird enclosure and an aviary, a beaver pond and a pool for otters; there were Mexican parrots squawking, bighorn sheep on artificial cliffs, an ocelot curled up in a rocky crevice and a sleek bobcat pacing restlessly. He passed a lush pollinator garden and a series of low and inconspicuous buildings; an elderly, white-haired docent stood with a watchful bird perched on her hand, waiting for interest. He wandered over and looked at the bird closely. It had large eyes in a beautiful face, and was compact but fierce looking.

"American kestrel," said the docent. "One of the smaller raptors. This gal is almost nine inches long, but weighs less than four ounces. Beautiful, isn't she?"

A few minutes later he stood bracing himself with his hands on a low wall over a moat. Across the moat slept a black bear on a sunny ledge. This was a zoo of animals native to the region, and though bears did not live in the hot flat-lands a handful of them still roamed the piney mountains that rose above the desert floor. He had read that every so often a bear was found dead atop a power pole, where it had climbed suddenly in terror, escaping from a car or a noise, and been electrocuted.

He watched the bear sleep, and in the lull of the sun and the heat and the stillness felt like dozing off himself.

Then the stillness was disturbed by yelling boys, hitting each other in the face. The father, in shorts, stood at T.'s elbow, looking down into his camera and adjusting a ring on the lens. A projectile—someone had lobbed a balled-up piece of litter. It hit the bear a glancing blow on the ear and he stirred, disoriented, turned around once and then settled down again.

"Too soon, I wasn't set up yet. Missed the shot," said the man, shaking his head. "Go again."

The wife looked around for something else to throw and T. felt heat filling his face. A tension bowed in him: he felt a rush of fury.

"Are you kidding?" he asked, turning to the wife. She wore large mirrored sunglasses. "You're throwing garbage at the bear? For a *picture*?"

"What's the big deal?" said the family man.

"Don't do it," said T. His shoulders were fluid and nervy, his face shining. He was enraged. Or excited. But all here, he thought: and *I will kill them*. Even though he knew it was a posture, he felt the anger and relished it.

The man shrugged and the wife began rifling through her purse, apparently ignoring him; a few feet away one of the

flailing children, a thin boy in khaki camouflage pants, was already lofting a second missile, a foam cup half-full of brown slush. The cup missed the bear and fell into the moat below, and the slush slung out of the cup as it arced past and dimpled the bear's dark coat. The bear reared up again, doubly confused.

The thin boy jeered.

T. turned to the father, who was still fumbling with his zoom lens. A split second of hesitation. "You let your kid do that again, I swear to God I'll grab that camera and break it open on the cement," he said.

He realized his molars were grinding. He had never done this, never. Never anything—. He was thrilled and at the same time he hated the man, hated his wife and even his children.

"Mind your own business," said the family man.

"I'm dead serious. I'll smash it to fucking bits."

"I'll sue you!"

"What are you thinking? Seriously. What does someone like you think? Do you think?"

"Stupid bear!" jeered the camouflage kid.

"Mind your business," said the family man again.

"It *is* my business," said T. "Just like it would be if you threw garbage at my sister. What don't you get about that? Is there an argument for what you're doing?"

"Let's just go, Ray," said the wife.

"I got a squirt gun," said the kid, and pulled it out: the size of an assault rifle, bright pink.

"Don't even think about it," said T., and looked at the father. His neck tensed, his hands flexed. "Tell him to put that thing away. I'll punch your face. I mean it."

The man was squaring off, his eyes narrowed. He let his camera rest against his chest, the dangling lens cap swinging.

"Tell *me* how to handle my kid? He can squirt his water gun at the bear if he wants to."

"You disgusting. Piece. Of shit," said T.

The wife tugged urgently on her husband's sleeve.

"Come *on*, Ray."

After a moment the family man turned, his wife beside him and the kids ranging around them both; as they turned a corner the kid in camouflage pants whipped around and sneered, sticking up the middle fingers of both hands before he disappeared.

T. felt the adrenaline surge fade but still he burned. He wanted to hunt them down and punish them. But he did not. He did not utter a word of complaint to the zoo's management. He was flooded with elation.

He was elated. This was who he was, he thought; he was a person who would defend, who would swear and threaten and feel the heat and the cliff-edge of opinion. He felt good—better than good. He stood there for seconds, or was it forever?—stood there partway in rapture, struck.

On its flat rock the bear was still turning blearily round, tossing its head as though trapped in a nightmare. Finally it resettled itself and laid its chin on its paws to go back to sleep.

He went back that night when the zoo was closed, thrilled, as if he was lightly drunk, at the illicitness in himself. It was new. What arrested him in the zoo was the wildness it contained— how far this was from the realm of his competence. He wanted to meet it. He knew the zoo animals lived in cages but nothing more about them except that they were alone, most of them, not only alone in the cages, often, but alone on the earth, vanishing. Their condition was close to what he was trying to grasp, lay somehow at the base of his growing suspicion that the ground was no longer fixed, was shifting beneath him.

Empire only looked good built against a backdrop of oceans and forests. It needed them. If the oceans were dead and the forests replaced by pavement even empire would be robbed of its consequence. *Alone*, he thought—a word that came to him more and more, in singsong like a jeer. In the zoo the rare animals might have been orphaned or captured or even born in captivity. He had no idea where they came from, could not know their individual histories. But he knew their position, as he knew his own: they were at the forefront of aloneness, like pioneers. They were the ones sent ahead to see what the new world was like.

Would they tell what they saw?

The rarest animal in the zoo was a Mexican gray wolf, the one pictured in the tourist brochure, an animal that was apparently frail and aging. Its fur looked mangy; it had been asleep when he was there earlier. The wolf's pen, as the sign posted on it told him, was a temporary setup during construction of a new exhibit. It was nothing more substantial than a chain-link fence near the road, with barbed wire curling along the top.

He looked at his shoes: round toes. He should be able to wedge them into the holes. He shoved his flashlight in his pocket, hooked his fingers through the mesh and pulled himself up, kicking for purchase. His feet flailed against the fencing and his fingers were already bruising, imprinted with purple lines. Speed was the key, he thought, move quickly. He always had reasons for each single action, but he had no good reasons for doing this. Was he irrational? But it lifted him. He would follow the question to its resolution, even if the question was unconscious.

He was not even all the way up the six-foot fence when he regretted his tactics. He had to get down from here, the pressure on the pads of his fingertips, which he feared were

going to be sliced clean through. In a scramble he grabbed
the metal frame the wire was stretched on and went up and
over it, catching barbs on his chest and thighs. His leg, half-
way over, was tangled in the wire, and struggling he lost his
foothold. Falling he tried to launch himself forward, away
from the barbs.

When he recovered, on the ground with an aching neck
and shoulders, he had a sharp pain in his leg. Sitting up he
saw he had grazed his calf on a cactus as he fell. Through the
thin cotton of his pants it was bleeding, and in the dark he
could see white spines sticking through the fabric. He stood
unsteadily, bracing himself against the fence; he could make
out almost nothing. He walked around the cactus, lifting his
flashlight. In the dark he could imagine not only wolves but
almost anything, a secret menagerie. He was filled with the
rush of this, with the idea of myriad creatures materializing
from the blackness. Their coats glowed, their faces were both
benign and predatory. The faces of animals were amazing in
that, tongues of velvet and claws of ice. What were they?

There was a gate, padlocked; a metal box built into the
base of the fence; a dry log, a thin tree. Doves rose suddenly
from the tree, a flurry of hysterical wingbeats. He jumped.

His leg was aching.

He began to point his beam at bushes and the bases of
trees, where holes might be tucked. Finally he flicked off the
light and squatted down. Without the glare his eyes adjusted
and finally he apprehended a shape that was not a bush or
tree, hunkered down against the fence, low and dim.

He got up silently and picked his way closer, still without
the flashlight on, his eyes on the ground while he threaded
his way between bushes. Closer and closer till he pointed the
flashlight toward the ground in front of the wolf's hunched
shape and touched the switch with his thumb. A quick yellow

flicker of eyes and then the wolf moved fluidly, fleeing along the fence. It went away from him, into a corner where it remained.

He would not get closer. The wolf would not allow it.

The next morning he removed the small spines from his leg. The wound was throbbing, but he did not mind; there was something he savored in it, pinching the hair-thin fibers hard between the tweezer edges. The sensation was fine and sharp as a grass blade. It satisfied him.

He took two aspirins and showered. In his socks and his shirt, standing in front of the in-room coffeemaker, he thought of the old wolf again. Animals were self-contained and people seemed to hold this against them—possibly because most of them had come to believe that animals should be like servants or children. Either they should work for men, suffer under a burden, or they should entertain them. He had strained against the wolf's aloofness himself, resenting the wolf for its insistence on distance. He had felt it almost as an insult, and inwardly he retaliated.

But then he was self-contained too: he had a private purpose, a trajectory, and no one had license to block it. It might be obscure even to him, but that obscurity was his own possession. The old wolf's unwillingness to be near him was fully forgiven by the light of day and in fact the joke was on him. Wariness was simply its way of life, having nothing to do with him. It had not been robbed of this quality, though it was caged and it was solitary: it retained its essence. It did not attempt to ingratiate itself. It did not have diplomacy.

He thought he recalled feeling, in the flash of its eye-shine, a similar flash in himself—a fleeting awareness that in the wolf's gaze there was a directness unlike the direct-ness of men.

Wolves were gone, the educational sign on the cage had read, from most of the country. They were the villains of fairy tales, and there had been vast campaigns to exterminate them all across the continent. A slaughter of the wolves, along with the buffalo. Long before that in the late Pleistocene, according to the sign, the Clovis people had caused the extinction of the cave bear, the giant beaver, the saber-tooth tiger, the horse and the mastodon.

He buttoned his shirt without looking at his fingers, eyes on a weather map on the television, a smiling weatherman pointing and gesturing. He had wanted the old wolf to come close to him, head down, softening. As though all wild animals could one day be tamed — as though this was an aspect of all of them, this one-day-tamable quality, and their wildness was nothing more than coyness or a mannerism. As though other animals should not only submit to people but behave like them, comport themselves with civility.

Privately, he thought, at the heart of it, you wanted animals to turn to you in welcome. It was a habit gained from expecting each other to do this, from expecting this of other people and only knowing people, not knowing anything beyond them. That was another kind of solitude, the kind where there was nothing all around but reflections.

And what about the endless differences of the animals, their strange bodies? Many legs, stripes, a fiery orangeness; curved teeth or tentacles, wings or scales or sky-blue eggs . . . Instead of looking at the wolf as an animal he never knew and never could, as with the sacred and the divine, he had fallen into the trap. He had wanted it to lick his hand and lope along beside him.

•

Beth was finished being dead, with her departure accom-
plished and her absence complete. There was the memory of
her but that had nothing to do with death, or at least was a
willful opposition to it.

The animals on the other hand were in the middle of
dying, not only one at a time but in sweeps and categories.
This he found increasingly distressing. He began to comb
newspapers for the latest word about animals vanishing; he
began subscribing to magazines. In magazine pictures he saw
animals far away, in the places where they had been born and
either continued to live or were beginning to die off. Some
were in backgrounds of green, others yellow, others a bright
turquoise. White now and then, Siberia or the Antarctic.
These were the places of the animals' origin, warm green, dry
yellow, the wet deep blue.

Then there was the gray of human habitation. The blue
places were turning to brown, the yellow places to dust, the
green places to smoke and ashes. Each time one of the ani-
mals disappeared—they went by species or sometimes by
organizations of species, interconnected—it was as though
all mountains were gone, or all lakes. A certain form of the
world. But in the gray that metastasized over continents and
hemispheres few appeared to be deterred by this extinguishing
or even to speak of it, no one outside fringe elements and
elite groups, professors and hippies, small populations of little
general importance. The quiet mass disappearance, the
inversion of the Ark, was passing unnoticed. The flocks of
passenger pigeons that had darkened the sky, Teddy Roosevelt

on safari shooting hundreds of animals from a train . . . he saw a list from one of Roosevelt's trips to Africa in 1909. Five hundred and twelve animals shot, including seventeen lions, eleven elephants, twenty rhinos, nine giraffes, forty-seven gazelles, eight hippos, and twenty-nine zebras. George V of England had killed a thousand birds in one day for sport; in a year the Roman emperor Titus had nine thousand captured animals killed in popular displays.

He soon learned to recognize the signs of an animal's imminent disappearance. Some were tagged or collared or photographed, some monitored by bureaucrats. Sometimes a group or individual took up the cause of an animal or a plant and could muster the rationale for a lawsuit, and often the courts favored the victim; but the victim remained a victim and for each victim whose passing was noted thousands more slid away in the dark. From where he stood they succumbed with great ease; from where he stood they had always been invisible anyway.

In his own case it had not required strength or merit to make the authorities take his side. The judiciary was harder for industry than the executive but still the case had been a rote one—he himself had not even been there, had been ignorant of the stakes and indifferent to them—a few lawyers paid, a few dates, phone calls and briefs and filings. That was all, and he won, and the pavement spread in a flood and now he was richer and the universe was simpler by one. But it should not have been so easy, either for him or for his competitors. He thought of the other people he knew in real estate development, mostly middle-aged men with solid tans who inclined toward arrogance. There was entitlement, of course—he knew this and had always accepted it, in practice if not in theory, for in theory he cleaved to merit, held merit in high esteem.

But alongside entitlement there also had to be good information — information about supply and demand, history and the future. In this matter of mass extinction, he decided, there was a scarcity of information.

His competitors had done no more than he did, he knew this, except insofar as they could be represented by points further out along the same arc: most of them were older, better capitalized. But they were no worse than he was, in substance, and yet he resented them now as he resented the racewalker, for reasons he recognized were hypocritical — as though they had done an injury to him personally. His own profit seemed beside the point, seemed to exist within the realm of the personal and the trivial, while the profits of others exemplified a trend.

He was a name on a list, a long list. It was not necessarily that he should have been outright prevented from realizing his object, but there should have been resistance. There should have been a fair fight and he should have been in the thick of it. His position was a curious one, certainly — he had a living to make, he had his plans and projects. But there had to be reason, balance. There had to be, at the very least, recognition.

•

Animals in the outside were far from his life, but zoos were close at hand. Zoos would be his study.

His practical lessons took place at nighttime, which left his days free for commerce. At first he read mail-order manuals but soon they left him at loose ends and he hired a locksmith to teach him. The locksmith, a Brazilian, came to his apartment

twice a week and brought his full toolkit: hooks, rakes, diamonds, balls, tension wrenches. They practiced on T.'s doors and cabinets, on a variety of locks the locksmith installed for the purpose.

After the lesson the locksmith would often stay for a nightcap; T. had assured him that he would not use his hard-won knowledge to commit crimes against persons or property, and though he had the impression the locksmith could not care less whether he used his powers for good or for ill the friendly assurances served as a bridge between them. Criminal trespass would be the limit, he said jokily. The Brazilian stayed to drink with him on Fridays and sometimes played a few hands of cards.

His nights were not always free, however. He was still not delivered of Fulton despite the fact that he had professed bursitis to get out of playing racquetball; Fulton's wife had taken him under her wing.

As a young man with no clear defects or blemishes, with his health and his wealth and a full head of hair, he was apparently eligible. He was a sad and noble sufferer, apparently, and from this position—an invalid minus the illness, with all his parts in working order—he became an object of desire for many women newly introduced to him. Still others, who had met him before and deemed him cold or distant then, now viewed him with excessive generosity. Possibly they imagined themselves as Florence Nightingales; possibly they saw in him a soulfulness brought to the fore by loss.

It was Janet's calling to bring him and these wanting women together. Janet did not believe it was feasible to be single; to Janet a bachelor eked out his living on the margins of society, orbiting the married couples wild-eyed and feral as a homeless man at a polo party. A single man, to Janet, was superior in the social hierarchy only to a single woman—this

last a life form that was repellent but fortunately short-lived, naked and glistening as it gobbled its way out of its larval cocoon.

Because Fulton was an investor T. could not refuse his hospitality on every occasion, and so at least once a week he found himself a dinner guest at Fulton's house in Brentwood. It was an article of faith with Janet that when men brought wealth to the table women must bring good looks; and since this was Los Angeles there was always someone sitting across from him—not too much older than he, for Janet had imposed a limit of thirty to allow time for courtship, engagement, and a brief honeymoon followed by reproduction—whose hair had been bleached, breasts lifted, or nose pinched into narrowness above delicately flared nostrils.

Janet was a homemaker by choice, a Texas debutante whose father had gifted her with a dowry that had made her attractive to a legion of Fultons; what distinguished her own Fulton was chiefly that he had beaten other suitors to the punch. So the women she brought to meet T. were seldom burdened by such useless accessories as an academic record or a sense of social purpose. They tended to be certain of their attractiveness and accustomed to admiration; they were eager to begin a conversation with him but not always sure where to take it. One of them asked him what he did for a living and then, after he told her, smiled, twirled her hair around a finger and gazed at him glassily, as though fully expecting him to run with the discussion from that point onward.

At first he tried to be polite to show deference to Janet, but as the dinners wore on over the weeks he saw he had to discourage the women, smoothly and cannily, without allowing them to say precisely what it was in his manner that had pushed them away. Janet should see only that the women, despite their initial surge of interest, would never quite warm to him.

He applied himself thus to the task of quiet repulsion; and as he grew competent at lock-picking the pace of Janet's dinner invitations began finally to slacken.

"I don't know what your problem is, man," said Fulton as he was leaving one night, following an encounter with an interior decorator named Ligi who had wished to talk only of upholstery. "Why don't you make a move for once?"

"Listen, Janet needs to stop setting me up," said T. gently. "I appreciate her good intentions. But I'm not in the market."

"Jesus, you don't have to *marry* them," said Fulton. "But they're better than K/Y and carpal tunnel."

"Not to me," said T.

"That's hardcore," said Fulton.

In New York for a business meeting he drove to the Bronx at night. The lock was easy. A low metal gate in a grove of thin trees, then a walk across a dark, wide square. Lights reflected on a sea-lion pool.

On the second lock his fingers slipped nervously, but soon he was in. His neck was wet and his heart rate rapid; he heard the rush of blood in his ears. He slipped the tools back into his pack, stood still and made himself slow his breathing. He had read a zoo press release. "The most endangered mammal in the world, the Sumatran rhinoceros has not bred in captivity since 1889." Penlight beam focused, he read the card: *Dicerorhinus sumatrensis*. It was the only one in captivity in the United States and it was a dinosaur; its species had lived for fifteen million years and there were only a few hundred left. A female.

She hauled herself up as he stood there, hauled herself up and walked a few steps away. She was nosing hay or straw, whatever dry grass littered the floor of her room. She gave an impression of oblong brownness. The Sumatran rhinoceros, he had read, liked mud wallows. Here there was nothing but floor.

He was standing where any zoo patron could stand, and there was no danger or special privilege. Still, no one was around—he was alone with her—and he was content. It was not to claim the animal's attention that he was here but to let her claim his. She was the only one of her kind for thousands of miles, across the wide seas. What person had ever known such separation?

The Sumatran rhinoceros reportedly had a song, difficult for the human ear to follow; its song had been mapped and similarities had been found between this song and the song of the humpback whale. It was not singing now.

Sight was less important to a rhinoceros than to him, he knew that, but she still had to see. He put his hand to his nose, blocking sight between his own two eyes, closing one and then the other. He had read that the vision of many animals was dichromatic; they saw everything in a scheme based on two primary colors, not three. Were they red, he thought, red and blue? He closed his own eyes, heard the rise and fall of his chest and nearby a rustle whose nature he could not discern. Behind the eyelids it was thick and dark but impressions of light passed there, distracting. They passed like clouds he found himself idly drawn to interpret, to fix into the shape of rabbits or swans.

After a while the rhinoceros sighed. It was a familiar sound despite the fact that they were strangers. He knew the need for the sigh, the feel of its passage; a sigh was not a thought but substituted for one, a sign of grief or affection, of putting down something heavy that was carried too long. In the wake of the sigh he wondered exactly how lonely she was, in this minute that held the two of them. Maybe she saw beyond herself, the future after she had disappeared; maybe she had an instinct for the meaning of boundaries and closed doors, of the conditions of her captivity or the terminus of her line, hers and her ancestors'.

Maybe she had no idea.

He put a hand against the cool wall and felt almost leaden. No other animal could have eyes shaped like these, see the ground and the trees from this place with this dinosaur's consciousness. No other hide would feel the warmth of the sun wash over these molecules, and neither he nor anyone would know how it had felt to live there, in both the particulars and the generalities, the sad quiescence of the animal's own end of time.

•

His mother had always been punctilious about hygiene but now she neglected to bathe; timely about bills, but now she neglected to pay them; anxious to read her mail, but now she neglected to pick it up from her box. The lapse of her mania for cleanliness was the most glaring change, making of her inward switch an ongoing outward pageant. Once she had watched milk expiration dates like a hawk but lately, neglecting to purchase new food, she settled for eating butter without bread, ketchup on stale crackers, aged baby carrots excavated in surprise from a rancid puddle of red-leaf lettuce at the back of the crisper.

A new frugality had taken hold. Although her savings were sufficient for a comfortable retirement she did not like to draw upon them; instead, before T. even knew her intent, she had sold all her jewelry and commissioned her former neighbors in Darien with the sale of the family heirlooms she had left in the house.

"You don't need to do this," he told her when he found out, perched on the arm of her sofa with his arms crossed.

At work on a puzzle of cavorting dolphins, she showed no interest in turning to face him. "If you're worried about money I can help you. There's no reason you should deprive yourself."

"I didn't want those old things anyway," she said, and fit in a puzzle piece. "The armoires and the tables. Who needs them?"

"Someone else in the family might want them. That desk from 1680, for instance. Maybe that second cousin that sends you those long family letters at Christmas? The one in Salt Lake City?"

"Betsy?"

"Right. Betsy."

"I don't like Betsy. She's obese. And Mormon."

"Still, might as well keep it in the family. We're not hurting here, you and me. I'm rolling most of my profits back into investment, but I have plenty left for you to live well."

"A penny saved is a penny earned."

"You don't need to earn pennies. I paid six million in taxes last year."

"Don't brag. You could end up in the Pancake House."

"I'm not saying it's a big deal. I'm just trying to make you see."

"I'm doing just fine, honey. Really."

"Yesterday when I came in you remember what you were drinking? The vinegar from a pickle jar? It had pieces of stem and peppercorns floating in it."

"It was good. If you like pickles, why not the juice? People are so finicky."

"And the cereal you were eating Tuesday? With the maggots in it?"

"Those weren't maggots, T. Don't be ridiculous! They were mealworms."

All he could do was hire a nurse, who kept the refrigerator stocked, cooked and cleaned, and made sure his mother remembered to bathe. A strong and matronly woman from Yugoslavia, the nurse took her charge out once a day to walk through the streets to the beach; she was a staunch believer in the restorative powers of locomotion.

•

In celebration of his nation's birth Fulton had pulled out all the stops, resulting in Fourth of July festivities so red, white and blue that heads spun from the impact of spangles. In his three-acre backyard a band in cowboy gear played traditional favorites: for Fulton liked gangsta rap but Janet listened exclusively to country. Thus the lyrics of "I'm a Yankee Doodle Dandy" were belted out by a woman with long, elaborately curled red hair who swayed back and forth in an agitated fashion from one high-heeled foot to the other; as the afternoon wore on she began to caress the microphone with a frantic obscenity, groaning "The Battle Hymn of the Republic" as though straining under the lash.

T. was prevented from leaving by the promised arrival of a new investor whom Fulton had invited to meet him. He watched the redhead stagger back and forth across the front of the stage and felt battered; across his horizon Janet paraded a number of sacrificial virgins, each of whom required civil handling. During a foot-stomping rendition of "Clementine" there was a blonde from Indiana; when the sheet cake was cut—a giant flag in the shape of the country, with Hawaii and Alaska as bundt cake satellites—there was a dark-haired woman with a long face.

"This is Tanya," said Janet. "She's a real estate agent! You guys have so much in common!"

"I'm sorry," said T., smiling affably. "What would that be?"

"You know! Real estate things!" effused Janet, and steered her friend forward with a viselike grip on her arm.

"I'm really sorry to hear about your loss," said Tanya, but wavered between a frown and a smile.

"Tanya just got divorced recently," said Janet.

"Well then *I'm* sorry," said T., and meant it.

"It was actually a very positive step," said Tanya.

"She was wasted on him," said Janet.

"I don't doubt," said T.

"So, you're in real estate too?" asked Tanya, and T. nodded very slightly before turning back to the redhead, who was now wailing, "Hang down your head, Tom Dooley, hang down your head and cry-iy-iy . . ."

"I develop resort properties," said T.

"Hang down your head Tom Dooley; poor boy you're going to die-iy-iy."

"Oh, wow. Yeah. I'm a buyer's agent. Residential. I'm actually new to the whole racket. I just started a year ago. When I was married, you know, all I ever did was the Home Shopping Network, basically."

"Listen," said T., because he could not bear to look at the singer a moment longer and did not want to make small talk either. "Can I confess something? Janet's always trying to set me up, and her intentions are good, but I don't want to be set up. I'm basically still in mourning. I don't want to meet anyone."

Tanya nodded eagerly, as though what he said had nothing to do with her.

"You're probably totally sick of it," she said. "Am I right?"

He hoped she would impart the tidbit to Janet, but this must not have occurred; for after the triumphant finale, namely "The Lord of the Dance," he was served up the redhead herself.

His second break-in after the rhinoceros was a Monkey House near San Diego, where his research failed him. The Monkey House was equipped with a silent alarm.

Making his way down a narrow corridor between the cages of the smallest monkeys—marmosets, tarsiers and golden lion tamarins, their small homuncular faces beadily watchful in the foliage behind the thick glass—he felt the shock of security guards bursting into the building, one from the front and one from the rear.

He heard the crash of the metal doors and the racking of slides on two guns; thoughtless and rushing, he leapt over the wall of an open enclosure and shimmied down a palm tree. The rough bark tore at his legs and he tumbled onto a tussock and hid behind a fake rock, his thighs burning so hard he had to grit his teeth at the sting.

Within hearing distance the guards met; they came together in the walkway between his enclosure and another.

"See anything?"

". . . bird got in earlier? And just tripped the thing now? Like with the myna at the fundraiser."

"I betcha it was Galt. Couldn't raise him before. Heard he's off the wagon."

They stumped heavily toward the front of the building, the beams of their flashlights scoping but giving him a wide berth. When their footfalls faded he climbed out of the exhibit as quietly as he could and scurried out the rear service door. He wanted to apologize to the monkeys, to tell them he was sorry for the intrusion. He had not meant to bring them

the loud men with guns—behind him, unseen, a monkey had squealed at the noise, startled out of its sleep.

Attacks had occurred in the past, he learned; a young female baboon had been shot in the stomach by a hunter wanting to take home her skull for a trophy. The zoo in question was under pressure. But the incident led him to research animals who were not always closed within buildings, who could not be sealed off so easily with electronic systems. It was not that he was afraid of the awkwardness of an arrest—victimless trespasses like his tended not to draw much publicity—but more that his experience would be trivial if it revolved around awareness of risk.

And how arbitrary it was that certain authorities ruled over zoo animals, decided which persons could draw near to them—authorities vested by neither the state nor any other body, handed permits with a near-infinite laxness by the Department of Agriculture. There were almost no standards for the treatment of the animals unless the zoo they lived in belonged to the American Zoo Association—some two hundred out of two thousand. The other zoos could do almost anything to their charges.

He had standards. He only broke into accredited zoos. In the others he knew he would see nothing but misery. They held no appeal for him.

When he first met Susan's daughter he was hitching a ride with Susan to the dealership where his 560 was being serviced. He had finally traded in the 190.

Her daughter lived in an apartment building hemmed in by smaller buildings on the Marina's narrow peninsula. Herons and ducks alit on a dirty-looking canal; wide ramps led up to the front doors. The building's functionality, he thought as he passed through the foyer, gave an impression

of coldness, as though the Herculean effort of making the premises handicapped-friendly had drained those in management of all their energy reserves and left them no choice but to decorate the lobby with two dead philodendrons and a stained brown carpet.

Casey seldom left the building, Susan told him as they waited for the elevator, not because she was not able to do so but because she was angry and depressed. Susan brought her food and supplies twice a week and had done so, she told T. as they stepped into the freight elevator, ever since the accident nearly six years before.

The apartment felt temporary, with plywood on bricks for bookshelves and ripped pieces of cloth tacked over the windows. Susan set down a grocery bag on the counter and the two of them passed into the dining room and the hall, where dirty beige indoor-outdoor carpeting bore deep gray grooves from thin wheels.

"She won't let me make improvements," whispered Susan.

"I hear you, Mother," called Casey. "Don't apologize for me, OK? If I want to live in a shithole that's my choice. I'm not sorry."

"I wasn't apologizing, honey," said Susan calmly as they turned a corner and stood at the bedroom door.

"You were making excuses for the paraplegic. Same thing."

T. saw a thin, pale young woman sitting in her rumpled bed. She had her television on with the sound muted; on the nightstand sat a fish tank containing a single blue-and-gold fish, its long fins waving. She scowled at him.

"This must be the boss," she said. "COLA raises plus five percent."

"T., this is Casey. Casey, T."

"I'm a bitch. Did she tell you?"

"Not in so many words," said T.

"Yeah well. You can't say bad things about a cripple."

Susan had warned him she was outspoken. He went with it.

"True," he said.

"The best thing about this room is the view," said Susan cheerfully, and opened the blinds over a wide window. "Would you look at that? Beautiful!"

"I forget the Pacific is even there," said Casey to T. "I look at Oprah and Jerry Springer. And my betta fish. At night sometimes, when I'm moisturizing my atrophied legs, I look at the test pattern. You should give her a *ten* percent raise this Christmas. She has a cross to bear."

"Indeed," said T.

"Did you bring the batteries for the remote?"

"Everything on the list, dear. Like always. Mind if I clean this up here?"

"Go for it."

He watched as Susan picked up balled tissues, brown apple cores, coffee mugs full of mold and glasses coated with the residue of old juice. Oddly he was relaxed, even sleepy. He felt content in the room. Susan gathered the detritus into a waste basket and carried it out.

While she was in the other room Casey glared at him.

"Is this a staring contest?" he asked, amused.

"It was. You just lost though."

"I'm devastated."

"You should be. Staring contest performance is a measure of social anxiety. Losing means you're even more spineless than me."

He cocked his head, waiting for her to continue.

"Get it? Spineless?"

"It's not funny."

"Tell me about it. Hey. Pass me that chapstick, would you?"

Before the car accident, Susan said on their way out, her daughter had been quiet, gentle, somewhat passive. She had been seventeen then, a good student, popular; she had been accepted to Stanford, but then came the accident, a pileup of cars on the freeway in an ice storm outside Denver. When the school semester began she had still been in the hospital.

Later she refused to attend, though the school was willing to make accommodations for her. She was stubborn, said Susan. All she had left was speech, and speech stood in for action. She magnified herself through bold talk; she put her words where the rest of her couldn't go.

"And she's still my baby. I love her just as much as I ever did," said Susan, backing out of her parking space.

Fruiting olive trees were planted on the parking lot islands, and beneath them black ovals littered the asphalt. He could hear the tires crunch them.

"No, that's not true," went on Susan, muted. "I love her more."

He watched her tired profile as she looked over her shoulder and then turned back to the steering wheel. He felt a sympathy that made him wince and then a wash of gratitude.

"I know I'm lucky to have you," he said.

After that he began to pay visits to Casey almost every week. He ran up and down the beach five or six miles on weekday mornings, his dog loping beside him on the path, and half-marathons by himself on Saturdays and Sundays, along the firm sand near the waterline. Part of him still resisted running, and when he started he doubted he would persist; but then he ran longer distances, and by the time he went eight or

nine miles he was often filled with euphoria. It flamed up through his calves and his chest and along his jaw to what felt like a trembling membrane beneath his skull, a rush of adrenaline that delivered him to elation.

Sometimes he ran down the beach from Santa Monica to Venice to the peninsula and stopped in at a convenience store to buy a small token for Casey, a newspaper or a bag of chips. Sometimes he stopped at a neighborhood pet store to pick up a plant or a new snail for her tank. He could not purchase anything but snails, for hers was a male fighting fish and would fight other fish to the death.

He was amused by her pugnacity. She was only a couple of years younger than he was but she seemed like a teenager. She did not mind that he showed up with sweat stains in the armpits of his T-shirt; she was not reminded by this, as he feared at first, of her own debilitation.

"Are you kidding?" she said when he asked her this. "I hated that shit. Sports and jocks. Only time I ever ran was to catch a bus."

Her mother had persuaded her to attend support-group meetings and she liked to mock these; but she also knew they were helpful, and attended them faithfully. T. sometimes drove her there in her car, which was modified for hand operation and to hold her wheelchair. She taught him to drive it. At the third meeting to which he drove her, in late November, she confessed there was a man at the meetings who intrigued her; he was an ex-policeman, shot in the back by a rookie.

"You can't tell my mother. She wouldn't approve of him," she said. "He obsesses about CIA covert operations and collects weapons. He buys some of them on the black market. They're not even legal. Also he drinks malt liquor, and on special occasions he does crystal meth."

"But you like that about him," said T.

"Sure, hell," said Casey, looking out the window. "I don't care. Whatever works, right?"

"It's not enough for you to have a paralyzed boyfriend, you want an addict too."

"Don't knock it till you've tried it."

Waiting to pick her up afterward, leaning against the window of her car, he watched the wheelchair-access door for her emergence and felt like an elder brother, waiting to take his sister home from a school dance. Yet Casey had a family already, her mother and her father, a soft-spoken, kindly man. He was a bureaucrat of some kind who liked to discuss taxes. Whenever Congress attempted to reform the income tax code he shook his head sadly, as though heathens were trampling on hallowed ground. Despite the fact that T. reserved his reverence, such as it still was, for other agencies— the Department of State, for instance, and the Library of Congress—he felt a certain kinship.

The door cranked back on its circuit and a gray-haired woman in a wheelchair appeared; behind her was Casey, followed closely by a gaunt, grizzled man in a filthy peasant shirt with an old army blanket covering his lap.

"T., this is Sal."

"Good to meet you," said T. But when he reached for Sal's hand his own was slapped, grabbed and flipped in some complex high-five maneuver he failed to follow.

"So who are you, Casey's big brother?"

"I don't have a brother," said Casey. "Big or little. Ever listen to me in there?"

"I meant *Big Brother*. Don't they have 'em for gimps? How come just the inner-city black kids get their own guilt-ridden Yuppie motherfucks? Get *me* a Big Brother. Take *me* to the park, shoot some hoops. Buy *me* an ice cream cone. I could use one. Shit. Get me a double-ass Rocky Road."

"If you're really nice to him he'll bring you some pink cotton candy," said Casey. "See you, Sal. T., could you get the car door please?"

"I can't believe you're into that guy," said T. as he drove. "Does he ever shower?"

"When the mood takes him. This was a low day."

"You might want to rethink."

"Like it's your business?"

"It's my business if the guy's an asshole."

"Please."

"I mean it. That handshake? Passive-aggressive."

"More like aggressive-aggressive."

"He's got a lot of anger."

"So would you if you had to piss through a catheter for the rest of your life. He's not going to beat me up, T. He's got a hollowpoint lodged in his spinal cord."

"Excuses, excuses."

"That's better. You sounded like a jealous husband."

T. cuffed her on the arm.

"Flatter yourself."

"Ow. That hurts."

His mother approved of his friendship with Casey, whom she referred to as "that little paralyzed girl." Partly she believed it was an act of charity, and as such would help to keep him safe from an afterlife in the Pancake House; partly she liked the fact that it gave him a social outlet. And she was eager to introduce Casey to the jigsaw puzzle.

"It's the ideal thing for that little paralyzed girl!" she said earnestly, twisting in her dining room chair to look up at him. "It keeps your mind active."

"I think her mind's active enough already," said T.

"I can give her some of my old ones. I have more than forty in the closet. Please, T. It's such an opportunity!"

"I'll ask her," said T. "OK? I promise."

He kissed the top of his mother's head and waved to her nurse, soaping dishes in the kitchen.

Outside group therapy Casey did not socialize with, as she put it, other pathetic shut-ins; he suspected his mother would fall into this category. Casey preferred the company of those she could abuse, and was uncomfortable in situations that seemed to call for civility. But when, after delaying for several weeks, he finally conveyed his mother's invitation, she was surprisingly gracious. They went to the apartment on a Sunday, and as T. took the wheelchair off the back of the car his mother stood at her door, hands clasped, smiling and waiting patiently.

"I am so glad to meet you!" she cried as Casey rolled up her front walk. T. could hear her stage-whisper as she leaned down to the chair, "You are having a very healthy effect on my son!"

When they left, after stale graham crackers and tea, he was struggling to heft a stack of puzzles deep enough to impair his vision. Casey, he assumed, had no intention of even opening the boxes, but had nodded and smiled with a semblance of interest as his mother laid them out on the table.

"Thank you," he said, backing out of the driveway. "You didn't have to do that."

"Do what?" she asked, looking at him blankly.

"Be so nice to her."

"It wasn't, like, hard or anything," said Casey sharply. "I liked her. Don't be so condescending."

"How did I condescend to you?"

"To her, idiot."

True, he thought. But his mother was so often childlike.

"That woman is the only reason you're living. When you were born she could have thrown you in a garbage can. Many do."

"I never saw it that way."

"You should."

•

The pupfish lived in a small rocky pool in the desert uplands of Nevada, a few miles from Death Valley. Since long before the rise and fall of the Roman empire they had lived in the pool, only a few yards across, spawning and eating on a single ledge on the wall of the pool, beneath an overhang. There were no others like them in the world.

He drove to the pool with his dog on a three-day weekend; the dog sat in the passenger seat. They sped through a small town that contained almost nothing but an opera house, and they stopped for gas on a road that led to a nuclear test site. He had read a scientific paper that said the pool the fish lived in was fed by water from the test site, so-called fossil water; but the water would take ten thousand years to reach the fish's hole, so the radioactivity that now tainted it had not yet reached the fish.

Pebbles clanged against the undercarriage of the Mercedes and as the car lurched on the dirt road the dog lost her footing. Before them rose craggy hills, brown grasses and yellow wildflowers. Farmers had tried to grow alfalfa here. Finally he parked and walked up an incline, his dog watching him from the car. A plaque on the rock had a picture of the fish, blue and tiny, possibly an inch long.

But the walls of the hole were almost sheer, and even if he were able to rappel down he would risk hurting the fish, kicking the fragile outcrops where they ate. He had read that divers went in sometimes, but it was highly skilled work and he was neither trained nor equipped. The water was murky and he could not make out the fish beneath the surface. All he could see was a line of plastic funnels on a string.

But there was another place: the scientists had moved some of the fish to a refuge, not open to the public.

It was a concrete tank.

He peeled back a loose flap in the fence and crawled through; no cactus to navigate this time, only clumps of gold grass. The tank was built under a roof to protect it from the desert sun, and set low into the floor. He knelt down on the rim and leaned over the placid water, then flicked on his flashlight. He could make out brown scum, yellow algae. He waited.

Finally the fish came. They were tiny but their eyes were large, and for this reason even the adults looked like babies. They darted back and forth on the edge of his beam as he watched them, appearing to have no goal. Possibly they went back and forth because the light was disorienting them.

After a while he clicked it off. The floor was cement, and cool beneath him. To stave off extinction generations upon generations were bred and died in this concrete tank, where they were reduced to nothing—darting energy between straight walls. The cave where they had evolved, which looked from above like a dull puddle perched in a nest of rocks, was in fact the narrow mouth of a body of water that went hundreds of feet down, no one knew how far. Divers had descended to several hundred feet but still not touched the bottom. It was a deep, pinhead-narrow fissure in the earth, and water filled it from a profound source.

Back in the cavern, he thought, possibly the fish had a reason to live—no less or more than its fellows, anyway—and possibly there was even a civilization. Save the algae they ate on the ledge, there were no other species in the hole. The fish were alone, with only each other for company—not one animal but hundreds of them, alone as a whole kind, in a world without others.

Each fish lived for less than a year in the hole: once in a fish generation there might be an event. It might occur that a bird lit on the rock near the ledge with a flapping of wings, or a leaf was blown into the water from a shrub on the nearby ground; clouds might gather over the cave opening and rain might fall, dappling the surface and bringing molecules from afar, molecules from factories, cars, people's skin.

He closed his eyes and thought of swimming in the deep, armless and legless with only a streamlined slip of a form, swimming with nothing around him. He was in cool water: he flowed and was nothing: nothing was around him.

It was easy to think of the fish existing in pure monotony, to assume their brains were so small they did not even register this. From there it was easy also to see them as crude bundles of nerves that moved through their medium by reflex and instinct. He recognized the philosophy.

He put out a hand and touched a fingertip to the surface of the water. This alone was a disturbance for them; this was a pollution. Rolling onto his front again he looked over the ledge at them, propped on his elbows. To see them closely he had to stare, had to fixate on their minuscule bodies, the gestures of their movement. How good it must have felt to glide through the depths of the same water they knew through the eons, apprehend the slanting of long

beams of sunlight through the depths. Feeling must have filled their bodies there, under the sky, over the depths; feeling must have overwhelmed the small motes that they were.

After all they depended on their own decisions to survive and needed feelings to guide them; they needed fear, for instance, for this purpose. Fear they knew. And if they knew fear why not the inverse too, the glowing comfort of safety, the warmth and closeness of other fish; and why not lone-liness too, even if it moved through them like one more ripple of light.

6

He never spoke of his incursions and guarded carefully the difference between himself and the self that was available publicly. This was a clear benefit of being alone, because if Beth were still living he could never have done it. She would have broken the seal.

On occasion he had the sense that he was celebrating her through his dedication; though he knew she was gone he also allowed himself the conceit that she had special knowledge of his activities. With meticulous care he planned his business trips in relation to sanctuaries and captive breeding facilities, finding reasons to fly to these places even when profit was unlikely. Undetected he entered a bird sanctuary in San Diego, a rescue center for manatees scarred by boat propellers, a butterfly habitat in New Hampshire, a laboratory in Rhode Island where American burying beetles were bred and released. He was a regular at the best zoos in California, Arizona and New Mexico and he also flew to others—St. Louis, Seattle, Cincinnati. Each night he reserved for a single enclosure.

And he took a course in basic first aid that stood him in good stead. His thighs stayed lightly scarred from the tree in the Monkey House, whose superficial but stinging cuts had proved slow to heal; his knees scabbed over from multiple abrasions he tended to reopen, and his right calf bore the purple marks of teeth from a young Morelet's crocodile. It had been a fairly fortunate encounter in fact—the baby crocodile had let go almost right away, allowing him to drag himself out of its pen sheepishly, hurting but mostly ashamed of his carelessness. The punctures were not deep and did not require stitches; he slathered them in antibiotic ointment and left it at that.

So that Casey would not notice the marks he ran his half-marathons in long pants; to her and to his mother he was rock climbing, in the mountains and at the gym. Thence came the battered kneecaps, the scrapes on his elbows and knuckles and cuts on his fingertips.

At the beginning he was afraid of the predators, and though he chose with great care, avoiding animals known to be highly territorial or prone to aggression, he was still wary. They were not pets. But he soon lost this novice fear. It was not his habit to stalk the animals, merely to enter their enclosures and sit in one place to observe them. So he waited for each animal to show itself, and over time he grew tired, then bored; he was amazed at the depth and reach of his boredom, the way minutes and hours wore on uneventfully. For the animals too the greater part of captivity was waiting: when their food was delivered the last animals fed, slept and briefly forgot, he believed, the urgency of hunger. Then they awoke and the waiting started again.

He wished he knew if they got impatient. Expectation struck him as a human impulse, but then he thought of his dog. Her days were entirely given over to expectation, it seemed to him.

Waiting for a feeding the animals paced or swam or leapt from branch to branch, as their natures dictated, with a bat now and then at a so-called enrichment tool or a peck at an errant insect. Their lives were simple monotony. They slept to use up time; this was how their days were spent, the last sons and daughters.

In the wild, he thought, there would be almost no waiting. Waiting was what happened to you when you lost control, when events were out of your hands or your freedom was taken from you; but in the wild there would always be trying. In the wild there must be trying and trying, he thought, and no waiting at all. Waiting was a position of dependency. Not that animals in the wild were not watchful, did not have to freeze in place, alert and unmoving—they must do so often—but it would hardly be waiting then. It would be more like pausing.

Time must run more quickly there, matching heat and cold to the light of day and the dark of night. Familiarity with this pace would spin out through long days, as though it would never change: now and then would come quick fear or a close call, but mostly the ease of doing what had always been done. For a second a prey animal might grow complacent, and then in a rush the end came. As the animal moved where it had always moved, a scent on the wind might stop it. The last surge of adrenaline, the light-headedness of a bloodletting: sleep again in the fade, in the warm ground of home.

And how different could it be when the death was a last death? Say an individual was the very last of its kind. Say it was small—one of the kangaroo rats for instance—and ran from a young fox through a hardscrabble field, towering clouds casting long shadows over the grass. The run lasted a few seconds only; no one was watching, no one at all because there was no one for miles around, no one but insects and

worms and a jet passing high overhead. Say neither of them knew either, the fox or the rat, that the rat was the last, that no rat like him would ever be born again. Was it different then? Did the world feel the loss?

The field stayed a field, the sky remained blue. Any pause that occurred as the action unfurled, any split-second shifting of the vast tableau would have to be imagined by an onlooker who did not exist. The fox started to run again, looking for his next quarry since the last animal had been barely a mouthful.

And yet a particular way of existence was gone, a whole volume in the library of being. Others were sure to fall afterward—a long fly with iridescent wings that lived only in the nest of this single rat, say; a parasite that lived under the wing of the fly; a flowering plant whose roots were nourished by the larval phase of the parasite; a bat that pollinated the plant . . . it was time that would show the loss, only time that would show how the world had been stripped of its mysteries, stripped by the hundreds and thousands and millions. Remaining would be only the pigeons and the raccoons.

But it was not the domino effect he considered most often, simply the state of being last. Loss was common, a loss like his own; he couldn't pretend to the animals' isolation, although he flattered himself that he could imagine it. He was aware that in his search a certain predictable need was being answered. Still he thought he had a glimpse of something in losing Beth. If a being could be so singular to another, there was no doubt that there was singularity elsewhere, that the irreplaceable nature of being was not limited to his own small circle.

One day, he knew, it would be men that were last. In the silence of the exhibits he thought he could feel time changing him too, atom by atom. He was so bored one night that he lost resistance to falling asleep. It would be good to let himself go,

he decided: so he did. After that sleep was part of the routine, and sleeping he surrendered — it was up to the animals what happened. He was not protected anymore by the city and its installations. Lying down in the exhibits with them, awkward, uncomfortable, and finally overcome; creeping out before the keepers appeared for the morning feeding.

While he slept, as far as he knew, the animals did not mean to approach him. But when he woke up they were sometimes near him by happenstance. In this way he saw a ringtail nosing her young down into the entry of her den and a hyena tearing hungrily at the breast of a pigeon.

•

As a rule no one else came to his apartment. Since Beth had died and Fulton had kicked the dog it had welcomed no one: the rooms were a set of monastic cells, unseen by anyone but himself and the cleaning lady. And while his financial research was kept vaulted and secure at the office, indexed in spreadsheets and cross-referenced, his animal research was spread throughout the space he inhabited like debris at a crash site. Magazines were spilled over the arms and cushions of sofas, where the dog lay sleeping and shed her white hairs; printouts from library computers were piled on the kitchen counter where he never cooked; spilled water gummed the pages together in wavy blocks and blotted the type. Videotapes were perched in crooked towers, maps were laid out on the guest bed and over tables and desks. In disarray were his tools, the lockpicks for doors and gates, binoculars and night-vision goggles, cords and carabiners, wet suits and waders.

After Beth his apartment had been reduced to a closet, with a door he could shut to seal off the contents. It was only the presence of his dog that kept the place from wholesale neglect. He did not like to think of the dog living in squalor throughout the workday, even if it was unlikely she would share his preference for tidiness.

He meant to leave the apartment, which he had rented purely for convenience and to which he had never had a particular attachment. In time he would have to buy, he would need a show home. He lived so far beneath his means that Fulton ridiculed him. But when he bought he would have to move his office and his mother with him; so he delayed and delayed and the apartment felt less and less like a place he lived in and more and more like a storage locker.

Meanwhile his mother and Casey met almost every day to work on jigsaws. They seemed to be forging an alliance, because when he stopped by they contentedly ignored him and made jibes at his expense. At first he viewed this development with alarm but soon it felt, when he stepped into his mother's dining room, as though Casey was meant to be there, as though it was meant to be the three of them.

"Puzzles," he said to Susan at the office, and shook his head. "I don't get it."

"You know what it is? It's a miracle," said Susan. "It really is. You don't know the apathy I've been dealing with. I don't care what her new hobby is. It could be beekeeping or kung fu movies. Really. Whatever gets her out of her apartment. Believe me. It's a miracle, T."

In the past Fulton had left the planning decisions to him, but now he began to question the fundaments of the island

project with a marked belligerence. He suggested, for example, that they should attempt to attract mammoth cruise ships to their facility, despite the fact that there was no port for such vessels and no channels deep enough to accommodate them; he saw no obstacles to a high-volume, fast-turnover operation on an island off a coastline that boasted only a one-runway airport and no paved roads, where even a modest supply of fresh water had to be imported.

T. explained patiently the reasons for the modest scope of the development and its tidy benefits—the exclusivity appeal, the quick returns due to the fairly small capital out-lay—but Fulton only shook his head restlessly and accused him of "thinking small" and having "no cojones." He made this kind of remark most often in a group meeting with other investors, not when the two of them were alone; and though his protests were easily overcome, due largely to their senselessness, the suppressed hostility behind them was disruptive.

When T. took him aside and reminded him the enter-prise was only a boutique project, one of a large array of his current startups in which Fulton was free to invest, Fulton guffawed; when he offered him the opportunity to pull his funds Fulton ignored him. Clearly there was tension. Fulton had noticed that T. spent time with him only when he could not avoid it; it had dawned on him that T. preferred the company of others. Surprisingly to T. given his insensitivity in all matters, he appeared to be offended by this. He wished to draw T. back in, or failing that he wished to undermine him covertly.

Presently Casey liberated Susan from her long servitude. She left the apartment every day; she bought her own food, paid

her own bills, in short agreed to conduct her own life. For a while he drove her to buy groceries, to ease the transition.

They were in the produce section of a luxury food store in Santa Monica, Casey reaching up to a shelf of honeydew melons to touch them and smell them, when T. wandered away to pick up a bag of apples and found himself looking past the bag at a man's broad chest in a sport jacket, over a V-necked sweater.

It was Fulton.

"Shit, guy," said Fulton, and delivered a punch to the shoulder. "Look who."

"Fulton."

"What are you doing here? You don't buy food. You order out. I saw your refrigerator. One old jar of mayo that looked like earwax and a six-pack of Heinie."

"I came with my secretary's daughter."

"The dirty-blonde there? The quadriplegic?"

"Just her legs are paralyzed, actually."

"What I said, man."

He craned his neck to see past T.'s shoulder.

"She's not that bad. If you could get past the whole no-legs thing enough to just stick it in."

"Don't be foul."

"Good tits."

"End of conversation."

"You could always put a paper bag over the withered parts and go for the tittyfuck, I guess."

T. turned on his heel. He meant to steer them away from Casey but Fulton preempted him, striding past him to stick his hand out in her direction.

Caught off-guard, she dropped a melon into her lap.

"Fulton Hanrahan! Business partner of T.'s. Pleased as shit to meetcha."

"Casey."

He shook her hand far too hard; when he let go she rubbed it, wincing.

"So you two been keeping this whole thing real quiet, huh? He told my wife he was seeing someone but he wouldn't bring her over. Now I know why."

"Excuse me?" asked Casey.

"We're friends, Fulton. We're not in a relationship. I'm not seeing anyone."

"See Casey, my wife was trying to set him up with these hot women, and then he blows them off and goes for one with zero feeling below the waist. You like that, T.?"

Casey gaped. T. looked at Fulton sharply; his face was tanned and bland as ever.

"Shut the fuck up, Fulton. Casey. Let's get out of here."

"Are you kidding?" said Casey, and then smiled at Fulton. "I want to stay. Can I ask you something? So far what I'm thinking is Antisocial Personality Disorder. You may actually meet the diagnostic criteria for a sociopath. There's a handy checklist in the DSM-III."

"Great legs; nice personality, too."

"Number one on the checklist: Would you say you've exhibited, since roughly the age of fifteen, a pervasive pattern of disregard for the rights of others?"

T. looked at them both and an odd, dreary calm settled over him. He was aware of danger. It was like a tidal wave or a freeze: it was not up to him. Shoppers milled around and behind them in a blur.

Casey continued to smile coldly; Fulton picked up a piece of pale red fruit. At first T. could not recall what it was and then he thought *pomegranate*.

"Wait. I forgot. A sociopath typically fails to recognize his behavior as antisocial. You probably had no idea until I told

you. Right? This whole time you thought you were just a regular rich guy, I bet."

Fulton turned to T.

"This is one of those fruits where, if I ripped it open, there would be all those shiny red seeds inside. Right?"

"Leave us alone, Fulton."

He took hold of the back of Casey's chair, but she pushed off his hands. Fulton tossed the pomegranate back into the bin.

"I can't believe you, T. I knew you were a secret fag but I had no idea you would do sex on cripples. I mean that's sick. It's one step away from fucking rotting corpses. I mean half of this little lady is basically already dead."

T. felt stunned; the oranges and yellows of the produce aisle were dazzling. They fuzzed and vibrated in front of him. They were ancient Egypt in the tropics.

But Casey was still matter-of-fact.

"Among sociopaths the physically violent subjects tend to be the stupid ones. Did you know that? The ones who limit themselves to verbal abuse are smart by comparison. But that's obviously not you. Unless—wait. Are you physically violent too? Are you a wife-beater?"

There was a pause; Fulton seemed preoccupied suddenly, gazing over T.'s shoulder. T. heard his own voice, clipped and neutral. "He doesn't beat her, but he's been sleeping with the same prostitute twice a week since a year before they got married. He claims his wife is frigid. Every year he gives the prostitute a Christmas bonus."

"Fulton?"

Janet was staring wide-eyed at her husband from above a full shopping cart. A few feet behind her stood their preteen daughter.

Casey was the first to move, head slightly bowed, mouth solemn; she turned her chair and made for the row of check-out counters.

T. could not catch Janet's eye but he saw her daughter's face, alarmed. He was not sure what the daughter had understood: and if he made an apology to Janet it would only confirm the salience of what she had heard. He had to cut his losses.

"Janet," he said softly in acknowledgment, "how are you," as though nothing was happening. He raised a hand in greeting before he turned to leave.

If only the daughter had been out riding her pony.

At the front door he and Casey surrendered their grocery baskets without paying. They crossed the parking lot in silence. He was mulling over the damage to Janet's feelings and the loss of Fulton's money. For Janet—could she actually love him, or would it be mostly the shock? For himself, he considered whether he should be worried, because the funds were as good as gone already. Certainly their loss would be felt, he guessed, but it would not break him. He would go over the financials when he got home.

They got to the car and discovered Casey still had the honeydew, a symptom of their distraction. On her lap it lay pale and heavy.

•

The next business trip ended early. On his way to the zoo for daytime reconnaissance, listening to the news on public radio, he learned the pygmy chimpanzees he meant to visit had a newborn. He could not risk disturbing the group so with reluctance he turned back toward the airport.

He had left his dog in the care of his mother's nurse, since Angela could no longer be relied upon to remember to feed

and walk her, and when he got into his car in the parking structure at LAX—a new 600, for he had recently traded in the 560—and called his mother's apartment on the car telephone, the nurse was out.

His mother made him nervous.

"Your dog was here. But she's gone," she said vaguely.

"Gone? What do you mean, gone? Out? Is Vera walking her?"

"She went away. After we saw the man in the BMW."

"I'm coming there now," said T., anxious. "Stay home. OK? I don't understand what you're telling me here. Tell Vera to call me on the car phone if she gets there before I do."

At his mother's apartment Vera answered the door with a worried face. His dog had run away, she said.

"What do you mean? She never takes off!"

"There was a man in a car when we were on our walk. It was the three of us, your mother and the dog and me. We were walking on Abbot Kinney. This man parked his car. It was a nice car. Shiny black."

"Leather seats," said his mother, nodding. "Beautiful. And brand new. A death machine, of course."

"He said he knew her," said Vera. "He was a friend of yours."

"He was the one from the party," said his mother. "And I'll tell you what, T. You should steer clear of him. I know he's your friend but in the end that young man is headed straight for the Pancake House, no questions asked. I could tell right away."

"What party?"

"At your office at Christmas last year. You know. The big one with the muscles, and the very small wife. She wore pink."

"Fulton."

"I don't remember his name. He talked about tennis."

"Fulton. Oh no. Oh shit."

"Your mother needed to use the bathroom," said Vera, "so he said he would hold the leash for us while we went into a store. But then when we came out again he said she had run away."

"This is not happening."

Legs weak, he sat down on the arm of the sofa.

"I called the Humane Society," said Vera. "I called all of them. We went there to give a photo of her—from the picnic, where she was biting the rubber bone?—but no one knew anything."

He was stunned. He blinked and looked down at his knees. He had failed her. Was she dead? Suffering?

He held out his hands: they shook. He put the heels of his hands on his thighs and ground them in. He had done this to her.

"Oh, honey," said his mother, and put a hand on his shoulder. "It's OK. She'll come back."

Charges could be pressed but that would get him nowhere; it would not help his dog. Fulton would not respond to anything but abasement. Fulton must be granted the power, must feel he had won. And T. would do it gladly: he did not hesitate.

He called and asked Fulton to meet him, but Fulton said no. Fulton was busy. Fulton was seeing a marriage counselor, to stave off divorce. Fulton had no time for him.

"But you had time for my dog. What did you do with her? Tell me, Fulton. Please."

"The thing ran off, T. Not a damn thing I could do about it."

"I know that's not true. She isn't a runner. I know you're lying about this, Fulton."

"Didn't take to me. Trying to do a favor for a couple old ladies. Holding their dog while they hobbled up the steps. Thing lit off down the street like a bat outta hell. Who knew something so ugly could run so fast?"

"Tell me you didn't hurt her. Please."

"You fuck up my entire fucking marriage and now I'm the bad guy. Talk about blaming the victim."

"Listen. I'm very sorry for the effect my words must have had on Janet. I had no idea she was there. You know I didn't. Or your daughter. I deeply regret upsetting them. But I'm begging you here. Picture me on my knees. I'll give you whatever you want. So help me. Just tell me where she is. Let me have her, Fulton."

"What can I say. All I know is the thing took off down the street. All she wrote. And now I gotta go."

"Fulton. Please. I love that dog. You know I'm sorry. Help me out here, man. Please."

"See ya, T."

The dog had been missing three days when Casey rang his doorbell. In his distance he forgot the chaos and privacy of his space and opened the front door.

On her lap she held a basket full of rubber toys, a leash, a bag of dog biscuits.

"We're going to get her back," she said firmly.

The hopeful goods broke his heart.

"Come on," said Casey. "Let's go look. I'm ready."

He felt a dragging reluctance but she was determined; she turned her chair briskly and headed back to the elevator. Finally he grabbed a jacket and followed.

Casey had strong arms but even so, he knew, after a while they grew tired, and moving south along the boardwalk he thought of this: the farther, the longer, the more she must

ache. He felt guilty. Other dogs passed them, for the board-walk was popular among dog owners: now and then he or Casey petted one. At first they spoke but as they grew tired of walking their conversation dwindled.

"I'm exhausted," he said finally.

They had made a loop to the bottom of the Marina: it had been several hours. The soles of his feet were burning. Casey's stamina was shocking.

"I think we should cut in off the beach and get a taxi back to my place," he pressed.

"No," said Casey, and shook her head. "If you want her you have to pay. You have to pay for what you want. You know that."

"We're not going to find her just because we suffer," he said.

"Yes," said Casey. "We are."

"I should have worn different shoes."

"What are those, Ferragamos? Fulton was right. Some-times you dress really gay."

"It's not gay, Case. It's expensive."

On the way home along the bicycle path his feet hurt. A poodle with a tall bearded man in tight shorts, a Dalmatian with two lesbians, a pug with a fat man, a Chihuahua with an emaciated woman wearing too many bangles. All of them. But not her.

At the apartment door he remembered he should not let Casey in. On the floor in his dining room were the snarled, half-inside-out legs of his wetsuit; evidence was every-where. But he was too sore to keep up his guard. He had to collapse.

"It's a mess," he said wearily as he opened the door for her, and strode ahead to scoop up the most obvious traces and hurl them into a closet.

"What are you doing with an article about a rare tortoise and off-roading? You getting into ORVs suddenly?"

"Impact fees. A casino project," he mumbled, lowering himself onto the couch. He kicked off his shoes and heaved his feet up on the arm. "You need anything?"

"I'm hungry."

"Chinese takeout in the fridge," he said, closing his eyes. "But it's from yesterday. No, wait. Two days ago."

"Disgusting . . . really. What *is* this stuff?" said Casey.

"What?"

"About animals? All this material. Everywhere."

"Told you! Research for a project."

"A lot of it."

He shrugged. "Money at stake. You know me."

She gazed at him for a moment, then let it go.

They drank a bottle of white wine with the TV playing and then they drank another; they lolled on sofa and chair, drunk and still drinking. He felt relief that she had let him off so easy. His secret remained securely hidden.

"I'm going to go out on your balcony," she said after a while, and left him there, eyes glazed over: there seemed to be a prizefight on, men sweating. He looked around for the remote, but did not see it. He was tired.

What if his dog appeared below? Casey might fail to see her. Casey's view was limited from the chair, her seated position. His dog had always liked the pool, tail wagging as she moved and sniffed among the long knifelike leaves of the tiger lilies . . . he got up and went through the sliding doors to the rail.

Below the turquoise pool water glittered, empty.

"I thought she might be there," he murmured, and then looked over at Casey. Her face was turned from him.

"You don't know," she said. "You don't have a clue. You're not as arrogant as I thought, I guess."

"What?" he said sharply, a clutch of fear. "Know what?"

"It's damaging to say it," she said. "But it can't be helped. It's too bad. But without honesty I don't have anything. Once your body's taken from you, or at least your independence in the body, the only thing you have left is this, like, idea of yourself. It's an idea of character, or something. If I lie or hide, that's taken from me too. So I have to tell you."

"I don't know what you're talking about," he rushed. "Case, you're scaring me here. What is it? Are you sick?"

"No. Just pathetic. I love you."

"I love you too, Case. You know that. So tell me. What is it?"

"No, that's it."

She turned her face toward him finally, small and white with wide eyes.

". . . that . . ."

He felt nauseated. She studied him sadly: this was grim.

"Yes."

He turned and looked out at the palm fronds, still. He was glad of the lights, which gave him an excuse to look elsewhere.

"I thought it would go away. For Chrissake, you wear Ferragamos. And there's this one shirt you have with blue stripes on it that really dorks you up. No man should ever, ever wear a blue-striped shirt with a white collar."

"I'll take that under advisement."

"It should be federal law."

"Or maybe I should wear it more often. Then your crush will go away."

"It's not a crush, T. If it was I wouldn't bother telling you."

"Whatever it is."

"And don't feel you have to explain how deep but completely platonic your feelings are. It's obvious. I never expected

anything else. I know I'm like the cute paraplegic sister you never had."

"You like to speak for me."

"I'm good at it. Don't you think?"

He bent down and put his arms around her; she rested her forehead stiffly against his collarbone.

Inside she put on music and they drank more and danced giddily, she by moving her wheels on the slick kitchen floor. They went to his closet and she tore shirts off hangers, threw the shoes she disliked into a laundry hamper. He thought of the hundreds of dollars they represented, indeed thousands, and as he thought this she raced away from him toward the sliding doors with the hamper balanced on her lap. On the balcony she tipped it over the edge.

Right behind her he looked down and saw the shoes floating in the pool.

"I can't believe you did that," he said, but he could.

She was at her bag, pulling out a vial.

"Have some of these," she said. "They're for pain."

"I don't have pain," he said.

"Then take them for mine."

He thought of all that he had always forfeited, how he always kept control. How he never lost his hold on himself for even a moment.

He swallowed the pills.

"I want to go swimming," she said, and was already on her way out.

In the elevator she pulled off her sweater. Beneath she wore a cotton undershirt; her torso was surprisingly lovely, compact and muscular.

"I don't have my flotation device," she said.

"You're not serious."

"You're going to have to be my buddy," she said. "Never go swimming without a buddy, T.!"

"But it's three a.m. The sign says closed after midnight."

"Really, T.," and she shook her head, "who gives a shit? You're such a prig."

"Proud of it."

"Have you ever even been in this pool the whole time you lived here?"

"Once, in the first week."

"I'm going in the deep end."

"Wait!" he said desperately, but she was already out the back door of the lobby and headed for the pool deck. "How does this work?" he called after her, but she ignored him.

A few moments later she was rising in her chair, lifted on her strong arms: and then she fell forward into the water and sank like a stone. He jumped in, panicking.

As he heaved her head and shoulders above the surface, sputtering and soaking in his clothes, he thought she was crying but in fact it was laughter.

"I do pool physio all the time, fool," she said, water running down her face. "You didn't, like, save my life or some shit."

"Good. You don't deserve it."

She pushed his head under, holding the rim of the pool with the other arm. Submerged—he stayed because he wanted to: the lights on the sides of the pool were bright and hypnotic—he thought that he admired her. He looked at her ribcage, her flat, lean abdomen, his eyes smarting from the chlorine; her shirt floated above her belly. Behind her the pool lights wavered and dazzled him. Hard to keep his eyes wide; the eyeballs smarted. But he was busy seeing. He admired her bravery. She was a heroine.

In the water beneath them her legs receded, white and tapering to a distant point of feet; but here any legs would recede that way, pale and disappearing. Other legs would be moving in the water, that was all.

He saw his own legs; he could barely keep them down. They were not white because he was wearing pants and shoes. They were big and heavy. They wanted to be floating.

It did not matter how proud she was; still he had to admit to pity. No matter what, there was always pity, however her defiance might reject it . . . and yet the water was turquoise, flooded with white, and they were here within it like two parts of a whole—connected by liquid, only the membranes of their skin between them. What were legs, anyway? She could swim without them.

How specific each thing was to the need for it.

In the pool someone might see her and not know. Someone might catch sight of her floating and believe she had legs that walked; they might believe she was whole.

He could almost believe it himself.

He thought he was happy, for a second, but then how could he be?—he must be missing something.

In a haze he burst out, dripping. His shirt around his shoulders felt cold instantly in the air and he wanted to be submerged again. She was a sacrificial lamb; she was both great and small. He adored her. Dear friend.

She could hold him under; he would not protest.

Instead she studied him with a serious expression, frowning.

"I can, you know," she said.

"You can?" he asked stupidly.

He carried her upstairs, and only later went back for her chair.

It was the emotion of it that was piercing, a thing he could not have known. He would have guessed it would be difficult, the rawness of what was missing. Instead he was suffused by a sharp, rending emotion, unidentifiable to him. With Beth there had been warmth, but not this extremeness, tearing and erotic. Was it the effect of the pills? Afterward sleep together was like being in the water, where there was hardly a line between them. But then daylight was bleak. He raised himself on an elbow and gazed down. She was lovely at the top, fresh: down and down further she was sleek and firm: then she wasted into pale angles and bone. He felt sad and furtive. He should not be seeing this.

She was awake and studying his expression.

"I need to get out of here," she said. "Right away."

He helped her to her chair and waited while she used the bathroom; they rode down in the elevator, saying little. Her car was parked a block away and he walked beside her, glancing down at the top of her head. She never raised her face to look at him; even as he loaded the chair into the car he could not catch her eye. He watched her drive away standing where her car had been, on a grease stain.

It was barely dawn. The grass was dewy and the sky over the sea lavender. The skin on his arms pricked and chilled; he hugged himself and rubbed his upper arms with his hands.

Regret was nagging at him, even shame.

He was walking along the sidewalk back to his building, choked and empty, when he saw his dog.

She sat beside the front steps, waiting—thin and mangy, but alive. Alive!

He was floored by relief. He felt a splinter of pained love for Casey, shot through with remorse, as though his dog's

return was her doing somehow. He knelt down on the grass and laid his cheek against the dog's flank.

When he stood again and she rose off her haunches to walk with him he saw she was reluctant to move; she held up one of her back legs. She was lame.

The leg, it turned out, was broken and fusing incorrectly, and also badly infected.

"How did it happen?" he asked. He was still so grateful it was hard to be upset. She was alive.

"Can't really say. Some kind of blunt-force trauma; maybe a car hit."

"Are you sure?"

"Wait a second," said the veterinarian. "Oh . . . take a look. You see this wound at the ankle, with the pus and scabbing? The hair's gone. Looks like it was rubbed raw by a cuff or a chain. Same thing on this leg here. Let's see. She has wounds here too, under the hair. And there's tenderness here. We should do X-rays. She might have other injuries."

"What happened?"

"She was chained at the ankle, maybe jabbed and hit or beaten. She worried the chain with her teeth, trying to get it off. From the angle here I can tell the injury predated the chaining. Someone kept her chained up when she was already injured."

He felt a wave of faintness, bitter taste in his mouth. He saw Fulton's wine cellar.

A course of antibiotics could be tried, said the vet, but there was significant necrosis. He advised T. to let him amputate right away.

"You'd be surprised," said the vet, "how well they do on three legs."

The rooms of his apartment were full with the dog home again, convalescing. He was satisfied to know, even when she was out of sight, that somewhere in the apartment she was sleeping or eating or sitting watchfully. It was family, he guessed, more or less. Did most people want a house of living things at night, to know that in the dark around them other warm bodies slept?

Such a house could even be the whole world.

•

It was days afterward that he went to see Casey. She was not answering his phone calls and he felt increasingly nervous about this. He gave his dog a strip of rawhide before he left, pulled on his running gear and went down to the beach. He ran south. Beachgoers were out in force; some of them wore very small swimsuits, though the air was only mild. The surf was low but still kids on boogie boards paddled frantically.

When he got to her building the sun was setting. Standing in the foyer he pushed the call button once, then again; he peered into the camera lens. She had a monitor in her apartment, though she seldom looked at the screen—only listened, said nothing, and used the remote to buzz people in. But lately she had not been in bed as she used to; lately she was active.

After a few seconds of waiting he turned to leave, let down. One of her neighbors, a man with a prosthetic foot, was hobbling along the sidewalk. He lived two doors down on her floor and they sometimes nodded at each other in the elevator.

"You seen Casey around?" he asked on impulse, as the man came up the walkway.

"She was out here earlier. She was watching a couple of kids carry boxes for her."

"Boxes?"

"Moving."

"Moving?"

"Yeah. She gave me a plant. I don't even like them."

T. stared at him.

"But I just saw her a couple of days ago. She didn't say anything about it."

"What can I tell you."

The man was past, fumbling at his mailbox.

He would call Susan.

Running back north he wanted to know; he swerved inland off the beach and found a payphone.

Susan picked up coughing.

"She's moving?" he asked, when the coughing trailed off. No preamble. He felt agitated, even anxious. "Where to?"

"Thanks for your concern about my health, T. And in case you're wondering, it's pneumonia."

"Oh. I'm sorry. I thought it was just the flu."

"Walking pneumonia."

"Walking? What the hell does that mean?"

"It means you need to get a temp."

"Sure. Of course. Take good care of yourself."

"Here's the thing. I don't know what happened between the two of you. This is my daughter here, and my job."

"Yeah," he said, waiting.

"But she can't have any contact anymore," she said. "I'm sorry, T. You know how much I hate to be in this position."

"You're kidding."

Susan coughed, and the cough wore on.

"No."

"It doesn't—she's my best friend, Susan. I can't believe it. Is she really serious about this?"

"I think she's serious," said Susan. "Yes. I'm afraid she is, T. And I'm sorry, but I really do have to go," and she hung up still coughing.

He let his eyelids drop closed: a faint imprint of the great seal on the dollar bill, the glowing pyramid with its all-seeing eye.

He stood in the booth like a statue, testing the steadiness of his feet on the ground. He kept his eyes shut, and the sweat that had soaked his shirt cooled him in the night air. He started to shake. It came to him that beyond himself he had deprived his mother—she would be friendless once more.

He brought them to her and they were taken away again.

He needed Casey, he thought, because he liked her company, because her presence made him more than he was without it, but he could not deny that at the beginning he had also believed he was doing her a favor. *That* was where his arrogance had been. It was a mistake to think that because someone had fallen down, someone was injured or sick or less than complete, you were giving more to them by your association than they were giving to you.

It was a bad mistake.

He leaned for some time against the wall of the booth, still holding the receiver loosely till it occurred to him that he did not need to. The ears of unwashed men had greased the black plastic. Revolting. There was a sheen on the curving surface, the whorls and smudges of fingerprints.

He walked down to the waterline holding his hands out at his sides, feeling a need to wash them. But even as his legs moved him forward he knew a certain ambivalence or resistance, as though the leavings of strange men were also somehow the last touch of Casey, which would be washed off with the rest.

Still he plunged in his arms. The water was freezing.

7

His mother forgot him on a Thursday. On Thursdays they had dinner together; he brought over takeout and she turned from her puzzles. This time, when he knocked on her door in the early evening, pizza box in one hand, she tried to close the door in his face. He put a hand out to stop it closing.

"I didn't order one. It's not mine."

Vera stood behind her, shaking her head patiently.

"It's me," he said. "T. It's your son. It's our dinner."

He held out the box as though it might jog her memory.

"Yes," said Vera, and stepped through the door to stand next to him, an arm around his shoulders. "This is Thomas, Angela. Your son! He comes almost every day with his dog. Remember? You call him T."

"I don't . . ."

"Let's go ahead and let him in now, honey."

"Dog. The white dog? The one with white hairs on it?"

"Yes," said T., and nodded.

His mother turned her back and left the door standing open. She sat down on a stool close to the television and stared at it. She did not meet his eyes when he bent to kiss her.

Onscreen a man prodded another man's chest with a finger.

"Is this the only symptom?" he asked the nurse.

"She's fixated on hair. Dog hair, people hair. She looks for hairs on the furniture and picks them off one by one. She can spend hours doing this. And she keeps throwing away her hairbrushes. Then we have to buy new ones. I bought two in the last week. And I dug one of them out of the trash with yogurt all over it."

"Organic," said his mother, and squinted at him. "Fat-free."

She turned back to the television.

She had forgotten which room was her bedroom, said Vera; she had slept on the floor of the corridor and her hands and feet had been icy when Vera found her. She had omitted to put on a shirt in the morning and gone outside in nothing but underwear and a brassiere; she had made her way to the building's laundry room, where Vera found her picking the gray fluff out of the lint screens.

He went over to his mother and knelt down between her and the television; she leaned to her left and then to her right to see past him.

"You remember me, right? Mom. It's me."

Part of him thought that speaking close to her face, holding her wrists, fixing his eyes on her own would snap her to attention.

"Mom?"

"Are you a criminal?"

"I'm your son."

She was staring glassily and he turned to look where she looked; a man punched another man in the face.

"Is that a joke? Or a lie?" asked his mother, more speculative than accusing.

"Why would I lie about being your son?"

"Maybe you want to steal something."

"If I wanted to steal from you I would just grab your purse and run."

"You're a criminal. You have a criminal mind."

"I give up, then. I'm a criminal."

"Are you still my son?"

"Yes. I'm also your son."

"I must not have brought you up right. I did something wrong. Was I the wrong mother?"

"You were a great mother."

"Can you change the channel?"

"Sure. What are you looking for?"

"I just want to watch a show that's not about criminals."

He flipped through the channels, waiting for her to stop him.

"See? They're all about criminals. All the shows are about criminals. All of them."

"Do you want to watch the news instead?"

"All that is is more of them."

"OK. I'll let you have the remote back then. Here."

"Are you a criminal?"

He looked over at the nurse, who shrugged and bent down with a cup of tea for him.

"We've already been through that."

"I need to have a shower. I need to shave my armpits."

"Good to know. Go for it."

"It has sprouts in there."

She picked up a magazine from the end table and shuffled off toward the bathroom; he waited dranking his tea, and heard nothing. There was no sound of water running.

After he finished the tea he went to the bathroom door and knocked; his mother opened the door fully dressed and stood back slightly, waiting. Behind her the bathroom looked ransacked.

"Who are you?"

"I'm your son."

"The rapist? Or the murderer?"

"I like to flatter myself that I'm neither."

"I remember you. You like to do those crimes. The police come and solve them and have a trial with a pretty lady talking. You have to go to jail. Because sometimes you do killing, other times you do rape."

"I do mostly real estate."

She studied him suspiciously, at some remove.

"OK. I admit it. A little land speculation."

"I know you. I saw you there. You're the one from the program. Why do you even deny it?"

"Mom. I was with you in the living room, and we were watching TV. So let's not talk about me. Let's talk about you instead. I didn't hear the shower, is all. I wondered if you forgot. You said you wanted to have one."

"Oh," she said, and turned to look behind her. The floor was littered with toiletries and medicines; the cabinet doors were ajar.

"What are you doing there?"

"I thought . . ."

"Tidying up?"

"I wanted to get rid of them," she said faintly, and looked down at the spread.

He remembered the vial of pills. He looked down at similar vials on the floor.

"Let me help you," he said.

He knelt down and picked up the pills, slipped them into his pockets as she turned away and began to handle a hairbrush, plucking at the hairs that were caught in the bristles. Pink plastic razors were everywhere. He would not confiscate her razors, but he wished that he could.

"This is all over the place," she said, holding a tangle of hair she had removed from the brush. "It gets in things. It grows on you."

"It grows on all of us."

"Disgusting."

"You like to have it on your head, don't you?"

He put his hand on her shoulder and guided her to the mirror over the sink. They looked at their images: she was pale and old, he was smooth and young. She had not colored her hair in some time—since Beth, he guessed—and gray was woven through the yellow. He tried to keep his gaze on her worn features but it was hard and he was drawn back to his own reflection.

"See? It's good to have hair on your head," he said. "Isn't it? You wouldn't want to be bald."

"It should stay there, then," she said uncertainly. "It shouldn't fall off everywhere. It gets in the cracks. It sticks on things. It even gets on your tongue. Then you can't get it out! You can't even find it with your fingers. It's a finger tricker."

She was growing agitated.

"It's OK," he said. "Don't worry."

"It goes down your throat and makes you choke and throw up."

"You've been swallowing it?"

"Not on purpose," she said, indignant.

"Good. I'm glad to hear that."

"But it grows in the dark."

"At night, you mean?"

"In the body cracks. Under the arms. In the crotchal region."

He looked at her again. So much of composure, which he had till now believed to be a process of physical assembly, was in fact internal. His mother's hair had been combed, her face was clean, and yet she was dissolving. It was clearly visible.

"It also grows in the light," he said softly. "On the top of the head. Right? The sun shines right down on it. And on the legs and arms."

She cocked her head, considering.

"Let me run you a warm shower. Can I do that? Then I'll give you some privacy and you can get in."

In the kitchen he talked to Vera, keeping his voice low.

"Listen," he urged, helpless. "Maybe a specialist could help her. A neurologist? I'll make calls. I mean she's not even sixty."

"She still goes to church," said Vera. "Almost every day. She is not unhappy."

They turned to see his mother standing in the hallway, fully dressed but soaking. Her clothes dripped onto the floor. She had a comb in each hand.

Walking back to his apartment he tried to enumerate family members and came up with almost none. His father's parents had died before he had time to form a memory of them, his mother's mother had died when his mother was a small child, to be replaced by a stepmother who left again when his

mother was only twelve, and his mother's father, the cranky
Ukrainian who was the only grandparent he could remember,
had died a few years back of cancer . . . aunts and uncles were
estranged or distant. He had met a couple of them when he
was a boy or a teenager, but they had fallen away after. The
few cousins he had he would not even recognize if he passed
them.

His father had never seemed to remember the family
he'd grown up with, never seemed to think of them — as
though it was usual and correct to move ahead and leave
brothers and sisters behind you, unnoticed. His mother
had tried to encourage visits, he recalled vaguely, had
sent Christmas cards and gifts to his aunts and uncles
and cousins until possibly they stopped acknowledging
them.

Part of the growing estrangement from family, in the
end, was a simple product of freedom. It was the American
way to pick and choose from a range of possibilities, not to
be bound and obligated. Cut loose from a certain idea of
duty, it turned out, individuals did no great deeds but only
drifted apart.

Women left. There was a general feeling, he thought, a
preconception that men were the leavers, but in fact according
to statistics men rarely left. Mostly the leaving was done by
women. But it was men who drove them to it; it was the men
who misbehaved.

With each mammal it was different, with each bird, reptile,
amphibian, fish and invertebrate, but in the main it was the
males who went out, wandered, ventured, and were exposed.
They traveled further, died faster, and did not raise the
young. Meanwhile the females stayed. The females stored up
fat for lean times and lay low, in the hive, in the den, in the
nest, in the web. In the sandy hollow. Mostly the females

stayed, the males strayed, and so on down through the years. In the wild the males were more showy; they strutted and preened and the dull ones died off and the others fathered sons with magnificent plumage.

But among modern Americans, he had read in a magazine in his dentist's waiting room, three-quarters of divorces were instigated by women. More men betrayed their wives than vice versa: but finally it was the women who removed themselves, who went away completely, when it came to humans. In his case it was true, anyway—first her, then her, and even her. All left him in the end, whether by death or choice or defect. He couldn't blame them. They were otherwise occupied, or they were hurt.

Of course his father had left before anyone else, that was also true. His father was a man, and he had left both of them. But by his own admission his father had never been there in the first place.

•

The zoos were not new. What was new about them was the way the animals were valued as possessions more than symbols, the way the animals had become scarcer and scarcer as millennia passed so that they now were tradable. There had been zoos for thousands of years, for almost as long as there had been men who wanted to show their power through the jewels of their collections. More than two thousand years before Christ there had been, in the Sumerian city of Ur, vast collections of thousands of animals, gifts to the kings from their subjects—goods already, maybe, though still ripe for slaughter. Tuthmosis III let his

wild trophies pace the gardens of the temple of Karnak —
cheetahs, monkeys, deer and antelope with curling extrav-
agant horns.

He thought of these ancient zoos as he slept in the new
ones, so that some nights he was almost in both of them.

These days the zoos were full of final animals. Almost all
primates were on their way out, almost all the large carnivores,
the great cats and wild dogs and the bears, almost all the
wide-ranging and large herbivores, giraffes and pachyderms,
almost all the vast, intelligent mammals that lived in the
oceans. They were all on the clock, in the long moment of
going before being gone. The zoos were a holding pen: they
had the appearance of gardens, the best of them, but they
were mausoleums.

A child might believe a zoo was a small paradise — to a
child it might look like an Ark of creatures, in all their
splendid forms. When he went to a zoo by daylight, a visitor
like everyone else, he watched the children watching the
animals. He saw their captivation. Why should it not resemble
an Ark to them? In an Ark the animals were orderly, after all,
walking neatly in pairs and, for the purpose of their salvation,
submitting politely to the will of men.

The parents reassured each other and they reassured the
children. Here animals were separate from the hazard of
each other, their predators and their prey. They were safe
from men too, for in the wild there was always also the ruin
of the wild — new roads, earth-moving machines and fire
and chemicals that stripped the leaves off forests. Here the
animals were safe from everything but old age. It was widely
known that they lived longer in captivity.

In fact whole species were being protected as living relics,
given the honor of being almost extinct. This status was
posted on their exhibitions sometimes, as though it was a

blue ribbon. But even when the animals were relics they were less the last of their kind than a different kind entirely— a hybrid kind, he thought. A zoo kind. It had been observed since the nineteenth century that the mental fitness of zoo animals was seldom attended to by the zoo authorities, and this persisted. Where the large and wide-ranging animals were concerned, more often than not there was little to find there besides illness. Long ago they had lost everything and gone mad.

There were three elephants in the last zoo he broke into, all of them female and retired from circus life. It was still common for circus elephants to be beaten: for how else could an animal that weighed five tons be persuaded to stand on a stool on one leg? Domination had made the elephants resentful. Then there was their imprisonment, for in the wild they lived by walking. Walking was how they measured the passage of time. Here they were confined to cages; harassed by jabbering primates with long sticks; made to stand for end-less hours on concrete, to suffer the indolence and aching muscles of eating food off the ground. In the wild they rose to take their food from the treetops; they did not nose around for it in the dirt. All of this filled them with a massive and brooding rage.

Sometimes, for sixteen hours of the day, they swayed where they stood, rocked and swayed as though catatonic, and likely they were. But there were still things they enjoyed. They liked to be shown affection, to feel water coursing over their broad backs and to kick at the sand in their cages to find toys buried within. They liked to reach up for swinging bales of hay that hung from artificial trees.

They liked anything that was more than nothing.

The first time he went he felt their breath, a warm wind of eaten hay. The pale tips of their trunks were like digits, with a single finger knuckle that bent and clutched. When he came back the next night they recognized him and their pink, black-spotted foreheads vibrated. They rumbled. At night he took to sitting beside the bars, on the concrete. The floor was sloped in the barn where they slept, with a trough at the bottom to channel water and waste. The ceilings were high and there were no windows. He fell asleep against the cold wall with the elephants breathing in the dark a few feet away.

One morning he woke to the elephants pacing and felt he was pacing with them. A panic took hold of him. He was sinking into the torpor of the elephants himself, their permanent impoundment, and he had to get out. Their deep rage that was as heavy as they were, massive in its resignation—this lay over him in a swell, a contagion of misery. He almost thought they had conveyed it to him, had entrusted him with the purpose of getting out. There was nothing he could do but leave, get out and leave them here.

He would go.

As he was leaving it occurred to him that he would not come back, either to this zoo or to any of them.

With the elephants more than any of the others, he thought as he left them—as he left behind these great beasts who recognized him when he came, who rumbled and swayed sadly—he could feel them waiting. He had thought at first it was food they were waiting for. Here they were, the last animals, locked up and ogled, who had no chance remaining of not being alone. Here they were, and what he had assumed in his smallness was that they wanted food. It was possible to be fooled by the signs of their animation, in

the course of a day. But it was not food that interested them. Food was only a diversion for them, because they had little else.

They were not waiting for food, but they were, in fact, waiting. He had not been wrong about that. It was obvious: all of them waited and they waited, up until their last day and their last night of sleep. They never gave up waiting, because they had nothing else to do. They waited to go back to the bright land; they waited to go home.

8

Vera and his mother could not keep his dog again so he boarded her, recovered and walking well on three legs, in a luxury kennel. It claimed to be a resort for the dogs of the stars.

From the small plane that flew him down the peninsula in the morning the sky to the west was a light, full blue over the rolling forested mountains. He could see nothing but the green and the blue, which reminded him of a globe, a freshly printed textbook with perfect illustrations. He had a sense of beginning.

He sat next to the pilot and wore a headset; this endowed him with a sense of competence. He was equipped. If someone saw him now, they would have a false impression of mastery . . . he turned to look to the east, over the water, and saw thunderheads gathering. The pilot shook his head and said he would not fly again that day. A hurricane warning had been issued.

In the restaurant at the resort, where he always stayed when he came to supervise construction of his own, more

modest island facility, there were large televisions on the
walls. They ran a weather station constantly, but guests paid
little attention. The eye of the storm was approaching, pause
and swirl, pause and swirl; it was predicted to make landfall
by early evening.

He had heard nothing of this before he left home.

Still the island was not far and he had to see his own
place, so after a quick lunch he paid a young boatman to take
him out. As they crossed the shallows he sat happily on the
padded seat with the sun on his face; when his skin was hot
he bowed his head and gazed down through the turquoise
into the brown and orange of the coral. It was not, he realized,
as bright as coral he had seen in photographs: was there
something wrong with it?

A crowd of pelicans skimmed and flapped, drawn by tiny
silver fish in great schools that moved back and forth in
sweeps and flashes. He looked up from the water to the
horizon; before them was the delicate crescent of light sand,
the buildings' white facades, the thatch roofs beneath the
palms—everything as he had foreseen. There were the docks,
on their brand-new pilings, a single hammock swinging,
birds of paradise beneath the beachfront windows.

It was more than he had expected.

Two skiffs were tethered to the dock and as the motor cut
off he heard the high whine of a drill. Swiftly he left the
boatman waiting, walked to the end of the dock and touched
the edge of the thatch roof and the sturdy metal eye that
held the hammock. He craned his neck and stared into the
rafters, radiating like spokes from the high beam in the center.
Then he turned and strode up the dock to the beach, eager
to see the buildings. He looked at the sand under his feet:
old bleached coral cracked when he stepped—soft, porous
driftwood here and there—large green coconuts fallen from

the palms. The empty leg of a crab; the skull of a fish. Small young palm trees had been planted among the old.

One rule of thumb, a contractor had told him: tourists could never see too many palms.

The new white sand was full of vines and roots where the native mangrove was trying to find purchase; there were rake marks where the workers had scraped it back. Up ahead the main building, with its white dome and arches; off to the sides the flanks and the cabins. On the second floor, wide verandahs with thatch awnings. The doorways and windows had been roughed in but there was no glass in the windows and the doors had not been hung.

The buildings were still only shells, but lovely.

He could come here, maybe have a new life. His beach house, not for business but to be someone else, be different.

He felt a quick surge of euphoria; then there were pats of rain on his hair and he glanced upward. The cloud cover had lowered suddenly, a dark gray obscuring the distance. He was surprised.

Ahead the white buildings were backed up against the jungle. The sand was pocked with raindrops, more and more; palm fronds against the sky floated sideways. He zipped his windbreaker and stepped onto the patio. Behind a deep white wall two workmen were bent over electrical outlets, plying duct tape; the tarp beneath their feet was splattered with plaster and a radio played from a rickety stool. They turned and smiled politely when they saw him, wiping their hands on their shirts.

He shook their hands and asked in broken Spanish for his foreman; they answered in English and pointed him out, in the next room huddled over a circuit breaker.

A few feet away, through the rough arch, the rain began to fall faster. The sound of it filled his ears and the smell of it

filled his throat. As he crossed the floor toward the foreman he had a sense of tenuousness: there was a roof over their heads and there were walls, but there was no finishing. It was finishing that imbued buildings with their capacity to give comfort. Here there was no comfort yet; bare bulbs hung from the ceiling and burned with searing imprints.

They were practically outside. The rain fell harder.

T. stuck out his hand for a shake but Marlo embraced him. "Tomás," he said fondly. "We're just finishing. A storm is coming. A big storm, Tomás. What we do now is, we make sure we protect what we can. Stop the water damage. Then we go home. We got to go help the wife, you know? Help before the storm comes. Most of the men stayed home today. To help the wife and children."

"Go ahead," said T. "Please. Get home."

"High winds," said Marlo, nodding. "High winds."

He motioned to the others, preoccupied.

"You stay at the Grove, Tomás?"

"Always."

"Safe there. Very good."

They ran out then, Marlo with a plastic poncho on, the workers bareheaded and carrying between them a heavy tool-box. T. noticed they had brought their radio out with them, the cord wrapped carefully around it. They ran to their boats and got in. The palms were dipping and the canvas shelters on the boats whipped and flapped; the water was choppy and opaque.

Marlo stepped into T.'s boat and the captain started the motor. They huddled on a bench seat beneath the canvas. The deck was slick.

"Three generators," said Marlo, nodding, and patted T.'s knee. "Three backups. At the Grove."

"I'm not worried," said T.

Marlo nodded and said something to the boatman. Soon the two of them were yelling over the motor and T. heard nothing but noise; the prow of the boat lifted high and crashed down again over each wave, jolting him. He held tightly to the wet gunnel.

At the hotel dock he clambered out and watched them throttle away. When the boat vanished into the gray humid air over the waves he stayed where he was, his soaked feet planted firmly on the wood of the dock. He should have gone with them, should have helped them prepare for the storm. But likely it would pass, and tomorrow would be back to business. Still he was reluctant to go back into the hotel. Better he should stand here, wind-battered and shaking; better to feel this lassitude . . . his skin and clothes were waterlogged. Water ran down his neck and his nose and the thin windbreaker glued chilly to his arm skin.

The ocean and sky were one heavy mass without a line between them. His island was nowhere visible.

Soon he found himself retreating to the restaurant with the other guests, the restaurant with its gleaming copper-trimmed oak bar and rows of glittering bottles and large windows crisscrossed with tape to guard against shattering. Waiters moved among the tables, reassuring; they were used to hurricanes, which battered the coast year after year.

Rain flooded the swimming pool beyond the windows until water spread out over the pool deck and the lawn beyond. He put his face up to a triangle of taped glass, beside a long row of children who did the same until their parents pulled them back. The pool water was a muddy yellow, afloat with red flowers and brown palm litter and even a few lounge chairs, swirling and hitting each other. Nearby the trees moved and moved, bent low. Loose bark and fronds skittered

over the ground and caught on trellises and hedges, collecting at the base of low walls. Guests watched warily but tended to sit stiffly at their tables, as though the tables would protect them.

The televisions showed a weather map and at first the steadiness of the signal kept everything normal. Children ran and capered, restless; they hunched down by the windows until their parents noticed, twirled away from the windows laughing and shrieking. They played hide-and-seek, dashing back and forth across the room to conceal themselves behind potted plants and furniture.

Presently the signal was lost and the screens went snowy. In the moments afterward there was a pause in the room, almost a pause of fear. Quickly a waiter popped a movie into the VCR, and on every screen ran a movie about American astronauts with square shoulders and piercing blue eyes. Wind shuddered the walls as a great silver moon rose into the blackness of space; the elements outside and the space inside the capsule converged. On went the storm, and with pictures of wives and babies taped to the dashboards of their ship the handsome astronauts gazed out portholes in wonder, beholding an American universe.

In the late afternoon the wind abated and the rain slowed. Talk rose and there were a few barks of laughter, but then someone pointed out that the wait staff were all behind the bar, pretending to look busy there.

"The eye," whispered a woman at the table next to him. "We're in the eye."

In the quiet the wind shrilled and thudded again until it alarmed the children, who stood near their anxious parents holding onto their arms or legs, the small ones settling on laps. He heard glass shatter but did not see it. The taped windows let a white static of water sweep past; it pounded the

walls and the roof with new force and the windows shook in their frames.

How was his shell faring, the empty husks on the island?

Do not think, he told himself. Useless.

Anyway he was well insured.

Everyone else had at least a wife or a husband with them. Only he sat alone. Here was a whole life Beth had missed, a hole where a life should have been. But then, he thought, the universe was made up of holes—was it so terrible to be swept into one? After all. The holes were the black between stars, between constellations. It was holes that were the fabric of the galaxy.

At the thought he was calm, though someone nearby whimpered at the sounds of breakage and impact and a man in a light pink polo shirt sweated dark stains under his arms.

The storm blew itself out in the late afternoon and finally the guests wandered out of the restaurant, dispersing; they emerged into the half-light, into a patter of light rain. In twos and threes they walked quietly over the wet tiles and paved paths to their rooms and their cabins.

He smelled soil and humus and warmth made the air heavy over his shoulders. A few trees were down and lay across tennis courts but most of the buildings looked the same. He kicked a sodden raft of palm fronds from a doorway of a scuba shack near the beach and saw the basement had been inundated; above the thatch roof was in tatters, nothing left but the frame.

Only the gardens had fared poorly. They were flooded and muddy, bushes uprooted, flowerbeds flattened or washed out. And without its sculpted gardens the resort lost its stateliness, its reserve, even its authority. It was a victim now, a shabby and disordered outpost that was barely secure.

He went back to the crowded lobby to ask about the tele-
phone. Waiters and cleaning staff were leaving in droves, pil-
ing into beat-up vans and buses and jeeps to ride the rutted
roads home, even to walk. The manager threatened them.
But there were reports of devastation in the nearby town of
huts and shanties where most of them lived. They had to go.

"We will be understaffed throughout the rest of the dinner
hour," said the receptionist to T. "We regret this deeply."

The power was out, which they said was temporary; the
generator would soon come online again. At the door to the
lobby a waiter handed out candles.

No one was available to ferry him to his island; no one
could be reached by telephone because the lines were down.
He went to his room with his candle and his opened bottle of
wine; he lay on the bed with the door open to the wet dusk,
the candle guttering. He heard the other guests traipsing by,
the snatches of their conversation and the drip of palm
fronds.

Mastery was only a moment in the mind—of other men,
of yourself. Like the stock market, a consensus of opinion, a
pure abstraction; nothing to the tsunamis, the boiling sun,
the plate tectonics. The social compact was abstraction—
roads, buildings, and a temporary agreement about behavior.
That was it. The matter beneath it all was what lasted, and
meanwhile, always, the world of people was on the edge of
dissolution.

Soon, on a flimsy bed between thin walls, he had drained
the whole bottle of wine.

In the morning he waited in line in front of the hotel. It was
hard to press himself through the crowds; there was a second
wave of staff leaving, those who had worked through the
night and were now desperate. Vans and trucks left without

him again and again. Finally money talked, and he joined a
cook and two maids in a beat-up four-wheel-drive taxi.

The dirt roads were deeply braided with new ditches.
Cables lay across them, cars were mired deep in the drying
mud, and the taxi driver careened off the road at high speed
whenever there was an obstacle, splattering mud that
browned out the rear windows and the windshield. T. had to
get out and wipe the windshield for him whenever they
achieved dry ground and could stop the car without sinking.
Then they started up again and the taxi lurched over holes
and debris, leaving deep gouges in lawns that were already
swamped. When they got to their destination they were still
nowhere, because the center of the town was only a series of
piles in a field of mud. It looked like a landfill.

He glanced sidelong at the driver, who was stony. In the
back one of the young chambermaids started to cry, and the
other put an arm around her shoulders. The cook stared out
the window and shook his head.

Huts were mostly collapsed, wood and plastic and metal
piled on the wet ground. Here or there a lone stilt or two
leaned forlornly where a building had been. Water ran across
the road in what looked like a natural stream, it was so deep
and wide. As he got out of the taxi he smelled sewage; people
wandered wet and dirty, mothers with their babies on their
backs, men shirtless and shoeless and carrying piles of
belongings, shovels and jugs of water. Once the beach had
been hidden from the road by dwellings but now he could
see straight through where these buildings had been, straight
out through a hole to the sea. There had been no trees
among the shanties, no source of shade but the huts them-
selves, so now there was emptiness.

He set off on foot toward Marlo's house over piles of
twisted rebar and cinderblock and streams of sewage, sinking

into the mud past his ankles until his shoes and socks were boots of caked mud. He stopped to help a group of women lift a piece of cement wall off a chicken coop: the chickens inside were flattened, dirty white pads of feathers and beaks and talons. He wondered where the blood was.

After a while, a few false turns and circles, he saw the house ahead of him, intact. Everywhere else had been motion, the bustle and hurry of urgency: but Marlo's house seemed curiously still. In the yard beside it a black goat stood munching flowers, almost in slow motion. For a second he gazed at the goat as though both of them were similarly idle, similarly suspended. Then he broke the stare and started walking again. A fencepost had fallen down and the fence was sagging.

He knocked on the front door and waited and he knocked again. He was turning away when it finally opened, and a small girl in a red dress was looking up at him.

"Hola. Yo soy Tomás," he said, in his rudimentary Spanish. It was hard to know what to speak: some of them preferred English, some Spanish, some spoke English Creole or Maya or a language called Garifuna. "Está Marlo aqui?"

"Papi," called the child, turning.

Marlo stepped out from a door and picked her up; he held her as he spoke to T. He was different. For once he did not smile.

"Are you—are you OK here?"

"It is my son," said Marlo, in a monotone. "He was out on a boat. He has not returned."

"He might have had to put in somewhere," offered T. "Right? One of the atolls, or an island? Waiting till the storm passed?"

"He was at one of the atolls, where they take the tour boats," said Marlo. "They radioed in. They found his boat. But it was upside down. And he was not inside."

T. did not find words; he was inadequate.

"I don't want to intrude," he said.

"Come in. Please. Have coffee."

Marlo's wife sat with three teenage girls on the couch in their living room. They stood and smiled faintly when he entered, polite and miserable.

"The other boys, they are all looking for Javi," said Marlo.

"I'm very, very sorry for your situation today," said T., and Marlo translated. His wife bowed her head slightly and went into the kitchen, where she busied herself at the stove. The girls stood and followed her save the toddler on Marlo's lap, who played with a necklace of red and orange beads.

"Is there anything I can do? To help the search?"

Marlo shook his head.

"Let me know. The one thing I can offer is money. If that would help at all. To mobilize a larger search, anything. To help find him."

"That is generous, Tomás. But no, no thank you."

There was a glaze over Marlo's eyes; he was kind but not there.

"I just wanted you to know."

"Later, I will talk to Paolo," said Marlo, and nodded. "He will take you out in the boat. Maybe you want to leave after that, and come back other times. When the storm is cleaned up."

"What I want," said T., directly as he thought it, "is a guide. I want a guide with a good boat to take me up the river, to the preserve where the jaguars live."

"Jaguars?" asked Marlo, surprised.

His wife brought them small cups of coffee on an enamel tray. One of the girls in the kitchen burst into tears and the toddler turned in her father's lap to gaze at her sister.

"I am so sorry," he said again, awkwardly.

•

As the boat curved around the end of the island and his beach hove into view he saw the tall trees were down. He was looking at their root balls, straggly brown masses along the sand. He could see at least three thick trunks that had fallen across the white walls, caving them in.

The white sand was mixed with brown again.

"It's totaled," he said to Paolo the boatman. "I can see from here. I don't need to go there now. Go ahead, turn the boat. Turn the boat!"

They cut a wide U and headed back to the mainland. He could not force himself to look over his shoulder.

At the hotel he gathered his belongings; he had a couple of sweatshirts and a pair of good boots, but no tent or tarp or sleeping bag. He had very little. He lent his hotel room to the family of the maid who had cried in the taxi. Eight of them would stay in it—an old woman, five children, and the maid and her husband—along with the next-door suite, which he rented for them. They would stay there while the husband and the oldest son rebuilt their own two-room house; they would eat at the hotel restaurant on his tab, because they did not have transportation into town to buy groceries. It would help to assuage his conscience when he left the ruins.

He called his mother from a satellite phone at a medical clinic and got Vera, who went to look for her. There was a delay with the phone that made conversation desultory.

"Who is this?" came his mother's voice, wavering.

"It's T. Remember me?"

"—I can't hear them," he heard her complain to Vera. "It's staticky. It has an echo on it."

Vera took the phone again.

"She's having trouble hearing you," said Vera.

"We had a hurricane here," he said, enunciating. "I would have called sooner. There was a storm. It destroyed my new project."

". . . me to give it back to her?"

"No, you tell her what I say. OK? There was a big storm."

". . . big storm?"

"There was a hurricane here. I'm going to be out of touch for a couple of weeks. I'm calling now on a satellite phone."

". . . been going on the walks . . . little more fragile . . ."

"Tell her I miss her, and I'm thinking about her and hoping she's doing well. Tell her I'll be home soon."

"Who is this?"

It was his mother again.

"It's me, T. It's a bad connection. Can you hear me?"

"No one there," said his mother to Vera, fading in waves. "You know who it is? It's one of those crank calls. It's no one."

In Paolo's small metal motorboat, slapping the waves as they went south toward the mouth of the river, he felt flat but satisfied, equal to what came. Now that the buildings were gone and the telephone lines were down, he could not fly home anyway, not now. Nothing to do but go up the river toward the mountains. Was that where everyone would go, once the coastlines were gone? Higher ground.

The white lines spread behind the boat, further and further apart, disappearing into the gray of the deeper water as they grew separate.

His mother had loved him a long time ago, he thought. He squinted, trying to discern the precise moment when

the frothy lines of white were subsumed by the background of gray.

A long time past she had known him.

That was over. But it would be all right. Once the work of love had been hers, and she had done it. Now she was unable. It was not a turning, it was a simple erosion—what happened when the self fell away. It floated and sank, joined a deep well of souls, spreading. Where are you, rest of me? Fumble and glimpse but no worry; there was nothing to be done once it left. Child child, there there. And now I let you go.

It did not need to see itself anymore or be conscious of its boundaries. Vigilance fled in old age and man was like the other animals then, who science said could not see themselves. Here man was fully animal again, but he was still tender . . . you never lost what you were, never lost it fully. There was always the suspicion of a past life that faded and returned.

And you did not have to know yourself to be fully human. There were always those who did not, and no one said they were beasts.

•

Most of the roads were washed out so they traveled by water. From dock to dock, the open ocean to the wide mud-brown delta: and two days after the hurricane he lay back in a long, low boat moving slowly upriver.

There was a canvas shelter on the boat and the guide was quiet at the wheel. The two of them spoke rarely, so that birds would not startle. The guide, Delonn, was a gruff and modest old man, grizzled and heavyset with dark skin and a

light gray beard. He had worked for the national parks and attended a program for foreign students at Cambridge University; he spoke English with a clipped British accent. He had a vast knowledge of the rainforest, knew the common and the Latin names of plants and animals, the history of foods and medicines and poisons that came from the fruits and the bark and the leaves. He had reference to a long catalog of oddities and hazards.

They drank beers from a cooler. On the overhanging trees large green iguanas crawled lazily; on the bank stood a gray stork, and on a log sticking out of the water small bats were clustered sleeping. The water was torpid. When they came to a bend in the river, where the river's elbow reached out and flattened into a calm, sunny pool, Delonn encouraged him to jump from the boat and swim.

He shook his head.

"The crocodiles are very small," said Delonn, smiling.

T. stuck his foot up against the edge of the bench and pulled up his pant leg.

"I see you already know them!" said Delonn, and chuckled. "I thought you were a city boy."

"I am," began T., but the guide's smile fell and he leaned forward slightly, holding his arm.

"What's wrong?" asked T. "Are you OK?"

"A little heartburn," he said. T. waited while he breathed slowly for a few seconds and then smiled again. "You realize, Thomas, what the chances are of seeing a jaguar in the jaguar preserve?"

"Low," said T.

"Seventeen thousand to one. Approximately."

"It's OK," said T. "I just want to be where they live. I want to be in the theater. You know? But I don't expect them to give me a show."

There were a number of final animals here—crocodiles, parrots, turtles and anteaters. He knew he might not see any of them. He had mostly wanted to get away.

They jumped out of the boat around midday to walk through a forest thick with stands of bamboo, where T. stooped to inspect what Delonn said was a jaguar print. These were what most people saw of the jaguars, said the guide, and even then only in the rainy season. Black howler monkeys swung in the trees but were also difficult to see, fuzzy shapes in the canopy. At night they slept on the benches of the boat underneath the shelter, and T. listened to the whine of mosquitoes outside the net.

Mornings Delonn radioed back to his contact in the town, checking in; they drank bitter coffee and ate bananas and bread. They would only take the boat as far as the falls, after which they would travel by foot, leaving the beer and the ice behind in the boat and taking only what they needed. They would be carrying heavy packs, T. sixty pounds and Delonn eighty. He claimed to be accustomed.

After that they would wash off by splashing themselves from shallow creeks; they would eat mostly nuts and dried food and filter stream water to drink. This early leg of the trip was a pleasure cruise, said Delonn: T. should drink up.

The river narrowed and moved more quickly as they traveled; a light rain fell and pricked the water. When it let up the guide pointed out birds—a white-collared manakin made a clicking sound like two stones banged together and a bird called an oropendola screeched and rocked back and forth on its branch. There were tanagers and flycatchers and bat falcons; T. saw them fleetingly. It left him disoriented, all of them in the trees, so many.

Then the heat and the humidity. It laid him out.

He drank the last warm beer and fell asleep on his bench, the motion of the boat steady beneath him.

When he woke next Delonn was tying the boat to a strangler fig. Upriver was a series of white cascades, a fringe of thin streams threading their way down a pale gray escarpment. He watched as the guide prepared their backpacks, locked down the food hampers against scavenging animals, folded the shelter and tarped the boat. Then they swung their packs over the side and jumped down. His pack was heavy but this did not bother him; doggedly they tramped up a narrow, muddy trail away from the river, upward through dense foliage.

"Rain coming," said the guide. "I want to get to the campsite in time to set up beforehand."

Presently they stopped at a rocky outcrop, still in the shadow of trees. Up through the leaves he could barely see sky. It was late afternoon and the air felt thick. Delonn strung up the tarps overhead, tying complex knots with quick efficiency.

"I was only a Boy Scout for three weeks," said T. apologetically, watching. "They kicked me out for trying to sell merit badges on the black market. So I didn't have time to learn knots."

Just as Delonn tossed the sleeping pads through the open flaps of their one-man tents the rain started. T., watching from a perch a few feet away, brought the hood of his slicker up over his head. The wood in the forest was too wet to serve as fuel, Delonn said, so they would have no campfire. But he cooked for them over a small stove; he stirred soup and set it out in metal bowls. He poured whiskey into metal cups and they drank it under their vinyl roof, listening to the rain.

T. thought how comfortable he was in the company of Delonn, who was easy to be silent with. The guide spread his presence over them both, as much an umbrella as the tarpaulin. Falling asleep in his tent, stomach full of soup and bread and whiskey, he was glad to be where he was—in the midst of a thick field of sound with a thin, taut barrier between himself and the falling water.

He woke and realized the rain had stopped. He knelt and unzipped the door flap and got out; the guide's door was still zipped. He did not want to wake him so he scrawled a note and set off for a short walk up the trail.

Everywhere there were dripping leaves in a uniform shade of bright green. His shoulders and arms brushed wet branches and soaked his shirt instantly. He walked on, liking the feeling of being wet. He was wet all the time since he came to the tropics; he was never dry. He was steeping. The soil of the trail was so slick that he slipped and fell and soon his knees were pads of drying mud. Toes splayed on a tree was a bright orange frog; he almost stepped on a slug that was as long as his foot. He heard the sharp cries of something overhead and wondered if it was a bird or a monkey.

On his own he was barely equipped. To know that an animal was a last animal he needed other people, foresight and planning, research. He could not know it alone. He relied on data gathered by others; without the guide along he had none. For all he knew the frog was a last frog: but all he knew was nothing. When you knew the name of something that meant it was part of your life already. But here there were things he had never known. It was a new place and frightening, but it made him younger. The lightness was a boon, partly.

One frog—a golden frog was what he remembered, or maybe a golden toad—had lived in a misty cloud forest not too far from here. It had vanished only last year, or maybe the year before.

After an hour he turned back toward the small camp. The guide was still in his tent. T. consulted his watch: nine o'clock. He ate a granola bar and coughed loudly. Finally he walked up to the tent and spoke.

"Delonn? I think you might want to get started in there."

No reply.

"Delonn?"

He knelt and unzipped the flap. Delonn lay on his side, a sheet wrapped around his legs. T. reached out and touched a leg through the sheet; no movement, so finally he grabbed the sheet away. On the kneecap he noticed deep old scars, shining.

"Delonn! Delonn! You there?"

But Delonn was inert.

He climbed through the tent opening, up over the guide's prone body. He put his fingers against his neck, where he thought the pulse should be, but found none. Chest pains, he thought. Delonn had felt chest pains. He checked and re-checked, but still no pulse. He felt wired and nervy with alarm; his unfitness nagged at him. He was unqualified.

"Delonn. Come on. Don't be . . ."

He was playing a joke, possibly. At the expense of the rookie.

"Really. Not funny."

He shook Delonn's leg, then his arm, then rolled him onto his back and squatted beside him, looking down. The eyes were closed; the guide could still be sleeping. It was when the eyes were wide open and dull that you knew they

were dead. His fear for himself warred with disbelief . . . he had never been by himself. Not like this. With Beth at least there had been others there, the steady hand of the institutions.

He was lost. Nothing else had ever happened to him.

This was it.

For a time he lay in his tent, staring up at the orange and blue of the roof; several times, in a half-hearted gesture, he called out the guide's name. The silence confirmed him, but it was still not enough. Then he was suffocating; the tent oppressed. He went out.

He could not carry Delonn on his back, he knew that much for certain. It was at least five miles back down to the riverbank, five miles in slick mud, in dense foliage.

He would have to drag him.

He checked again and then again for signs of breath: could Delonn be in a coma? But the lips were drying. There was a dryness on the lips. He tried to pull Delonn into a sitting position; lamely, he tried CPR, vaguely recalling kneeling over his mother. He tried to press the feel of the dead lips away from him. He should have done this when he first found him. Now it was too late; it was sickening.

After several false starts he collapsed Delonn's yellow tent around the body and bundled it up. This tent, he noticed, was older and cheaper than his own, patched and taped at the seams. Delonn had let his client sleep in the good tent . . . he couldn't cover the face, for what if Delonn was not dead after all? What if the tent material blocked his mouth?

He cut a hole for the face.

He would pay them for the tent, he thought. Who was them? He saw Marlo's family. He would pay them for everything. He would cover them in money.

On Delonn's stomach he set down the second pack. He would need it, he thought. His own pack contained water and

food, maps in a plastic casing, a flashlight and a mosquito net. He found a bungee cord, which he attached to the package; then he tried pulling it over the ground. It was slow going, and the tent ripped and had to be retied and jerry-rigged frequently. Delonn must weigh more than two hundred pounds. The ground was slick in places, wet in others, then dry and crumbly. Wet was too wet: the package sank and got mired. Dry was too dry: the package snagged and bumped. Slick was good.

By his watch it was only eleven when he left the camp pulling Delonn, back down the narrow path the way they had come.

Once or twice, exhausted, he found himself weeping, though he did not feel grief. It was more like fear, fear and confusion. He had liked the guide but had no time to get attached; yet there was a shock to it unlike any he knew. Even with Beth it had not been like this: she had been contained by an institution, both of them had. Walls around them, walls humming with energy. In this he was abandoned. His limbs and nerves jangled with it, chaos under the skin.

He had never steered a boat before, never even pulled the cord on an outboard motor. He had watched it done but he had never done it. He did not know boats and he did not know rivers. He did not know corpses.

It took him a long time. He stopped for lunch, a chocolate bar he ate sitting on the ground, turned away from the guide's body. The afternoon wore on and his progress was painstaking; his palms were blistered from dragging and his fingers burned. His feet ached. The package was mud-splattered and torn. But he soldiered on with a lasting sense of incredulousness. It kept him separate from real things.

By night he would still be able to walk, he thought, but the flashlight batteries might not last. He recognized a stand of bamboo, the angle of a broken branch behind a black stump. A brown and blue butterfly flitted at the periphery of his sight. He was almost there. He thought of the skin of Delonn's back and the back of his head and shuddered—they must be ripped open, gaping. If the guide had not been dead when they started, by now he had murdered him. Maybe he should have left the body, spared him the brutal abrasion; maybe he should have run down to the boat alone, sped down the river and brought rescuers back with him. But there were carnivores in the forest.

Then he saw the boat through the trees, floating in the water. He was pacified; he was rewarded.

By the time he had taken the tarp off, erected the shelter and drunk fresh water it was getting dark. The boat had no spotlights. It had no light at all, only an electrical lantern Delonn had hung off the shelter to read by. In any case he was chilled at the thought of heading downriver by night. He would wait. With some difficulty he propped the package against the hull and then heaved it over the side onto one of the cushioned benches. He thought it was balanced but under his feet the boat rocked and it rolled off and fell heavily. He pulled it to the back of the boat and left it there.

He tried to honor it with a thought but was dull with fatigue. No strength left to hang the tarp or the mosquito net, so he wrapped the net around his head and torso and lay down, breathing thickly through it, on the bench he had slept on in better times. He and Delonn were both cocooned.

He had to shift his arms often to hold the netting away from his skin, for the mosquitoes landed on it directly; and trying to fall asleep in this awkward defensive posture he saw

poor Delonn waking, screaming suddenly at the recognition
of his flayed back and ragged scalp. He lay on his thin bench
in constant terror that Delonn might not be entirely gone
from his ripped body, that by accident or laziness he had half-
butchered him. It was a fear that he was lacking a center, or
he was a murderer.

He got up finally and pulled out one of his hairs. With the
flashlight he found the guide's lips, now blue; over them,
with great care so as not to touch them, he placed the hair.
In the morning he would be sure . . . but almost touching the
lips he feared he might also be dead, that deadness enfolded
both of them.

How could it not? They were so close.

With the first light he woke, nervous and shivering though it
was far from cold. Already the air was humid and he saw flies
buzzing over the package. Their presence actually reassured
him.

He had relaxed his hold on the netting during the night
and been bitten on his arms and his face. He itched from the
swellings, compelled to scratch at them right away.

The river was lovelier than he had seen it before, its water
slow and gold with a blue haze over the surface. Trees
hemmed the sky and made it small but there were pink
clouds over the tree line to the east. Around him on the still
boat were the sounds of crickets and birds; the water rippled
and sucked at the underside of the hull.

He was starved.

He drank water straight from a jug and found a small can
of black beans with a pull-tab, which he tipped into his
mouth and guzzled. Quickly it was over; his stomach was
heavy; he put the can in a plastic bag and looked at the tent-
wrapped package with its oval of face showing. He checked

the hair on the mouth, which was still perfect. The hair and the flies: he had not been wrong.

There was a gap between the lips, however, as though they were beginning to pull back off the teeth. The sight of it jarred him. He pulled the fabric sharply to one side so that the face was covered. He was almost antagonistic toward Delonn now, or at least Delonn's body. It had become an opponent, and a stubborn one.

He took a deep breath to steady himself. He tried the radio, though he was not convinced he was operating it correctly. He heard only static. Then he climbed off the boat again, jumping down onto the muddy bank, and untied the ropes from the strangler fig, fumbling with the guide's expert knots. Back on the boat, feet braced and arms trembling, he jerked twice on the cord and the motor started with a violent spit.

He exhaled shakily, grabbed hold of the wheel with wet palms and steered away from the bank.

Stay a course down the middle, he told himself, fewer snags there and greater depth. He did not want to let go of the wheel to grab the water jug or dig food out of the sacks; he did not want to cut the motor. So he stayed at the wheel steadily, wiping the metal with his shirt sleeve where his hands sweated, urinating once off the side of the boat. He was almost dozing at the wheel, his eyelids heavy in the heat of rising noon, when he heard something scrape loudly and the motor whined. The boat lost speed.

He walked to the back to look down. He had seen Delonn raise the propeller once or twice, why he had not known, but he knew it could be done. He leaned past Delonn at his feet, reached down and heaved it up. Two of the blades were sheared off and a third was broken. It must have hit a rock, he thought. Nothing could be seen through the turbid brown.

The current would still carry them downstream, but he had no way to steer. And the prow of the boat was pointed toward a bank already, moving steadily toward an eddy in the shallows. He glanced around in a panic and saw a white oar on a pair of hooks along the side. This he grabbed and grappled with and held out as they drifted; he stuck it over the side without judging distance, stuck it out and pushed away fiercely: and the boat slanted lightly away from the bank again.

For a while he used the oar on both sides of the boat, keeping afloat straight down the middle of the channel. It was tiring and his arms ached. As he rounded the meander with the still pool, where Delonn had offered him a swim, a large bird flapped over his head without warning; his hand slipped. The oar slid swiftly through the oarlock and into the water.

He watched it float away, hit a ridge of rocks and catch there as the boat moved downstream and left it behind. The boat stayed straight until it knocked into a low branch and slid up into a tangle of brush. A stick, he thought, and balanced tenuously on one of the side benches to reach up. After a struggle he was able to break a long branch off a tree and use it to push the boat off the bank, but the slant of the boat was hard to manage, the stick was awkward for steering, and at the next meander, where a short clay-red cliff rose on one bank, the boat lodged itself in the mud wall of the cliff.

He sat there for some time, listening to birdcalls and looking up at the clear blue sky.

•

When the current failed to dislodge the boat he decided to get into the water and push; he had to swim around and force

it off the bank. He peeled his shirt off and then his grimy jeans, perched on the gunnel and slid into the warm water gently. Feet in the mud, he pushed against the side of the boat until it seemed to loosen; as he pulled himself up a hard thing in the water slid down his calf. The cut was not deep but bled right away, freely. He left bloody footprints on the deck, which gratified him—as though someone else had finally acknowledged his injury. The blood collected into a thin ribbon.

River sand had gathered in the crotch of his boxer shorts and the crotch hung heavy like a sling, so he slipped out of the shorts and hung them from one of the shelter poles. For a while the boat moved nicely downstream; but then the river curved and despite his exertions it drifted into the bank again. He dropped into the water and pushed; again it drifted. Finally he was sick of the boat and furious.

He tied it to a tree and threw a full pack of food onto the bank, the water filter, his tent and sleeping pad and flashlight. He went to Delonn and touched the tent fabric at the shoulder. He laid a tarp over the body, covering the face, and tucked it carefully beneath.

He was sorry for Delonn but partly envied him too.

He clung close to the bank, wary of losing his bearings if he strayed too far into the jungle. At times there was no trail and the vegetation was thick where the trees were set back. He had to beat his way through. At times he had to stray from the bank, careful to keep the water in sight. Soon he had cuts on his arms and knees; he allowed himself small sips of bottled water but was eager to conserve it, and his head ached from dehydration. In the late afternoon he found himself at the edge of a large marsh that extended north from the river's edge.

He stood uselessly, despairing. The marsh reached far away from the river, too far to see—miles, clearly. He tried stepping

in and sank up to his knees; he almost lost a boot trying to pull his foot out. Better to swim the river, he thought. The river was not swift, but was the other bank a marsh too?

The further from the river he walked the further the swamp seemed to stretch. He got anxious. The sun was behind the trees. Finally he chose a hummock to set up his tent and struggled manfully with the tent poles until they held up the nylon. Inside he took off his bungee-cord belt and army pants, heavy with moisture, and sat down on his sleeping pad with his bare legs stretched out. He dabbed at the cuts with alcohol pads from Delonn's first-aid kit; then he found he was shivering and wrapped himself in his sheet. He had been wrong to leave the boat, clearly; for sooner or later, after the snags and the holdups, the spins and the drifts, it would have reached the coast.

It would have been safer than this.

He ate dry oatmeal from a plastic bag. The texture made him thirsty, parched his throat, but he took a single gulp from his small bottle of clean water and decided he had to save the dregs; he could not bring himself to glug from the flask of yellow-brown liquid he had filtered from the swamp. He studied it briefly with the flashlight, whose bulb was dimming rapidly. He believed he could see protozoans swimming, the whirring of their cilia.

Delonn was still on the boat, in his yellow wrap. The boat might be loose by now, loose but still tethered. He thought of it rocking lightly on the surface, Delonn bundled inside, and felt a pang of regret, almost fondness. Without Delonn's death he would never have known this fondness, the odd gratification of having, for a short while, guarded what was left of Delonn, the protector of his honor.

Of course he would also not have known the resentment, the disgust or the repulsion. Those were part of knowing.

Taking care of the deceased he had established a certain intimacy: they were not opponents after all but only companions.

He listened to the night; he curled in. Take stock, he thought, take stock. He would be fortunate if he got home at all. There were hazards beyond being lost, being hungry. Delonn had told him about a certain local tree species that grew near the stream bank and exuded a toxic sap. You could brush against the trunk or the branches unknowing and if the sap touched your skin it caused third-degree burns, raising welts up to six inches long. Delonn had been able to identify the trees; of course he himself had no idea what they looked like. For all he knew he was surrounded.

He had had a strong faith once that the world was, at its best, its warmest and most glowing, a network of cities. He recalled a map of the continent at night—a map or a time-lapse satellite photograph—anyway the North American continent seen from the sky, with lights winking on all over, the clusters of population like beacons in the blackness of space. This had seemed to him once to be the epitome of the real, of the hopeful and the farseeing. A night starred with fires, with the fires of habitation. The world had been buildings, he had always believed, and the invisible structures that imbued these buildings with roles, keeping some persons outside them and others within. The whole world had been the systems of men, and he recalled faintly what a comfort it had been to admire it.

And it was not—as he considered now, huddled and wretched and further from cities than he had ever been— that these systems and the rules that bound people to them were not close to the core of life: but the life they described was a narrow life, a fast life. It was a small life, the life of certainty and straight paths, that life of crowds and buildings.

And look. Look!

It had passed.

9

More than anything he wished he could just glance up at the sky and see an airplane or a helicopter, the sun reflecting off its silver skin, solid and ready to descend.

But all he got looking up was eyeshock.

By the time he had ringed the marsh and returned to the riverside he had tired his throat with tuneless singing; he had kept himself steady by impersonating a soldier, tramping forward step after step, slogging. There was another marsh, then another. There were nights and mornings. How many miles was it now? He wished he knew; he wished he had an accounting of them, a tally. Then at least he could be sure of an accomplishment. He was weary of the sweaty air, the low gray skies, the crowding of brown and green: he moved as quickly as he could and let the wet air fall to the sides. He had rubbed insect repellent through his hair, stared at the label and then poured it down the back of his neck, N,N-diethyl-meta-toluamide 100%.

These were the only written words he had seen in a while, he reflected—although how long had it been? Only a few days: but already it was a lost country. Aside from the tags in his clothing they were the last proof he had of English . . . certainly he was nearing the mouth of the river now. Certainly he would be there in a matter of minutes, see a sedate tourist boat motor up the channel, old ladies seated pleasantly on the shaded benches. He imagined their pastel-colored visors and wraparound sunglasses, how they would smile blindingly and point in amazement when they caught sight of him. He would strike them as a woodsman or a hermit; they would be able to tell he was a person undergoing a hardship far from their experience, undergoing a trial by fire and a transformation. Once recovered from their initial exuberance—a man who came out of nowhere! A Tarzan, a Doctor Livingstone!—they might well be frightened.

This at least was something to find pride in, obscurely, a secret sense of himself as a man made rugged by adversity, a rough primitive.

He found a trail, finally, following the river, and at first he was encouraged, thinking he must be nearing the town. But the trail was narrow and often seemed to fade and then reappear: it was not, he realized presently, maintained by humans. It was an animal trail. There were piles of scat here and there; there were gnawed tree trunks and broken twigs; there were the husks of fruit thrown down from the trees and once, in the scat, a pile of bones.

He retreated into the trees around lunchtime, seeking a place with fewer insects. Sitting on a log where a stream of sun filtered down he ate more of the dry oatmeal and drank the warm river water: it left silt in his throat but he did not think it would make him sick. When he came to the delta, he knew, he would meet a crisis of questions: they would

clamor at him. People there might have been close to
Delonn, there might be children and grandchildren, a sister
or a wife.

He peed in a bush and was tying his bungee-cord belt
when he heard a scratch and looked up: there was an animal
perched on a branch. It was small and brown with large eyes
and round ears, a thick coat of fur and a long thick tail; it
sprang away chattering. He watched it jump and climb until
it was too far from him to see.

He had no idea what it was. This pleased him: maybe
there was hope yet. How was it that his own ignorance was a
comfort? But it was.

Expecting to reach the coast, expecting to reach the town, he
became indignant as he failed and kept on failing. Anger rose
fiercely in his chest and subsided again. At least to see
someone, someone who could help him, but no one came.
No one appeared. He had always been on the bank of this
sluggish river; he had always been walking here, always been
this person. The rest had been a mirage.

He started walking at six in the morning and by four in
the afternoon his feet hurt too much to persevere. Blisters
bubbled and ripped on his heels and his toes; they bled
through his socks, forced him to whistle sharply to forget the
pain.

He began talking to himself. He wandered, he was bored,
but he had no other diversion and after a while he was forced
to invent a companion.

"So are we going to die?" he asked him.

"Unlikely," said the friend, and paused. "Possible," he
admitted.

"This is ridiculous," he told him. "Could it be we went off
along a tributary? Or another fork of the river as it braids at

the delta, a fork that takes longer to reach the coast? But we're still headed east. I know that from the sun. So sooner or later we have to come to the ocean."

"Too bad you got kicked out of the Scouts before Orien-teering."

"East is all we have to know," he insisted stubbornly.

Together they recalled moments from youth—kids he knew, things that happened. Who was in the closet with Kate Bonney, in sixth grade? French-kissing? The story circulated for weeks . . . Eric K., that was it. It was the first-ever kiss for both of them and Eric K. was determined to make it a French one; he had read up on technique. But he was overeager and had put his tongue so far down Kate Bonney's throat that it touched her stomach. That was the story and they had circulated it without mercy. He himself had had a tendency to bribe the girls at that age, bribe them for the favor of a feel or a kiss: Blow-Pops in watermelon, cherry, or grape. The pink flavors were the favorites . . . small tokens, nothing extravagant: they were gifts, not payment. He had a soft touch even then. He stopped walking as he recalled this, could almost taste the sharp tang of the globes of sugar.

He recalled all these people as an elegy, since he was removed from them. Not only now, he thought, but forever. He might still seek people out, talk to them—of course he would, they were part of him—but his eyes would be fixed on a point beyond them. His craftiness in boyhood, his single-minded enterprise—all was for the sake of gain, for gain was his religion, simple and stunning. No grown man could love accumulation as fully as a boy did. Indeed he never recaptured the joy of that love, and it passed out of his grasp.

And the infrastructure: he had drawn cities, first, and plastered his walls with them; he had built cities of Legos and lined the shelves of his room with their red platforms,

their blue and yellow rectangular monoliths. There were Lego helipads, gas stations. Then he made his parents buy him miniature trees, tiny street signs, other items that architects used to build their dioramas, and built his own replicas from kits—the Capitol building, the Washington Monument, Mount Rushmore. He had hastily disassembled the babyish Lego structures in favor of these, had enlisted his father's help in lighting them so that the buildings of state cast long shadows, and as he slept they towered over him.

With the sun setting at his back he dropped his pack on a rippled hump of sand that rose out of the river. The river must be low: at times the sand bar was underwater, he could see from the dark contours. Now it was dry. It had not rained since Delonn was alive, since he became alone. Even the rain had forsaken him. Maybe he could tempt it; he would use only the mosquito net for shelter instead of his tent. Let the rain come, he would welcome it. He draped it over a jutting tree limb and propped it up from beneath with four long sticks. Fit for a dignitary, he thought. He could sit underneath and watch the flow of the river as the sun went down.

Before he retired into the shelter he took a bath and stood in shallow water in sunlight until he dripped dry. His cut legs stung but he was pleased to be washed. Dusk fell over the river with him sitting on his sleeping pad behind the translucent white screen, his pack and the rest of his meager belongings arrayed around him. He had not wanted to put his clean self back into the filthy army pants; instead he had washed them and hung them on the tree limb beside his netting. He sat wrapped in the sheet. It was a balmy night. He flipped the switch on the flashlight and saw the bulb dim away to nothing.

Scrounging in the pack he found a packet of soup powder, which he tipped into his mouth; stale crackers, which he

gobbled. And then: the plastic flask of whiskey! He shook it: still an ounce or two left. He had forgotten it completely. Thanksgiving.

He drank and watched the light of the sky change. If he were not so hungry, he thought, he could almost be happy here. He had left the settlements now, all the old geographies. For so many years they had been the only thing; you did what you did and whatever it was consumed you, as though your actions were the heart of experience. As though without a series of actions there would be no story of your life.

Those who loved stories also loved the human, to live in cities where there was nothing but men and their actions as far as the eye could see. Once it had been believed that the sun revolved around the earth; now this was ridiculed as myopic, yet almost the same belief persisted. The sun might be the center of the planets and then the sun might be only one star among galaxies of them: but when it came to meaning, when it came to being, in fact, all the constellations still revolved around men.

He had been drawn to cities, had considered no alternatives—cities and buildings, buildings and institutions. The lights across the continent. But what if, from his childhood on, he had imagined not the lights but the spaces between them? He would do so now, to make up for all the years behind him.

Forget the buildings and the monuments. Let the softness of dark come in, all those light-years between stars and planets. Cities were the works of men but the earth before and after those cities, outside and beneath and around them, was the dream of a sleeping leviathan—it was god sleeping there and dreaming, the same god that was time and transfiguration. From whatever dreamed the dream at the source, atom or energy, flowed all the miracles of evolution—tiger, tiger,

burning bright, the massive whales in the deep, luminescent specters in their mystery. The pearls that were their eyes, their tongues that were wet leaves, their bodies that were the bodies of the fantastic.

Spectacular bestiaries of heaven, the limbs and tails of the gentle and the fearsome, silent or raging at will . . . they could never be known in every detail and they never should be.

When time moved, mountains rose from the plains and the miracles multiplied, infinitely lovely. The miracles were the beasts.

•

Lying on his back, gazing up past the tip of the bough at the spectrum from blue to black in the sky, he heard a clinking and scraping off to his right.

He sat up abruptly. White in the dimness, white bearing down on him. It was the boat. It floated downriver.

His bad knots.

He dropped the flask and tussled with the mosquito net: the boat was approaching rapidly. It was almost already there, almost at the sand bar. Was it not his duty to scramble aboard? Was it not what he was supposed to do?

He pulled the netting up and ducked through, the sheet falling around him; naked and tottering he stood on the edge of the sand bar, his feet sinking. The prow loomed past him: he splashed out into the water and grabbed the side, tried to heave himself up: he was clinging, legs thrashing, looking down into the boat, halfway over the side. His feet trailed in the water. He could not get in: the boat was still moving fast: over the side he could see.

Delonn was not inside. The yellow bundle was not there at all.

Then something sharp hit his back and the shock made his fingers slip off the gunnel. He fell and sank under, nose full of water: he had bashed into a tree. Splashing and choking he retreated onto his sand bar, the boat a light wraith as it moved off down the river, faint and fainter, glowing in the darkness and fading away. He was breathing hard. The branch had gouged his back. And he was being bitten savagely by insects: he shook himself off and ducked back under the net.

How could Delonn have been moved?

Something must have moved him.

Now the boat would sail into the delta like a ghost ship; the boat would arrive and be empty of both of them. He had missed it.

He sat back down beneath the net; he brushed the wet sand off his calves and ankles. The boat was out of his reach for good, he knew, trembling with the suddenness of it: but it was all right, actually. It was right. Delonn had loved the river and the forest. Delonn would not have minded staying there, disseminated among the elements that he knew. Let the vessel float, let it vanish quietly. He was leaving all that; he was letting it go.

He thought of his mother. She let things go, he thought, but not because she chose to. And yet there was something right in her devotions, despite their idiosyncrasies. Despite the fact that the origin story was all about people and their passion and their sex, a tale in which animals and the rest of creation were window dressing at best . . . her story was a romance. But at least she had a love interest other than herself.

And the mother of God knew how to put herself second. Not second to men, though some might see it that way, but second to everything.

He had begun by idolizing the men, he saw now. Not so much his own father, who had been of limited interest to him, but the fathers of nations. It had been natural to begin with these men, wanting to emulate them, wanting to walk, as they did, wearing the luminous cloaks of their authority . . . no boy wanted to imitate his mother. No boy aspired to that yielding, self-effacing kindness, that quality of service. Boys wanted either to break things or to build them. But now it was his mother who stayed with him, not for what she was to others but for what she had always been to him alone, one small being where all her affection was concentrated—for how she had loved when it mattered most.

He was fortunate. He had ended up here, in the middle of what was real—not what came easiest but what turned out to be closest to the center. He ended up here, under the black of the sky, wanting to copy his mother's love. The affection she had given him when she was still herself, before she was robbed of it, the sense of protection and loyalty.

This was the knowledge that mattered, he thought: simple, simple, simple.

●

He had nothing but the sheet to dry himself with. After he did this and wrapped himself in it again it was still damp, and a chill took hold of him. If he came, finally, to the mouth of the river, what would they think of him? If he told them what had happened to Delonn, would they even believe him? To think of this was a luxury; to think he might be suspected of crime or negligence was to assume he would see the ocean again. And yet it could not be more than another day's walk.

The river was simply not long enough to keep him walking until he fell down.

He drank the rest of the whiskey. It warmed him a bit, but still he was shivering. He settled down on the sleeping pad as the song of the crickets rose around him; he held the empty flask close to him, inside the sheet. Good to have something to hold, he thought, even something empty.

When a thing became very scarce, that was when it was finally also seen to be sublime and lovely. It had happened with wild nature in England in the nineteenth century: nature that had been despised and avoided before it was destroyed by cities and farms and pollution became, when there was almost none of it left, the subject of poems and paintings, the highest access to the divine. Now some few persons, he thought, marginal persons in their marginal groups, knew the value of the animals and their world, and he was one among them.

He was as farsighted now, he thought with a flush of his old conceit, as he had ever been in his stock predictions, in his speculation for his own profit. He saw what was coming. Whether it was wheat futures or neighborhoods or the Nikkei or this; for the market had failed to see the animals for what they were, the animals in their own places with the ancient networks of their culture and landscape intact. Worth far more than single commodities.

The lapping water was like a lullaby. Uncountable wealth, he thought, not the kind that was superfluous but the kind that kept you alive, down through the generations.

But the market would take too long to recognize it; the market already had. The market had failed them.

10

When he felt it he did not move at all, not even—second nature—to look at the place on his wrist where his watch used to be. It was still night, not a glimmer of dawn. There was no moon; it was pitch black. He only woke up because it was lying on him. He had been on his side with his right arm flung out and his left clutched around his stomach; the animal lay on the right hand and arm through the mosquito net. It lay on top of his hand and arm, trapping them, and against his stomach.

His first thought was that it wanted to hurt him. But it did nothing, only shifted once or twice after the first settling-in, shifted and took a breath. He tried to picture it from its breathing but was unable to. Beneath the dirt-smelling, musky coarse hair, through the very thin net, he could feel the movement of joints against him as it settled in on its haunches. What was it doing?

There was heft to it, but it was not huge: it was neither large nor small. It was a mammal, certainly. It was not a

jaguar, not an ocelot or a margay, nothing feline and sly—more likely a young tapir or a paca, large, stout, snouty and ground-dwelling. There were many herbivores here, more than he knew how to name. If it was a tapir, the lowland species that lived in the region, it was one of a kind that was soon to die off.

Lying stiffly, the crushed arm pricking pins and needles, he wondered if it had lain down on him because it was wounded or hungry, because it smelled the vestiges of food on his person: but the pacas and the tapirs ate tubers, grasses and fruits, Delonn had told him. It could not be seeking warmth, not in the swelter of the tropical night. Even the sheet was almost too much for him. He did not dare to move; he kept his breathing regular; he would not turn over, would not give it cause for alarm.

He remembered his dog. He remembered the feel of her paw in his hand, her knobby knuckles and smooth claws under the pad of his thumb. He had to get back; he had to take care of her. It was a small responsibility but it was his.

The animal stayed: it breathed and wheezed: and though he was beyond exhausted he held himself rigid for a while. But the night wore on and on and he started to let himself slide. He still had whiskey in him. Drifting off he was confused about where and even when he was—in an orange place somewhere, that held memories? Here was Beth, for one thing; after all that had happened and not happened, she was faithful and she had stayed with him. She was not sad to have died, she said. She said that when you died what happened was you made room for the new. Young ones were born, occupying the space where your old self had been.

She was not as selfish as he was, he thought. He still wanted to be there himself, wanted to be at the party. He still wished; he was not giving up. And the coyote he killed was

there, and his dog. They ignored him but he was glad to see them. He was surprised, in fact, at how happy he was. He remembered his dreams, he knew them. Was this a dream, or was it a decision? Beth was far away but content. She smiled, still to reassure him. She had never forgotten what he needed from her, her happiness even after she was dead.

He would let go, but never give up. A name, a life, the street he lived on when he was ten: goodbye then soon, to all of them. This was what was occurring all over, as the world dwindled and its colors were stripped from it. People kept busy on the surface but underneath it they were sleeping, sleeping in their billions. They were sleeping simply, as the other animals did, sleeping and dreaming of the life that might once have been.

As the animal slept its way through time until the end of it came, so would he.

What could it want from him? What it must have felt once — an imprint of touch on the other bodies, how they wriggled close there, in the den. He could almost feel them on his own sides. A mother and a small brother, a new one. On and on it was warm: it was warm, it was good. They were made to be close; they were made to be together. That was what mammals were. Not all animals, true, but his kind. Some of them.

But the mother left then, and she never came back.

They went out to find the mother again. The brother strayed from him and ended up somewhere else. It was strange without the others so close: it was strange and far too open. He imagined he knew the coldness of this, of walking for the first time alone.

Looking for the mother the animal went down to the mud, went down to the wet grass and slippery ground. The silty water washed over him. His legs went pedaling; his eyes

were above the surface as he pedaled with all four legs. It was warm in the water, as it was in the den. Better there than the air. He was looking for the mother, looking, looking: instead there was the brother, floating and not so warm. Why cold, brother? The brother floated and floated away.

When the others left and they were all that you had, when all the ones that you loved had died: so it was, for last animals and for him. What did anyone do, when they were left alone?

They found a way not to be.

Think the thought and he would know how it was; he would see the past and with it the future, not only of them but of him. Angry, a person might thrash and fight—even against himself, because he did not know who he was, or who the others were either. Later he would have to sit, crying crumple-faced in the pile of the dead. This was how it would be with the men, after they finished their work. They would have to be alone after that, and for so many years. On and on they would live, surrounded by gray. Complexity would be gone, replaced with dull sameness that stretched out unending . . . and when they had killed all their friends and everywhere was empty: only then would they see how terribly they had loved them.

•

So an animal had come to him, in the end. He was lucky: he recognized this again and again, as though each time was the first recognition. He was contented in this luck, which at first he had mistaken for a tragedy. But he was not done yet. In the morning, he could tell, he would get up again and he would walk to the sea.

The tough skin, the coarse hair. The animal breathed thickly. For a time he did not know what he felt. In out, in out, they breathed and breathed. They both had lungs, they loved to sleep, they liked to be alongside each other in the comfort of their rhythm. He slept, or thought he slept; he dreamed, or thought he dreamed. Did it matter? If the animal was speaking to him, fine: if it was only what he believed was the animal, that was fine too. To know was to be.

The animal was glad, he saw. The animal trusted, and its trust was simple but it was not crude. It had found something, a protector. And then he knew: it was thinking of its mother. That was why it was here. The mother had left and been killed, the mother had disappeared: how the animal missed her!

It had made a mistake, though it did not know this yet. It believed it had found its mother, found its mother again. It came down to the river searching for her and because it wanted to find her, wanted desperately, here she was. It believed it was not alone anymore. He was close, a real and breathing body: so at long last it was sleeping soundly.

Sleeping here it could feel safe again, and this thought of safety was the same as it had always been. The good thought was the same thought wherever you were. Faced with being the last, faced with being alone, the thought was still the same, still and always the same. When it came to the future the animal might not have plans, might not need them—what it had was an impression, almost a whimsy. An impression of seasons, the smell of the rain; of the ground and the wind, the sun and the moon, towering clouds, the great sky in flight. The feel of others like itself here close, of others not itself further out; the feel of rushing youth and the

feel of slow growing old, of misery and joy. This was one breath, first stifled and then freed: one soft and glancing touch that was the memory of life.

Back to the beginning and on to the end—home was flesh, was nearness. Poor animal. It thought he was its mother, but its mother was gone.

As, after a while, all the mothers would be.

Acknowledgements

I want to thank Kierán Suckling for his talent as a critic and his knowledge of endangered plants and animals. I'm very grateful to Richard Nash for his unflagging enterprise, Maria Massie for her excellent instincts, Kate Bernheimer for her generous editorial help, Julie Miller for her time and talent with photographs, Chris Dietz for his reading, and my brother Joshua for his intimate understanding of the capitalist spirit.

For their own writing, particular thanks to David Hancocks, author of the lovely and necessary *A Different Nature: The Paradoxical World of Zoos and Their Uncertain Future*; Joy Williams, author of the groundbreaking essay "The Animal People," among other works, for her inspiration; and Jeffrey Moussaieff Masson and Susan McCarthy, authors of *When Elephants Weep: The Emotional Lives of Animals*.

For their kindness in allowing me close to zoo creatures, many thanks to Jeff Williamson and Steve Koyle of the Phoenix Zoo, as well as Nancy Biggins-Adams, keeper of mammals at the Arizona-Sonora Desert Museum.

To the memory of the West African black rhinoceros, which disappeared from the world in the time it took to write this book. And in honor of the rarest species in the United States, any of which may vanish in the blink of an eye: the Alabama beach mouse, Alabama lampmussel, Alabama sturgeon, Attwater's greater prairie chicken, Berkeley kangaroo rat, Buena Vista Lake ornate shrew, Cahaba pebblesnail, Carolina elktoe, Catspaw, Devil's Hole pupfish, Florida panther,

Florida salt marsh vole, Fosberg's love grass, Franciscan manzanita, giant Palouse earthworm, Guam Micronesian kingfisher, Hawaiian crow, Hawaiian monk seal, interrupted rocksnail, Key Largo woodrat, Lange's metalmark butterfly, and Miami blue butterfly.

photo by Kierán Suckling

Lydia Millet is the author of five novels, most recently *Oh Pure and Radiant Heart*, which was shortlisted for Britain's Arthur C. Clarke Prize and named one of the best books of 2005 by publications such as the *Christian Science Monitor*, *Time Out Chicago*, *Booklist*, and Canada's *Globe and Mail*. Her 2002 novel *My Happy Life* won the PEN USA Award for Fiction. She lives in Arizona with her husband and daughter.